'A comic tour de force, a biting satire on the hypnotized world of artificial wants and needs that Huxley predicted, a moving study of brotherhood and family failure, *F* is an astonishing book, a work of deeply satisfying (and never merely clever) complexity' John Burnside, *Times Literary Supplement*

'What a strange and beautiful novel, hovering on the misty borders of the abstract and the real. Three brilliant character studies in the brothers – religion, money and art. What else is there? The answer, Kehlmann suggests, without ever saying so, is love, and its lack is the essence of the failures of all three men' Ian McEwan

'With the wizardry of a puzzle master Daniel Kehlmann permutes the narrative pieces of this Rubik's Cube of a story – involving a lost father and his three sons – into a solution that clicks into position with a deep thrill of narrative and emotional satisfaction. Kehlmann is one of the brightest, most pleasure-giving writers at work today' Jeffrey Eugenides

'*F* is an intricate, beautiful novel in multiple disguises: a family saga, a fable, and a high-speed farce. But then, what else would you expect? Daniel Kehlmann is one of the great novelists for making giant themes seem light' Adam Thirlwell

'Kehlmann's world is fully convincing while being philosophically challenging. H˙ ˙   ˙   ˙˙˙g us with his storytelling ˙   ˙s of our own' Toby Lichtig

'. . . this   ˙ls – a work   ˙ible beauty   ˙ew Adams,

'Daniel Kehlmann's subtly yet masterly constructed puzzle cube of a new novel . . . with its sly Möbius-strip-like connectedness, doesn't just hint at the possibility of a plan behind the scenes; it enacts that plan in the very telling, its elegant, unfolding construction revealing the author's intended pattern by book's end; a sign of hope, perhaps, or even faith' *New York Times*

'Like its two most obvious influences, Franzen's *The Corrections* and Foster Wallace's *Infinite Jest*, *F* isn't a comedy in the traditional sense: it jumps between genres, toying with melodrama here, riffing on the gothic horror story there . . . reminiscent of Franz Kafka or Elias Canetti – both laugh-out-loud funny and so uncomfortable that one occasionally needs to put the book down to get a breather' Philip Olterman, *Guardian*

'It cannot be an easy thing to write a comic novel about the death of God. Still, Daniel Kehlmann may just have pulled it off . . . In a godless world, love counts for a great deal. And failing love, ordinary human decency goes a long way. Since Kurt Vonnegut died, there has really been no one to tell us this; the reminder is welcome' Simon Ings, *Guardian*

'Daniel Kehlmann braided art, religion and finance into a typically effervescent but heartfelt comedy-of-ideas about faith and fakery' Boyd Tonkin *Independent*, *Books of the Year*

'Compelling combination of digestible philosophy and buzzy page-turning thriller . . . the ideas in this book are big, exciting, an irresistible puzzle, and the prose flows like the Rhine – increasingly dramatic, occasionally soulful' *Big Issue*

Daniel Kehlmann was born in Munich in 1975 and lives in Vienna, Berlin and New York. His works include *Measuring the World*, *Me & Kaminski* and *Fame*, and have won numerous prizes, including the Candide Prize, the Literature Prize of the Konrad Adenauer Foundation, the Doderer Prize, The Kleist Prize, the WELT Literature Prize, and the Thomas Mann Prize. *Measuring the World* was translated into more than forty languages and is one of the biggest successes in post-war German literature.

Carol Brown Janeway's translations include Bernhard Schlink's *The Reader* and *Summer Lies*, Jan Philipp Reemtsma's *In the Cellar*, Hans-Ulrich Treichel's *Lost*, Zvi Kolitz's *Yosl Rakover Talks to God*, Benjamin Lebert's *Crazy*, Sándor Márai's *Embers*, Yasmina Reza's *Desolation*, Thomas Bernhard's *My Prizes* and Daniel Kehlmann's *Measuring the World*, *Me & Kaminski* and *Fame*.

F

Daniel Kehlmann

Translated from the German by Carol Brown Janeway

Quercus

First published in Germany in 2013 by Rowohlt
First published in Great Britain in 2014 by Quercus
This paperback edition published in 2015 by

Quercus Publishing Ltd
Carmelite House
50 Victoria Embankment
London EC4Y ODZ

An Hachette UK company

A CIP catalogue record for this book is available
from the British Library

PB ISBN 978 1 78429 623 0
EBOOK ISBN 978 1 84866 752 5

10 9 8 7 6 5 4 3 2 1

Typeset by Jouve (UK), Milton Keynes

Printed and bound in Great Britain by Clays Ltd, St Ives plc

For A

F

The Great Lindemann

Years later, long since fully grown and each of them enmeshed in his own particular form of unhappiness, none of Arthur Friedland's sons could recall whose idea it had actually been to go to the hypnotist that afternoon.

It was 1984, and Arthur didn't have a job. He wrote novels that no publisher wanted to print, and stories that appeared occasionally in magazines. It was all he did, but his wife was an eye doctor, and that paid the bills.

On the way there he talked to his thirteen-year-old sons about Nietzsche and different brands of chewing gum. They argued about an animated movie that had just opened starring a robot who was also the Redeemer, they traded theories about why Yoda talked so weirdly, and wondered whether Superman was stronger than Batman. Finally they pulled up in front of a line of terrace houses in a street in the outer boroughs. Arthur honked the horn twice, and within seconds a front door flew open.

His oldest son, Martin, had spent the last two hours sitting at the window waiting for them, dizzy with impatience and boredom. The panes had misted over with his breath, and he'd drawn faces with his finger, some solemn, some laughing, some with their mouths screaming wide. He had wiped the glass clean again and

3

again, watching his breath spread a fine haze back over it. The clock had ticked and ticked – what was taking them so long? A car, then another car, then yet another car, and still it wasn't them.

Then suddenly a car pulled up and honked twice.

Martin raced down the corridor, past the room into which his mother had retreated so as not to have to see Arthur. It was fourteen years since he had tiptoed swiftly out of her life, but it still tormented her that he could exist without needing her. Martin ran down the stairs and along the main hall, then straight across the street – so fast he didn't even see the speeding car coming at him. Brakes squealed inches away from him, but he was already in the passenger seat, hands clasped above his head, and only now did his heart let up for a moment.

'My God,' Arthur murmured.

The car that had almost killed Martin was a red VW Golf. The driver kept up a pointless honking, perhaps out of a feeling that such an incident couldn't go unremarked. Then he stepped on the accelerator and drove on.

'My God,' Arthur said again.

Martin rubbed his forehead.

'How can anyone be so dumb?' asked one of the twins from the backseat.

Martin felt as if his existence had split in two. He was sitting here, but he was also lying on the asphalt, crumpled and still. His fate seemed as yet undecided, both outcomes were still possible, and for a moment he too had a twin – one there outside, slowly fading away.

'He could be dead,' the other twin said matter-of-factly.

Arthur nodded.

'But is that really true? If God still has a purpose for him? Whatever. In that case nothing can happen to him.'

'But God doesn't have to have a purpose for him. It's enough if

4

He knows. If God knows he's going to be run over, he'll be run over. If God knows nothing's going to happen to him, nothing will happen to him.'

'But that can't be right. That would mean it doesn't matter what anyone does. Daddy, where's the mistake?'

'There is no God,' said Arthur. 'That's the mistake.'

Everyone went quiet, then Arthur started the engine and drove off. Martin felt his heartbeat slow. Another couple of minutes and he'd be able to be certain that he was still alive.

'And school?' asked Arthur. 'How's it going?'

Martin looked sideways at his father. Arthur had put on a little weight and his shock of hair, which still had no grey in it, looked, as always, as if it had never been combed. 'Maths is hard, I'm not sure I'm going to pass. French is still a problem. But not English any more, thank goodness.' He spoke fast, so as to get out as many words as he could before Arthur lost interest. 'I'm good at German, we've got a new physics teacher, chemistry is the same as usual, but during experiments . . .'

'Ivan,' asked Arthur, 'have we got the tickets?'

'In your pocket,' one of the twins answered, so now at least Martin knew which one of them was Ivan and which one was Eric.

He eyed them in the rearview mirror. As always, something in their absolute identicalness struck him as false, exaggerated, even unnatural. And this was some years before they started dressing identically too. This phase, in which they liked people to be unable to tell them apart, would only end when they turned eighteen, a short interval during which not even they themselves were entirely sure which of them was which. Thereafter they would repeatedly be overcome by a feeling that they'd each lost themselves at some point and were now leading the other's life, just as Martin from now on would never be able to rid himself entirely of the suspicion that he had died that afternoon on the street.

5

'Stop staring like a moron,' said Eric.

Martin turned around and made a grab for Eric's ear. He almost succeeded, but his brother ducked, seized his arm, and twisted it upward with a jerk. He screamed.

Eric let go and announced cheerfully, 'Now he's crying.'

'Pig,' said Martin shakily. 'Stupid pig.'

'You're right,' said Ivan. 'Now he's crying.'

'Pig.'

'Pig yourself.'

'You're the pig.'

'No, you are.'

At that point they ran out of things to say. Martin stared out of the window until he was sure that his tears would stop. The shop windows that lined the street gave back the reflection of the car as it passed: first shrunken, then elongated, then bent into a half-moon.

'How's your mother?' asked Arthur.

Martin hesitated. What was he supposed to say? Arthur had asked this same question right at the beginning, seven years ago, the first time they met. His father had seemed enormously tall, but also weary and somewhat absent, as if enveloped in a fine mist. He had felt shy in front of this man, but also, in some way that he didn't quite understand, a kind of pity.

'How's your mother?' the stranger had asked, and Martin had wondered if this really was the man he had encountered so often in his dreams, always in the same black raincoat, always faceless. But it was only that day in the ice cream parlour, as he dug around in his fruit sundae with chocolate sauce, that Martin had realized just how much he enjoyed not having a father. No shining example, no predecessor, and no burden, just a vague image of someone who might show up one day. And now this was him? His teeth weren't exactly straight, his hair was all over the place, there was a stain on his collar, and his hands looked weathered. He was a man who could have been any other man, a man who looked just like any other man on the street, on the train, anywhere.

'Just how old are you now?'

Martin had swallowed and then said, 'Seven.'

'And this is your doll?'

It took Martin a moment to realize that his father was asking about Miss Miller. He had brought her with him, as he always did; he was holding her under his arm without even thinking about it.

'So what's she called?'

Martin told him.

'Funny name.'

Martin didn't know how to reply. Miss Miller had always been Miss Miller, that was simply her name. He realized his nose was running. He looked around, but Mama was nowhere to be seen. She had left the ice cream parlour silently as soon as Arthur came in.

No matter how often Martin thought back to that day, and no matter how much he tried to summon up that conversation from the shadows of his memory, he always failed. The reason was that he had imagined it too often before it took place, and the things they actually said to each other soon merged into the things he'd imagined so often over the years. Had Arthur really said that he didn't have a job and was dedicating himself to thinking about life, or was it just that later, when Martin knew more about his father, he simply attributed this answer to him as the only one that seemed to fit? And could it be that Arthur's answer to the question of why he had walked out on him and his mother, was that anyone who gave himself over to captivity and the restricted life, to mediocrity and despair, would be incapable of helping any other human being because he would be beyond help himself, succumbing to cancer, heart disease, his life cut short, rot invading his still-breathing body? It was totally plausible that Arthur would give such an answer to a seven-year-old, but Martin didn't really think it likely that he would have felt confident enough to ask the question in the first place.

It was three months before his father appeared again. This time he picked Martin up from home in a car with two eerily similar boys in the backseat; at first Martin thought they must be an optical illusion. In turn, the pair had looked at him with great but rapidly diminishing curiosity; they were totally focused on themselves, ensnared in the riddle of their doubleness.

'We always think exactly the same thing.'

'Even when it's complicated stuff. Exactly the same thing.'

'When someone asks us a question, we both come up with the same answer.'

'Even when it's the wrong one.'

Then they both laughed exactly the same laugh, and a shiver ran down Martin's spine.

From then on, his father and his brothers picked him up regularly. They went on roller coasters, they went to aquariums with fish that were half asleep, they took walks through the woods on the edge of town, they went swimming in pools smelling of chlorine and full of screaming children and sunlight. Arthur was always credited with making an effort, but he was never fully focused on what he was doing, and even the twins made little effort to disguise the fact that they were along for the ride because they had no choice. Although this was totally clear to Martin, these were the happiest afternoons of his life. On the most recent visit, Arthur had given him a brightly coloured cube, with sides you could twist in all directions, a new toy that had just come onto the market. Soon Martin was spending hours with it, he could have spent entire days, he was totally in thrall.

'Martin!'

He turned around again.

8

'Are you asleep?'

He wondered about trying to grab him again, but then decided it was better to leave things be. What was the point – Eric was stronger than he was.

Pity, thought Eric. He would like to have given Martin a whack on the ear, although he didn't really have anything against him. It just made him mad that his brother was so helpless, so quiet and timid. Besides which he still blamed him for the moment seven years ago when their parents had called them into the living room one evening to tell them something important.

'Are you splitting up?' Ivan had asked.

Their parents, shocked, had shaken their heads and said, 'No, no, absolutely not, no,' and Arthur had told them about Martin's existence.

Eric was so astonished that he immediately decided to behave as if this were a big joke, but even as he tried to draw breath and laugh, Ivan, who was sitting right next to him, started to snigger, which was the way things were if you were yourself and simultaneously one half of a pair, and no thought was ever yours exclusively.

'It's not a joke,' said Arthur.

But why not until now, was what Eric wanted to ask. Except that once again Ivan had already got out ahead of him: 'Why not until now?'

Things were sometimes complicated, was Arthur's answer.

He had cast a helpless look at their mother, but she had sat there with her arms crossed and said that even grown-ups were not always that smart.

The other boy's mother, according to Arthur, always bad-mouthed him and didn't want him to see his son, and he went along with that all too easily, if the truth be known, because it made things easier, and it was only recently that he'd changed his mind. And now he was off to meet Martin.

Eric had never seen their father nervous before. Who needed this Martin person, he thought, and how could Arthur have done anything so stupid to them?

Eric had known quite early on that he wanted to be different from his father. He wanted to make money, he wanted to be taken seriously, he didn't want to be the kind of person that people secretly pitied. Which was why on the first day in his new school, he had attacked the biggest boy in his class, without any warning, of course, so surprise had given him the necessary advantage. Eric had knocked him to the ground, then knelt on him, grabbed him by the ears, and banged his head into the floor three times until he felt his resistance give way. Then, just for effect, he had landed a well-aimed blow on his nose, because a nosebleed always made a big impression. And the big boy, for whom Eric was already feeling sorry, had burst into tears. Eric had let him get up, and the boy had groped and sniffled his way away with a reddening handkerchief pressed to his face. Since then Eric had been an object of fear for the rest of his class, and nobody noticed how anxious he was himself.

For it all came down to determination, he knew that already. Whether it was the teachers, or other pupils, or even his parents, they were all divided within themselves, all torn, all halfhearted. None of them could stand up against someone who had a goal and really went after it. That was as sure as sure could be, as sure as five times two equals ten, or that we're all surrounded by ghosts whose shapes are visible only occasionally in the twilight.

'I've made a wrong turn,' said Arthur.

'Not again,' said Eric.

'It's just a trick,' said Ivan. 'Because you don't want to go.'

'Of course I don't want to go. But it's not a trick.'

Arthur steered to the kerb and got out. Warm summer air streamed into the car, other cars raced past, and there was a smell of petrol. On the street he asked people for directions; an old lady waved him off, a boy on roller skates didn't even stop, a man wearing a large hat pointed left then right, up and down. For a while Arthur spoke to a young woman. She tilted her head, Arthur smiled, she pointed somewhere, Arthur nodded and said something, she laughed, then she said something while he laughed, then they said goodbye, and as she moved past him she touched his shoulder. He got back into the car, still smiling.

'Did she explain it to you?' asked Ivan.

'She wasn't from around here. But the man before her knew the answer.'

He made a couple of turns, then they were at the entrance to a parking garage. Eric stared anxiously into the darkness. He would never be able to tell anyone how much he hated every tunnel, every cavernous opening, every closed space. But apparently Ivan knew it anyway, just as it always happened to Eric too that he found himself thinking his twin brother's thoughts instead of his own, and words surfaced in his mind that he didn't know. It also happened frequently that when he woke up, he remembered strangely Technicolor dreams – Ivan's dreams were brighter than his own, somehow more all-encompassing, and the air in them seemed fresher. And yet they could still hide things from each other. Eric had never understood why Ivan was afraid of dogs when dogs really were among the most harmless of creatures; he didn't understand why Ivan liked talking to blondes more than brunettes, and it was a mystery to him why the old paintings that just bored him in museums awakened such complicated feelings in his brother.

They got out. Long fluorescent bulbs gave off a wan light. Eric crossed his arms and stared at the ground.

'You don't believe in hypnosis?' asked Ivan.

'I believe people can persuade each other of anything,' said Arthur.

They got into the elevator, the doors closed, and Eric fought to control his panic. What if the cable broke? Such a thing had happened before, it would happen again, so why not here? The elevator finally stopped, the doors opened, and they walked towards the theatre. *The Great Lindemann*, it said on a banner. *Master of Hypnosis. Afternoon Performance.* There was a poster showing an unprepossessing man with glasses, obviously trying to look forbidding and penetrating at the same time. There were shadows across his face, the lighting was theatrical, it was a terrible photo. *Lindemann*, it said to one side, *will teach you to fear your dreams.*

A young man yawned as he checked their tickets. They had good seats, close to the front, in the third row. The stalls were almost full, but there was no one up in any of the circles. Ivan looked up at the heavily decorated ceiling and wondered how anyone could paint that. The artist had used skilled trompe l'œil effects to conjure up a nonexistent barrel vault. How did you draw this when you wanted to show that there really was both no second space there and simply the illusion of one? There was nothing about it in any book.

No one to help you. No book, no teacher. You had to figure out everything important for yourself, and if you didn't, you had failed your life's purpose. Ivan often wondered how people with no particular gifts put up with their existence. He saw that his mother wished some other life for herself and that his father was always somewhere else in his thoughts. He saw that his schoolteachers were sad little souls, and naturally he knew about the apparitions that tormented Eric. Whenever he got caught up in one of Eric's dreams, he found himself in a dark, sticky place where no one would want to be. He also saw Martin, who was too weak and spent too much time alone with his mother. Ivan sighed. Hypnotism didn't interest him, he'd rather have been at home again, so that he could draw. Just keep drawing until you finally get better at it, that was all that counted, it was the only thing he wanted.

The light dimmed and the murmur of conversation died away. The curtain opened. Lindemann was standing on the stage.

He was plump and had a bald spot that was made all the more noticeable by the few sparse hairs combed over the nakedness of his skull, and he was wearing black horn-rimmed glasses. His suit was grey, and there was a little green handkerchief in the breast pocket. Without preamble, without so much as a bow, he softly began to speak.

Hypnosis, he said, was not the same as sleep, but rather a state of inner wakefulness, not submission, but self-empowerment. The audience would witness astonishing things today, but nobody need have cause for concern, for nobody could knowingly be hypnotized against their will, and nobody could be made to perform some act that in the depths of their soul they were not ready to perform. He then paused for a moment, and smiled as if he'd just delivered some rather abstruse joke.

A narrow set of steps led down from the stage into the audience. Lindemann descended them, touched his glasses, looked around, and walked up the centre aisle. Obviously he was now deciding which people to take back up onto the stage. Ivan, Eric and Martin lowered their heads.

'Don't worry,' said Arthur. 'He only takes grown-ups.'

'So maybe it'll be you.'

'It doesn't work on me.'

They were about to see something big, said Lindemann. Anyone who didn't want to participate mustn't worry, he wouldn't come too close, the person would be excused. He reached the last row, ran back surprisingly nimbly, and jumped up onto the stage. For starters, he said, something light, just a joke, a little something. Everyone in the first row, please come up here!

A murmur ran through the theatre.

Yes, said Lindemann, the first row. All of you. Please be quick!

'What does he do if someone says no?' whispered Martin. 'If someone just stays in his seat, then what?'

Everyone in the first row stood up. They whispered to one another and looked around unwillingly, but they obeyed and climbed up onto the stage.

'Stand in a line,' Lindemann ordered. 'And hold hands.'

Hesitantly, they did so.

No one was to let go of anyone else, said Lindemann as he walked along the line, no one would want to, so no one would do it, and because no one would want to, no one would be able to, and because no one would be able to, it wouldn't be wrong to declare that everyone was literally sticking to one another. As he was talking, he reached out here and there to touch people's hands. Tight, he said, hold hands tight, really tight, nobody step out of the line, nobody let go, really tight, indissoluble. Anyone who wanted to should try and see what happened now.

Nobody let go. Lindemann turned to the audience, and there was some timid applause. Ivan leaned forward to get a better look at the people onstage. They looked uncertain, absentminded, somehow frozen. A little man was clenching his jaws, the hands of a lady with hair pulled into a bun were shaking, as if she wanted to tear free but was finding that her neighbour's grip, just like her own, was too strong.

He would count to three, said Lindemann, then everyone's hands would let go. 'So one. And two. And . . . ,' he slowly lifted his hand. 'Three!' and snapped his fingers.

Uncertainly, almost unwillingly, they let go, looking at their hands in embarrassment.

'Now go sit down again quick,' said Lindemann. 'Down. Quick. Quick.' He clapped his hands.

The woman with the bun was pale and swayed as she walked. Lindemann took her gently by the elbow, led her to the steps, and spoke to her quietly. When he let go, she was more sure-footed, went down the steps, and reached her seat.

That had been a little experiment, said Lindemann, an opening trick. Now for something serious. He went to the front of the stage, took off his glasses, and squinted with his eyes scrunched up. 'The gentleman in front over there in the pullover and the gentleman right behind him, and you, young lady, please come up.'

Smiling awkwardly, the trio climbed onto the stage. The woman waved at someone, Lindemann shook his head in reproof, and she stopped. He positioned himself next to the first of them, a tall, heavyset man with a beard, and held his hand in front of the man's eyes. He spoke into his ear for a while, then suddenly called, 'Sleep!' The man fell over, Lindemann caught him and laid him down on the floor. Then he stepped over to the woman next to him and the same thing happened. And then again with the other man. They all lay there motionless.

'And now be happy!'

He must explain, he said. Lindemann turned towards the audience, removed his horn-rims, pulled the green handkerchief out of his breast pocket, and began to polish them. They were all only too familiar, were they not, with the stupid suggestions that mediocre hypnotists – pretentious and untalented incompetents of the sort you encounter by the dozen in any profession – love to instil in their guinea pigs: freezing cold or boiling heat, bodily stiffness, sensations of flying or falling, not to mention the universally beloved forgetting of your own name. He paused and stared thoughtfully into the air. It was hot in here, wasn't it? Terribly hot. So what could be going on? He mopped his brow. Such idiocies were familiar to everyone and he would skip them without further ado. My God, wasn't it hot!

Ivan pushed his wet hair back off his forehead. The heat seemed to be rising off the floor in waves, the air was damp. Eric's face

15

was all shiny too. Programmes were flapping the air all over the audience.

But something could surely be done to fix it, said Lindemann. Not to worry, the theatre had capable technicians. Someone would turn on the excellent air-conditioning at any moment. In fact, it had already been done. Up here you could already hear the humming of the machinery. You could feel the rush of air. He turned up his collar. But now it really was blowing terribly. The equipment was astonishingly powerful. He blew on his hands and shifted from foot to foot. It was cold in here, very cold, really very, very cold indeed.

'What's going on?' said Arthur.

'Haven't you noticed?' whispered Ivan. His breath was rising in clouds, his feet had turned numb, and he was having trouble inhaling. Martin's teeth were chattering. Eric sneezed.

'No,' said Arthur.

'Nothing?'

'I told you, it doesn't work on me.'

But that was not enough, said Lindemann. Over. The end. As he'd already said, he didn't want to waste anyone's time with such tricks. Now he was going to get to something interesting without any further delay, namely, the direct manipulation of the powers of the mind. The lady and the gentleman here on the floor had already been following his instructions for some time. They were happy. Right here and now, in full view of everyone, they were experiencing the happiest moments of their lives. 'Sit up!'

Awkwardly, they hauled themselves up into a sitting position.

'Now look,' said Lindemann to the woman in the middle.

She opened her eyes. Her bosom rose and fell. There was something unusual about the way she was breathing and the way her eyes moved. Ivan didn't really understand it, but he recognized something large and complex. He noticed a woman in the row in front of him turning her eyes away from the stage. The man next to her shook his head indignantly.

'Eyes closed,' said Lindemann.

The eyes of the woman on the stage closed immediately. Her mouth was open, a thin stream of saliva was running out of it, and her cheeks shone in the spotlights.

Alas, said Lindemann, nothing lasted for ever, and the best things always ended first. Life could seem immense and miraculous now, but the truth was that nothing lasted, everything rotted away, everything died, without exception. One almost always repressed that fact. But not now, no, not at this particular moment. 'Now you know it.'

The bearded man groaned. The woman slowly sank backward and held her hands over her eyes. The other man sobbed quietly.

But, said Lindemann, one could still feel cheerful. Life being a short day between two endlessly long nights, one should enjoy the bright moments even more and dance for as long as the sun still shone. He clapped his hands.

Obediently this trio stood up. Lindemann clapped the beat, slowly at first, then faster. They leapt like marionettes, throwing their limbs this way and that, and spun their heads. There was absolute silence, no one coughed, no one cleared their throat, the audience seemed transfixed by horror. The only sound was the stamping and panting coming from the stage, and the creaking of the boards.

'Now lie down again,' said Lindemann. 'And dream!'

Two of them immediately sank to the floor, while the man furthest to the left still remained standing, and seemed to grope with his hands – but then his knees also buckled, and he stopped moving. Lindemann bent down and looked at him closely. Then he turned to face the audience.

He said he now wanted to conduct a difficult experiment. Only

17

a handful of practitioners could pull it off, it required the highest skills. 'Dream deeply. Deeply, deeper than ever. Dream a new life. Be children, learn, grow up, fight, suffer, and hope, win and lose, love and lose again, grow old, grow weak, grow frail, and then die, it all goes so fast, and when I tell you, open your eyes and none of it will have happened.'

He folded his hands and stood there silent for a long moment.

This experiment, he finally said, didn't always work. Certain subjects woke up and had experienced nothing. Others, by contrast, begged him to erase their memories of the dream because the experience was too disturbing, in order to regain the ability to trust both time and reality. He checked the time. But meantime, in order to occupy themselves while they were waiting, a couple of simple things perhaps? Any children in the audience? He went up on tiptoe. That boy there in the fifth row, the little girl on the end, and this boy in the third row, the one who's the spitting image of the boy right next to him. Come up!

Ivan looked to the right, then the left, and behind him. Then he pointed to himself questioningly.

'Yes,' said Lindemann. 'You.'

'But you said he only calls grown-ups onto the stage,' whispered Ivan.

'Well, I was wrong.'

Ivan felt the blood rush into his face. His heart pounded. The other two children were already on their way to the stage. Lindemann fixed him with his eyes.

'Just stay where you are,' said Arthur. 'He can't order you around.'

Ivan slowly got to his feet. He looked around. Everyone was looking at him, everyone in the auditorium, every single person in the entire theatre. No, Arthur was wrong, there was no way to refuse, it was, after all, a hypno-show, and whoever had come had to take part. He heard Arthur say something else, but he didn't understand it, his heart was thumping too loudly, and he was already starting towards the stage. He pushed past the knees of the people in the seats and went up the centre aisle.

How bright it was up here. The spotlights were unexpectedly powerful and the people in the audience mere outlines. The three grown-ups were lying motionless, no sign of life, no sign of breath. Ivan looked out into the stalls but couldn't locate Arthur or his brothers. Lindemann was already right there in front of him, down on one knee, pushing him back a step very carefully, as if he were a fragile piece of furniture, and looking into his face.

'We're going to do it,' he said softly.

Up close, Lindemann looked older. There were furrows around his mouth and eyes, and his makeup was sloppy. Anyone painting his portrait would have had to concentrate on the eyes, deep-set and hooded behind the horn-rims: restless, unreadable eyes, giving the lie to the cliché that hypnotists stared so intensely that a subject would lose himself in their gaze. In addition, he smelled of peppermint.

'What's your name?' he asked in a slightly louder voice.

Ivan swallowed and told him.

'Relax, Ivan,' said Lindemann, his voice now loud enough to carry to the people in the front few rows. 'Fold your hands, Ivan. Clasp your fingers.'

Ivan did so, wondering how anyone was supposed to relax on a stage in front of so many people. Lindemann couldn't mean it seriously; he was just saying it to confuse him.

'That's right.' Lindemann was now addressing all three children, loud enough to be heard anywhere in the theatre. 'Absolutely quiet, absolutely relaxed, but you can no longer separate your hands. They're stuck to each other, you can't do it.'

But it wasn't true! Ivan could easily have separated his hands, he felt no resistance and no blockage. But he didn't feel like blaming Lindemann. He just wanted it to be over.

Lindemann talked and talked. The word *relax* kept being repeated, and he kept saying something about listening and obeying. Maybe it was working with the other two, but it was having no effect on Ivan. He felt no different from before, there was absolutely no question of a trance. It was just that his nose itched. And he needed to go to the toilet.

'Try,' said Lindemann to the boy next to Ivan. 'You can't let go, you can't, try, you won't be able to.'

Ivan heard a deep rumbling noise; it took him a few moments to realize that it was laughter. The audience was laughing at them. But not at me, thought Ivan, he must have noticed that it's not working on me, that's why he's not asking me questions.

'Lift your right foot,' said Lindemann. 'All three of you. Now.'

Ivan saw the other two lift their feet. He could feel all eyes on him. He was sweating. So what could he do? He lifted his foot. Now they'd all think he was hypnotized.

'Forget your name,' said Lindemann to him.

He could feel the anger rising in him. It was all becoming truly stupid. If the man asked him again, he'd show him up in front of everyone.

'Say it!'

Ivan cleared his throat.

'You can't, you've forgotten it, you can't. What's your name?'

The problem was the situation, it was so horribly bright and also really hard to stand on one leg in front of all those people, it took all your concentration to keep your balance. It wasn't his memory that was letting him down, it was his voice. It stuck in his throat and wouldn't come out. Whatever anyone asked him now, he'd have to stay silent.

'How old are you?'

'Thirteen,' he heard himself say. So by sheer will he could do it.

'What's your mother's name?'

'Katharina.'

'Your father?'

'Arthur.'

'Is that the gentleman down there?'

'Yes.'

'And what's your name?'

He said nothing.

'You don't know it?'

Of course he knew it. He could feel the contours of his name; he knew where it was in his memory; he felt it, but it seemed to him that the person this name belonged to was not the person Lindemann was asking, so none of this really hung together, and it was completely irrelevant when set against the fact that he was on one leg on a stage with an itchy nose, his hands squeezed together, and he needed to go to the toilet. And then the name came back to him again, Ivan of course, Ivan, he drew breath and opened his mouth . . .

'And you?' Lindemann asked the boy next to him. 'Do you know your name?'

Now I've got it, Ivan wanted to shout, now I can say it! But he stayed silent, it was a relief that the whole thing was no longer about him. He heard Lindemann ask the other two something, he heard them answer, he heard the audience laugh and clap. He felt drops of sweat running down his forehead, but he couldn't wipe them away, it would have been embarrassing to move his hands now when they all thought he was in a trance.

'It's already over,' said Lindemann. 'Not so bad, was it? Separate your hands, stand on both legs, you know your names again. It's over. Wake up. It's over.'

Ivan lowered his foot. Of course it was easy, he could have done it the whole time.

'It's okay,' said Lindemann softly, putting a hand on his shoulder. 'It's over.'

Ivan went down the steps behind the other two. He would have liked to ask them what it had been like for them, what they'd seen and thought, how it felt to be genuinely hypnotized. But he was already back in the third row, people made room for him, he pushed past their knees, and dropped into his seat. He let out a breath.

'How was it?' whispered Martin.

Ivan shrugged.

'Do you remember, or have you forgotten it all?'

Ivan wanted to answer that of course he hadn't forgotten anything and that the whole thing had been a silly trick, but then he realized that the people in the rows in front of them had turned around. They weren't looking at the stage, they were looking at him. He glanced around. The whole theatre was looking at him. Lindemann had lied. It wasn't over.

'Is that him?' asked Lindemann.

Ivan stared up at the stage.

'Your father. Is that him?'

Ivan looked at Arthur, looked at Lindemann, looked back at Arthur. Then he nodded.

'Would you like to join me, Arthur?'

Arthur shook his head.

'You think you don't want to. But you do. Believe me.'

Arthur laughed.

'It doesn't hurt, it isn't dangerous, you might even like it. Give us the pleasure.'

Arthur shook his head.

'Not at all curious?'

'It doesn't work on me,' called Arthur.

'Perhaps not. Maybe that's right, it can happen. All the more reason for you to come up here.'

'Take someone else.'

'But I want you.'

'Why?'

'Because that's what I want. Because you believe you don't want to.'

Arthur shook his head.

'Come!'

'Go on,' whispered Eric.

'They're all looking at us,' whispered Ivan.

'So what?' said Arthur. 'Let them look. Why do children find everything embarrassing?'

'Let's all say it together!' called Lindemann. 'Send him up here to me, show him, clap if you think he should come. Clap loud!'

Wild applause erupted, with stamping of feet and calling, as if nothing were more important to everyone than getting Lindemann's wish granted, as if none of them could imagine anything more satisfying than seeing Arthur up on stage. The noise achieved a crescendo as more and more voices joined in: people were clapping and yelling. Arthur didn't budge.

'Please!' cried Eric.

'Please go,' said Martin. 'Please!'

'Only for you,' said Arthur, and got to his feet. He worked his way through the howling crowd to the centre aisle, walked to the steps, and climbed them. Lindemann made a rapid gesture and the racket ceased.

'You're going to have bad luck with me,' said Arthur.

'Possibly.'

'It really doesn't work.'

'That nice boy. That was your son?'

'I'm sorry. I'm the wrong person. You want someone who feels awkward at first, and then chats with you and tells you things about himself, so that you can turn him into a joke and make everyone laugh. Why don't we skip all that? You can't hypnotize me. I know how it works. A little pressure, a little curiosity, the need to belong, the fear of doing something wrong. But not with me.'

Lindemann said nothing. The lenses of his glasses glinted under the spotlights.

'Can they hear us?' Arthur pointed to the three motionless bodies.

'They're busy with other things.'

'And that's what you'd like to do with me too? Give me another life?'

Ivan wondered how his father was managing to let them all understand every word he said. He had no microphone and he was speaking softly, yet he was completely audible. He stood there calmly as if he were alone with the hypnotist and allowed to ask whatever he wanted. Nor did he seem to be absentminded anymore. He seemed to be enjoying himself.

Lindemann, on the contrary, looked unsure of himself for the first time. He was still smiling, but frown lines had appeared on his forehead. Gingerly he took off his glasses, put them on again, took them off once more, folded them up, and pushed them into his breast pocket behind the green handkerchief. He raised his right hand and held it over Arthur's forehead.

'Look at my hand.'

Arthur smiled.

The sound of giggling spread through the audience. Lindemann grimaced for a moment. 'Look at my hand, look at it, look at my hand. Just my hand, nothing else, just at my hand.'

'I don't notice anything.'

'Nor should you.' Lindemann sounded agitated. 'Just look! Look at my hand, my hand, nothing else.'

'You're focusing my consciousness on itself, aren't you? That's

24

the trick. My attention is focused on my own attention. A slip-knot, and suddenly, it's impossible . . .'

'Are those your sons down there?'

'Yes.'

'What are their names?'

'Ivan, Eric and Martin.'

'Ivan and Eric?'

'The Knights of the Round Table.'

'Tell us about yourself.'

Arthur said nothing.

'Tell us about yourself,' Lindemann said again. 'We're all friends here.'

'There's not much to say.'

'What a pity. How sad, if true.'

Lindemann lowered his hand, bent forward, and looked at Arthur in the face. Everything was very quiet, the only sound was a faint hiss, perhaps from the air-conditioning, perhaps from the electrical current to the spotlights. Lindemann took a step back, a board creaked, one of the sleeping bodies groaned.

'What do you do for a living?'

Arthur said nothing.

'Or don't you have a job?'

'I write.'

'Books?'

'If what I write got printed, they'd be books.'

'Rejections?'

'A few.'

'That's bad.'

'No, it doesn't matter.'

'It doesn't bother you at all?'

'I'm not that ambitious.'

'Really?'

Arthur said nothing.

'You don't look as if you'd settle for a little. You might want to believe that of yourself, but actually you don't. What do you really want? We're all friends here. What do you want?'

'To get away.'

'From here?'

'From everywhere.'

'From home?'

'From everywhere.'

'It doesn't sound as if you're happy.'

'Who's happy?'

'Please answer.'

'No.'

'Not happy?'

'No.'

'Say that again.'

'I'm not happy.'

'Why do you stick it out?'

'What else is there to do?'

'Run?'

'You can't just keep running.'

'Why not?'

Arthur didn't reply.

'And your children? Do you love them?'

'You have to.'

'Right. You have to. All of them equally?'

'Ivan more.'

'Why?'

'He's more like me.'

'And your wife? We're all friends here.'

'She likes me.'

'That wasn't the question.'

'She earns money for us, she takes care of everything, where would I be without her?'

'Free perhaps?'

Arthur said nothing.

'What do you think of me? You didn't want to come up onto the stage, and now you're standing here. You thought it wouldn't work on you. What do you think now? For example, of me?'

'A little man. Insecure about everything, which is why you are what you are. Because without all this here, you'd be nothing. Because you stutter whenever you're not up here.'

Lindemann was silent for a while, as if giving the audience the chance to laugh, but there wasn't a sound. His face looked white and waxy; Arthur stood very straight, his arms by his sides, stock-still.

'And your work? Your writing? Arthur, what is it with all that?'

'Not important.'

'Why not?'

'A hobby. No reason to fuss about it.'

'It doesn't bother you that your work doesn't get published?'

'No.'

'That you aren't any good? It doesn't bother you?'

Arthur took a small step back.

'You think you have no ambition? But maybe it would be better if you did, Arthur. Maybe ambition would be an improvement, maybe you should be good, maybe you should admit to yourself that you want to be good, maybe you should make the effort, maybe you should work at it, maybe you should change your life. Change everything. Change everything, Arthur. What do you think?'

Arthur said nothing.

Lindemann moved even closer to him, went up on tiptoe and

put his face close to Arthur's. 'This superiority. Why make the effort, is what you've always thought, isn't it? But now? Now that your youth is over, now that everything you do carries weight, now that there's no time to be casual any more, what now? Life is over very quickly, Arthur. And it gets squandered even more quickly. What needs to happen? Where do you want to go?'

'Away.'

'From here?'

'From everywhere.'

'Then listen to me.' Lindemann put a hand on Arthur's shoulder. 'This is an order, and you're going to follow it because you want to follow it, and you want to because I'm ordering you, and I'm ordering you because you want me to give the order. Starting today, you're going to make an effort. No matter what it costs. Repeat!'

'No matter what it costs.'

'Starting today.'

'Starting today,' said Arthur. 'No matter what it costs.'

'With everything you've got.'

'No matter what it costs.'

'And what just happened here shouldn't bother you. You can think back on it quite cheerfully. Repeat.'

'Cheerfully.'

'And it really isn't important. It's all a game, Arthur, just fun. A way to pass the time on an afternoon. Just like your writing. Like everything people do. I'm going to clap my hands three times, then you can go and sit down.'

Lindemann clapped his hands: once, twice, three times. There was no sign of any change in Arthur. He stood just as he had before, back straight, his neck tilted slightly backward. There wasn't a sound to be heard. Hesitantly, he turned around and went down the steps. Gradually timid applause broke out here and there, but once Arthur had reached his seat, it crescendoed into a thunder. Lindemann bowed and pointed to Arthur. Arthur imitated him with an empty smile and bowed back.

That was what was so wonderful about his métier, said Lindemann when the noise had finally died down. One never knew what the day would bring, one could never foresee the demands that would be made on one. But now finally for the high point, the star turn. With a light touch on her cheek he woke the sleeping woman and asked what she had experienced.

She sat up, but after a few sentences the excitement took her breath away. She panted, sobbed, gasped for air. In tears, she described a life as a farmer's wife in the Caucasus, and a hard childhood in the winter cold, she spoke about her brothers and sisters, her father and mother, her husband, the animals and the snow.

'Can we go?' whispered Ivan.

'Yes, please,' said Eric.

'Why?'

'Please,' said Martin. 'Please, let's go! Please.'

As they stood up, there was the sound of snickering in the audience. Eric clenched his fists and said to himself that he was only imagining it, while Martin understood for the very first time that people could be mean-spirited and spiteful, taking malicious pleasure in things for no reason at all. They could also be spontaneously good, friendly and supportive, and both these qualities could exist simultaneously in the same person. But above all, people were dangerous. This realization would stay with him permanently, bound up for ever with a memory of Lindemann's face looking down from the stage at their departure, as he polished his glasses with the green handkerchief. At the very moment Martin, bringing up the rear, was leaving the theatre, he caught Lindemann's expression: eyebrows arched, smiling, wet tongue peeping from a corner of his mouth. Then there was a little click and the door closed behind him.

The whole way home, Arthur beat time on the steering wheel and whistled. Martin sat very straight next to him, while Ivan stared out of one window and Eric out of the other. Twice Arthur asked what on earth had upset them, why they'd wanted to leave, and why in the world children found everything so embarrassing, but when no one replied, he just said there were some things he'd never understand. That woman, he cried, that idiotic story about the Russian farm, all laid on far too thick, obviously she worked in cahoots with the hypnotist, childishly easy to see through, who would believe stuff like that! He turned on the radio, then turned it off again, then on again, and then, not very long afterwards, off again.

'Did you know,' he asked, 'that the condor flies higher than any other birds?'

'No,' said Eric. 'I didn't know.'

'So high that sometimes it's no longer visible from the ground. As high as a plane. Sometimes so high, that the distance above it is shorter than the distance below.'

'What's that supposed to mean?' asked Ivan. 'Above it to where?'

'You know, above it!' Arthur rubbed his forehead. For a few seconds he steered with his eyes closed.

'I don't understand,' said Martin.

'What's there to understand? I'd rather you tell me about school and how it's going, you never say anything.'

'Everything's fine,' said Martin quietly.

'No problems, no difficulties?'

'No.'

Arthur played with the radio again. 'So!' he cried. 'Out!'

Martin, Eric and Ivan looked at one another in surprise. Only now did they realize that they were in front of Martin's house.

Martin got out.

'Us too?' asked Ivan.

'Of course.'

The twins got out rather hesitantly; only Arthur remained sitting where he was. Eric looked down at his shoes. An ant was following a crack in the asphalt, and a grey beetle was crossing its path. Tread on the beetle, said a voice in his head, tread on it, quick – tread on the beetle and then maybe everything will still be all right. He lifted his foot, but then set it down again and spared the beetle's life.

Arthur wound down the car window. 'All my sons.' He laughed, wound the window back up, and put his foot on the accelerator.

The three of them watched the car drive off, getting smaller until it disappeared around the corner. For a while, nobody said anything.

'How do we get out of here?' Ivan asked finally.

'Five streets over there's a bus,' said Martin. 'After seven stops you change to another bus, then it's three stops, then you can switch to the subway.'

'Can we come in with you?' asked Eric.

Martin shook his head.

'Why not?'

'Mama's a bit funny about that sort of thing.'

'We're your brothers.'

'Exactly.'

But when they rang the doorbell anyway, Martin's mother came to grips with the situation surprisingly quickly. It was unbelievable, she kept saying, impossible to take in, like two peas in a pod. She gave the twins Coca-Cola and a plateful of sugary gummy bears, which they ate so as not to be rude, and of course she allowed Ivan to use the phone to call home.

After that they went to Martin's room and he got out the little air gun that Arthur had given him just a few months before and that he kept well hidden from his mother. The three of them positioned themselves at the window and took turns aiming at the tree that was slowly disappearing in the darkness on the edge of the street. Eric scored twice on the trunk and twice just leaves, Ivan hit the trunk twice but no leaves. Martin hit one leaf but not the trunk, and gradually they began to feel that they were related, and realized what it meant to be brothers.

And a car was already pulling up with a sharp honking of its horn to summon Eric and Ivan down the stairs and into the street. When their mother asked them what had happened and where their father was, they didn't know how to answer her. It wasn't until a telegram arrived from Arthur shortly after midnight that she got the two of them out of bed and made them tell her all about it.

Arthur had taken his passport and all the money in their joint account. There were only two sentences in the telegram: First, he was fine, no need for concern. Second, they shouldn't wait for him, he wouldn't be coming back for a long time. And in fact none of his sons set eyes on him again until they were grown up. But the following years did see the publication of the books that made Arthur Friedland's name famous.

The Lives of the Saints

The Lives of the Saints

I confess. I hear their voices, but see nothing because the sun coming through the windows is blinding. The altar boy next to me yawns. *That I have sinned through my own fault.* Now I have to yawn too, but I suppress it and clench my jaw so hard that tears form in my eyes.

In my thoughts and in my words, in what I have done, and what I have failed to do.

In a moment the light will fall at a deeper slant, and with it a little group of people emerges from the sea of shadows: the five old women who always come, the friendly fat man, the sad young woman and the fanatic. His name is Adrian Schlueter. He often sends me handwritten letters on expensive paper. He's obviously not yet heard of emails.

Forgive us our sins, and bring us to everlasting life. I can't get used to having to get up so early. The organ starts with a drone. *We worship You, we give You thanks.* I miss most of the notes, but that's a given in my profession, almost all priests sing badly. *We praise You for Your glory.* The organ falls silent. While we've been singing, the sun has risen higher, multicolours flicker brilliantly in the windows, thin blades of light flash through the air, each bearing a tiny blizzard of dust. It's so early still, and yet so hot. Summer is at its

35

merciless height. *With the Holy Spirit, in the glory of God the Father.* The yawning altar boy lays the missal on the lectern. If it were up to me, the poor boy would still be in bed. It's Friday, I don't have to give a sermon, so now I say: *The Word of the Lord.* The congregation sits, and Martha Frummel comes to the front, seventy-eight years old, she does the morning reading every second day.

First Epistle of the Apostle Paul to the Corinthians. *When I came to you, brothers, proclaiming the mystery of God, I did not come with sublimity of words or of wisdom.* Martha Frummel is a gentle, good woman, perhaps even one of the Just of the World, but she has a voice like a barrel organ. *For I resolved to know nothing while I was with you except Jesus Christ, and Him crucified. I came to you in weakness and fear and much trembling, and my message and my proclamation were not with persuasive words of wisdom, but with a demonstration of spirit and power, so that your faith might rest not on human wisdom but on the power of God.*

The Word of the Lord, I say again. Martha wobbles back to her seat. My congregation stands and sings: *Hallelujah! Hallelujah! Hallelujah! Hallelujah!* The sun is no longer dazzling, you can recognize the clumsy pictures in the stained glass: the Lamb, the Redeemer with his staring eyes and the loaf of bread in the cross of rays of light. This church is the same age as I am, the walls intentionally crooked, the altar a raw block of granite that for some reason is not at the east end but the west, so that at Early Mass the sun does not blind the congregation, as is the tradition, but me.

The Gospels. *As they were proceeding on their journey someone said to him, 'I will follow you wherever you go.'* My voice doesn't sound bad; I'm good at my job. *Jesus answered him, 'Foxes have dens and birds of the sky have nests, but the Son of Man has nowhere to rest his head.' And to another he said, 'Follow me.' But he replied, 'Lord, let me go first and bury my father.' But he answered him, 'Let the dead*

36

bury their dead. But you, go and proclaim the kingdom of God.' And another said, 'I will follow you, Lord, but first let me say farewell to my family at home.' To him Jesus said, 'No one who sets a hand to the plough and looks to what was left behind is fit for the kingdom of God.' I close the book. How appropriate, but it's a total accident, it's the prescribed passage for 8 August 2008.

And now the Profession of Faith. I clear my throat and declare what I wish I could believe. *God, the Father, the Almighty, Jesus Christ, the Only Son of God, crucified, died and buried; on the third day rose again, ascended into heaven; will come again in glory to judge the living and the dead. The Holy Spirit, the resurrection, the life of the world to come.* Yes, I wish I did.

The Prayers of Intercession. *We pray for the Dominicans, that they may diligently do God's work, for today is the Day of Saint Dominic. Hear us, we beg you. We pray for all those who search for the truth, hear us, we pray for all those who are sick, and for all who have strayed from the certainty of faith.* In our seminar for the study of the liturgy, we once discussed what sense it was supposed to make to beg an omniscient Being to grant a wish. Father Pfaffenbichel explained to us that the intercession itself was not important, it could always be omitted. But he didn't know my congregation. Two weeks minus Prayers of Intercession last year and they were already thinking God had forgotten them. Nine emails of complaint to me and unfortunately also three to the bishop and one official resignation from the church. I had to send Frau Koppel a box of chocolates and pay her two home visits to make her change her mind.

The Eucharist. The altar boy pours water over my fingers, the organ sounds the hymn, I lift the chalice with the Host. It is a moment of drama and power. You could almost think these people actually believe that a wafer is transubstantiated into the body of a crucified man. But of course they don't. You can't believe any such

37

thing, you'd have to be deranged. But you can believe that the priest believes it, and the priest in turn believes his congregation believes it; you can repeat it mechanically, and you can forbid yourself to think about it. *Holy, holy, holy*, I chant, and actually feel surrounded by a force field. Magical gestures, thousands of years old, older than Christianity, older than steel and fire. The first humans were already fantasizing about gods being torn limb from limb. Then later the legend of Orpheus, torn apart by the Maenads, then the tale of Osiris descended into the kingdom of darkness and emerging again reassembled as a living body, only eons later came the figure of the Nazarene. An ancient, blood-soaked dream, repeated day after day in countless places. It would be so easy to declare the whole procedure of transubstantiation to be mere symbolism, but that precisely is what constitutes heresy. You have to believe it, for so it is written. And you can't believe it. You must, you can't. *Lift up your hearts*, I say. *We lift them up to the Lord*, they say. *Dying you destroyed our death, rising you restored our life. Lord Jesus, come in glory.* The altar boy rings the little bell, its sound trembles in the air, the pews creak as my congregation goes down on its knees.

I lift up the Host. It is so quiet that you can hear the cars outside. I lay the wafers down again and perform the ritual genuflection. I immediately start to sweat, it's hard for me to keep my balance, I fell while I was doing it last week, it was dreadfully embarrassing. Hold on, Martin, keep your back straight, hold on! Shakily, dripping with sweat, I get back on my feet. *Let us pray with confidence to the Father*, I pant, *in the words our Saviour gave us.*

Our Father, hallowed be, Thy Kingdom, Thy will, our trespasses, phrases polished by a thousand years of repetition, *deliver us, amen.* I break the Host, push a piece into my mouth, and savour the dry, salty taste for a moment. It's not exactly God's body, but it tastes good. The organ begins the Agnus Dei, the five members of my congregation present themselves for communion. I'm afraid of the old people, who want the transubstantiated wafer laid on their tongues, the way it was always done before Vatican II; it's hard to lay something on a tongue without touching it with your fingertips. But I'm in luck today, three pairs of hands and only one wrinkled ancient tongue. The last one, as always, is Adrian Schlueter.

The body of Christ, I say.

Amen, he says, not looking at the Host as he does so, but straight at me, unblinking, as if he had to prove something to me. He will come back, this evening, early tomorrow, tomorrow evening, every day, he is my trial.

The organ ascends to the final chords and stops. I begin the concluding rite. *Bow your heads and pray for God's blessing.*

Go in the peace of Christ.

Thanks be to God.

I hurry to get to the exit first and position myself in the incoming blast of hot morning air. Martha Frummel's hand feels like sandpaper, and Frau Wiegner is all hunched over, her heart isn't good and nor is her back. Frau Koppel looks well, but as lonely as ever. Frau Helgner won't be back as often, she's very weak. Who does this to people? I'd really like to hug them, but I'm fat and I sweat, and they wouldn't like it. So I just shake hands and smile. They're gone already, only one person is still standing here.

'Dear Herr Schlueter, I'm afraid I'm in rather a hurry.'

'A question of belief, Father Friedland, it won't leave me in peace.'

I try to look at him as if I'm interested.

'The Trinity. I've read Tertullian. And Rahner. And His Holiness Ratzinger, of course. But I don't understand.'

'What don't you understand?'

'The Holy Ghost.'

39

I look at him despairingly.

'I understand the Son, I understand the Father, I also under-stand the difference between the Holy Ghost and the Son. But what is the difference between the Holy Ghost and the Father? Barth says God is the subject, the Spirit is the content, and the Son is the act of revelation.'

'It's a Mystery.'

It works. He blinks. Where would I be without that word?

'It was revealed to us!' I hesitate. 'Revealed' or 'made manifest'? I'd better check that one out soon.

'God has said to us that it is so. We can try to penetrate it by using our reason, but reason has its boundaries. And where we reach those boundaries is where we encounter belief.'

'I don't have to understand it?'

'You don't need to.'

'I shouldn't even try?'

'You mustn't.'

His hand is soft and dry, his handshake isn't even unpleasant. I've got away with it for today. He goes off and I head for the sacristy in relief.

The altar boy helps me to take off the chasuble. As soon as I'm standing there in my shirt, my eyes avoid my reflection in the mir-ror. All the same, it's not so bad: Chesterton, that great Catholic, was well nourished too, and I imagine even Thomas Aquinas as having been round and wise.

Compared with them, I can almost get by as being lean. I sit down on the couch. My Rubik's Cube is sitting on the arm; as always I'm happy to see it, and my hands reach for it of their own volition. The altar boy asked me recently what it was and why anyone needed one. *Sic transit gloria.* Twenty years ago it was the most famous object in the world.

'Do you have to get to school now?' I ask the boy.

He nods, and out of sheer sympathy I lean forward and pat his head. He flinches and I immediately take my hand away. How stupid of me. A priest must be careful these days, there are no such things as harmless gestures any more.

'I have a question,' he says. 'Last week in our religion lesson. It was about God's foreknowledge. How He knows what we're going to decide, even before we decide it. How can we still be free?'

The gauze curtains belly, flecks of light dance across the parquet floor. The cross on top of the cupboard throws a long shadow.

'It's a Mystery.'

'But . . .'

'Mystery means that it was reveal . . . I mean made manifest to us. God knows what you're going to do. But you are still free. That's why you're responsible for your actions.'

'That doesn't go together.'

'That's why it's a Mystery.'

'But if God knows what I'm going to do, I can't do anything else. So how am I responsible?'

'It's a Mystery.'

'What does that mean?'

'Don't you have to get to school?'

'Excuse me.' The acolyte is standing in the doorway: a Cistercian lay brother named Franz Eugen Legner. He has small eyes and is always badly shaved. He's been working for two months; before that he was buried somewhere deep in the Alps. He keeps the church clean, updates our website, plays the organ, and, I can't rid myself of the suspicion, reports on me to the bishop. I'm waiting for him to make a mistake so that I can lodge a complaint about him myself – a tactical preemptive strike. But unfortunately he doesn't make mistakes. He's very careful.

'You know what you did yesterday,' he says to the boy.

'So what did I do?'

'Never mind. You know. You remember.'

'Yes.'

'And yet you were free. You know, and still you could have behaved differently.'

'Because that was yesterday!'

'But for God,' says Legner in his soft, hoarse voice, 'there is no today and there is no yesterday. No now, no before, and no hundred years from now. He knows just as clearly what you're going to do as you know what you did yesterday.'

'I don't understand.'

'And you don't have to,' I say. 'It's a Mystery.'

Against my will, I'm impressed. Sixteen semesters, two of them at the Gregoriana in Rome, and I still wouldn't have come up with that.

Legner looks at me as if he's read my thoughts. Triumphantly he bares his teeth. In spite of it all, I pity him. Poor, desiccated schemer, where has all your cunning got you?

The boy picks up his school backpack and is already out the door. Seconds later I see him shuffle past the window and down the street. I close my eyes and quickly mix up the colours on the cube. Then I open them again and start to reorder the colours.

'The stops are whistling,' says Legner. He doesn't look at my hands, because if he did, he'd have to be impressed, and he's not going to cede his ground. 'On the organ. We should arrange for them to be repaired.'

'Perhaps the Lord can perform a miracle.' Why in the world did I say that? It wasn't even funny. The red side is now all completed.

He glowers at me.

'Just a joke,' I say wearily.

'He could do it,' says Legner.

'I'm sure.' Now the yellow side is done too.

He says nothing, I say nothing.

'But He won't,' I say. Now the white.

'It's not impossible.'

'No, not impossible.'

We're both silent.

'He could,' says Legner.

'But He won't.'

'You never know.'

'No,' I say, and put down the cube, which is now fully re-arranged. 'You never know.'

I had often stood in front of the mirror coolly but angrily reassuring myself that I didn't look bad. My face was symmetrical and well proportioned, my skin was okay, my body big enough, my chest and chin substantial, my eyes not too small, and I was also lean. So what was it?

Today I think it was all accidental. There is no such thing as fate, and for example, if I'd asked Lisa Anderson on another day, or at least asked her differently, everything might have turned out another way, and now I'd have a family maybe and I'd be a TV editor or a meteorologist.

Lisa was in my class and she sat diagonally in front of me. When she wore something with short sleeves I saw her freckles, and when the sun came through the window the light played on her smooth brown hair. It took me five days to come up with the right words.

'Shall we go to the theatre? *Who's Afraid of Virginia Woolf?*'

'Who's . . . what?'

Not that I would have enjoyed going to the theatre. I found it boring, it was always stuffy, and it was hard to understand the people on the stage. But someone had told me that Lisa liked it.

'That's the name of the play.'

She gave me a friendly look. I hadn't stuttered, and as far as I could tell, I hadn't blushed.

'What play?'

'In . . . the theatre.'

'What kind of play is it?'

'When we see it, we'll know.'

She laughed. Things were going well. I was relieved, and laughed too.

She turned serious.

Granted, something with my laugh hadn't been quite right: a little too loud and too high, I was nervous. I quickly tried to correct it and laugh the proper way, but I'd suddenly forgotten what that was supposed to be. When I realized how weird I sounded, I blushed after all: my skin tingled and went hot. In order to get past the moment, I laughed again, but this time it sounded even worse, and I suddenly saw myself standing in front of Lisa and staring at her and still laughing and watching myself standing in front of her staring and laughing. My skin burned red.

'Today's no good, unfortunately,' said Lisa.

'But you just – '

Unfortunately, she said. It had just occurred to her. No time.

'Pity,' I said hoarsely. 'And tomorrow?'

She paused for a second. Then: Unfortunately, she said, tomorrow was no good either.

'The day after tomorrow?'

Unfortunately she really had a lot on in the coming weeks.

After that I hardly even dared to look at her from behind. But I couldn't stop her from continuing to appear in my dreams. In them she was adorable, willing, and she hung on my every word. Sometimes we were alone in a wood, then again we were lying in a meadow, and sometimes we were in a room, so dimly lit that I could barely make out the curve of her shoulders, the outlines of her hips, and the soft sweep of her hair. When I then woke up, still riddled with lust and already tormented by shame, I couldn't come to grips with the fact that I could even have thought any such thing was happening in real life.

A few months later at a party, I fell into conversation with Hanna Larisch, who was in our parallel class. I had already drunk a second bottle of beer, the air seemed to be turning as soft as velvet, and suddenly we were talking about the cube. She had one too, everyone had one back then, but like almost all of them, she had only ever managed to sort out one side.

It was quite easy, I explained, it's best to begin with the white layer, then you make a T on each of the four side layers, then you permutate the corners, for which there are several alternatives: like this, and this, and this, I demonstrated the hand movements. The trick, I said, is to decide quickly how to rotate the corners, there's no formula for that, it's just practice and intuition.

She listened. The cube was at the peak of its popularity at that time, experts discussed it on TV, and magazines had articles about the people who won championships. My voice didn't even catch when I brushed her shoulder apparently absentmindedly; and when I took a step closer to be able to hear her better, because the music was so loud, she stroked her hair back and looked at me attentively. Yes, I suddenly thought, this is how it can go, this is how you do it. I took another bottle, it was easy to talk. And that was my bad luck. I talked and talked. I talked about how hard it was at the end to rotate the corners. I talked about having a shot at the state championships if I practised enough and maybe the national championships weren't totally out of reach. I could feel that time was passing and something was going to have to happen soon, and to hide how nervous I was, I kept on talking.

She stroked her hair back, looked at the floor, looked at me again, and now there was something stiff about the way she moved. This made me anxious so I talked more quickly. She stroked her hair again, but she didn't say anything. And I talked. I was waiting for some instinct to tell me what to do next, but this instinct was struck dumb. How did other people know how to behave, where was it written, how did you learn it? I looked at my watch to be sure that we still had time, but she misunderstood my glance and said she had to be getting home too. 'Already?' I cried, and 'No!' and 'Not now!' but then I couldn't think of anything else. We were both silent as the music blasted. Drunken fellow pupils were dancing beside us, their bodies squeezed against one another in the haze of cigarette smoke; over by the window two of them were kissing. Hanna hesitated and then left.

'Was it awful?' my mother asked. She was still awake. She usually was if I came home late. She sat in the kitchen and stirred lemon juice into a cup of tea.

'Was what?'

'I don't know, but I can tell from looking at you that it was awful.'

She set down the spoon next to the cup as though it were liable to break. 'There are some things you have to keep trying. Again and again. No matter how often they defeat you. You think it just happens to you, but it happens to everyone. It's absurd to keep on going regardless, but that's what you do – you keep on going.'

'What are you talking about?' I asked coldly.

She was silent for a moment. 'The championships. It'll happen. You mustn't let yourself get discouraged.'

Although she really wasn't old yet, her hair was already turning grey. She was a little plump, and she often smiled in an absent-minded, sad sort of way. At this moment, in the kitchen, after midnight, I thought a number of things all at once: I thought that of course she was right, and I thought that I couldn't talk about any of it with her, and I thought that in earlier times I would have been able to stay at home and live with her, freed from having to compete, safe from want, wrapped in her care, without anyone thinking it in any way peculiar. Only in the age of psychologists had this become frowned upon.

I fetched a cup for myself. In the room next door, where the record player was kept, piano music was playing softly. I poured myself some tea. Did everyone have to go out into the world? Could I really not live here, in this house, in this kitchen?

She shook her head, as if she'd read my mind. 'Don't give up,' she said. 'That's the whole trick.'

'But why not?'

She said nothing. I took my cup and went to bed.

On the other hand, a few months later I found myself in Sabine Wegner's apartment. We were alone, her family had gone out, we wanted to work on our Latin. Sabine was fat. She was a sweet girl, clever and warmhearted, but everything about her was fat: her face, her calves, her body, her hands. And I, who had no idea yet what I myself would look like one day, looked down on her just as mockingly as everyone else. Her whole appearance said that she wasn't a part of the game. She didn't come into it.

We sat at the dining-room table and deciphered Tacitus. Sabine drank peppermint tea, I drank apple juice. Finally we got to the end and I stood up.

'But the news is about to come on,' she said.

We sat down on the sofa. Gorbachev and Reagan shook hands, Honecker yowled into a microphone, Tom Cruise sat in a cockpit, a woman stood in front of a bluish background and announced rain, and then the ads were already starting: a housewife waved a cloth and told a proud man with a tie and a briefcase that things had never been cleaner. Then I put my hand on Sabine's neck.

In that first moment I thought it was some mistake. Why was I doing this, what was I thinking?

She sat there rigid. Out of the corner of my eye I could see that she didn't even turn her head. Take your hand away, I thought, there's still time. I leaned towards her. There was a roaring in my ears and my heart was thumping.

But she's so fat, I thought.

And I thought: But she's a girl.

Then she turned her head. Her eyes were strangely clouded. The large shadow made by her body. The sweetish smell of her perfume. My hand on her soft neck.

I felt dizzy. Really, I thought, she's not that fat. And her face, so close it was distorted, wasn't ugly. I saw that one of her eyelashes had fallen out and was lying on her cheekbone. I saw a little scratch on her temple. I saw that a tiny vein divided in the white of her right eye, and I saw the pores in her skin.

Her lips felt like cotton wool as she put them against mine. Uncertainly I put my hand on her hip and pressed down. Sabine pulled back, looked me in the face, wiped the back of her hand across her mouth, and came back to me. We kissed a second time, her mouth opened a little, and I felt a small living thing that was her tongue. Her breasts rose and fell, my heart pounded, I couldn't draw breath, but it seemed to be okay without oxygen. After a while she pulled her head back. I inhaled. She fumbled with my belt.

I stood up and let her pull down my trousers. Then she took hold of my underpants, pulled, and was looking at my nakedness. The opening credits for some crime series were blaring from the TV. I looked at her breasts. They were round, and large and full under her blouse. I reached for them, she leaned forward to meet me. The door opened and in came her father, followed by her mother and her sister, followed by a dachshund, followed by my mother.

Nobody said a word. In silence they watched as I pulled up my underpants and my trousers and buckled my belt. The dog grunted, lay down on the carpet, stuck its legs in the air, and waited for someone to scratch it. Getting dressed took longer than usual because of my trembling hands. The roaring in my ears was even louder than before, and the floor seemed to be a long way away. The dog heaved a pleading sigh, in vain. On TV a policeman with a moustache said something about ordering an arrest and the police force in Duisburg. I crossed the room, which seemed to be wobbling, picked up my Latin textbook, my notebook, dictionary and fountain pen from the dining-room table, and went to the door. Sabine's parents stepped aside to make room. Her sister giggled. My mother walked out ahead of me.

We went down the stairs.

'They were waiting for the bus,' she said. 'I happened to drive by, and offered to bring them home. Then I thought I'd take you home.' She paused for a few seconds. 'I'm sorry.'

She unlocked the car door and I got into the passenger seat. She carefully adjusted the rearview mirror and started the engine.

'I didn't think . . .' she said. 'I mean. Because Sabine. I wouldn't have imagined . . . ! She's not exactly . . . I mean, I wouldn't have just . . .'

I said nothing.

'When I got to know your father . . .'

I waited. She never talked about Arthur. But either she realized it wasn't the right moment, or she suddenly didn't want to divulge whatever it was, in any case she didn't finish the sentence. She didn't say another word before we got home.

Just give up – what was so bad about that? The thought was large and seductive. I came in second in the state championships, I qualified for the national championships, but I also knew along the way that the cube would never turn into a career. Against all my hopes, no government agency was interested in the services of cube experts, nor were the big firms looking for them, and even the creators of computer programmes and games favoured people with qualifications in maths or business.

But I liked being in darkened spaces, I liked listening to

49

Monteverdi, and I liked the smell of incense. I liked the windows in old churches, I liked the network of shadows in Gothic vaulting, I liked the depictions of Christ Pantocrator, the Saviour swathed in gold as ruler of the world, I liked medieval woodcuts, I also liked the sweet gentle humanity of Raphael's Madonnas. I was impressed by Augustine's *Confessions*, I felt instructed by St Thomas's exercises in hairsplitting, I was drawn to humanity in general, and I really had no desire to sit out my days in an office. Besides which I had no talent for self-abuse. There had been a time when I did it regularly, filled with anger and disgust and convinced I was committing an aesthetic transgression, a sin against beauty rather than against any moral code. I saw myself as if at a distance: a red-faced young man, already a little plump, laying hands on himself frantically, eyes almost closed, and so I soon cured myself of it. It's not something to admit in this age of psychologists, but the cube was actually more fun.

I'd get the thing with God worked out too. Or so I thought. It really couldn't be that hard. All it required was a little effort.

Secretly I expected it all to happen at my baptism. But when the moment arrived, the church was in the middle of being renovated: the walls were almost hidden behind steel girders, plastic sheeting hung in front of the altar, and unfortunately the organ was also out of action. The water felt like water, the baptismal priest looked like an obstinate muddle-head, and standing next to my mother with her sad smile, my brother Ivan was obviously trying not to laugh.

And yet I was confident that faith would arrive of its own accord. So many intelligent people were believers. You just had to read more, attend Mass more often, pray more. You had to practise. As soon as I believed in God, everything would fall into place, and my life would belatedly become my destiny.

*

I celebrated my twenty-first birthday with my fellow students Finckenstein and Kalm in a smoke-filled college bar.

'Augustine is a shrunken Aristotelian,' said Finckenstein. 'He's stuck in substance ontology, that's why he's been superseded!'

'Aristotle has never been superseded,' replied Kalm. 'He's the very essence of reason.'

You only ever have conversations like this when you're a student. Finckenstein wore thick glasses, had very red cheeks, and was as meek as a child. Kalm was a sweet-natured fanatic, Thomist, and clever champion of the Inquisition. On the weekends he competed in rowing events, he was interested in model trains, and had – and this made him an object of secret envy among his colleagues – a girlfriend. In front of him lay Arthur Friedland's book *My Name Is No One*. I pretended not to notice, and no one mentioned it. There was also nothing unusual about this, it was absolutely everywhere this year.

'Augustine's theory of time goes back much further than the Aristotelian tradition,' I said. 'Everyone quotes his remark that we know what time is as long as we don't think about it. It's beautiful, but as a theory of knowledge, it's weak.'

'But the paradigm wasn't the theory of knowledge,' said Kalm. 'The paradigm was ontology.'

We fell silent in exhaustion. I put some money on the table and stood up.

'What's bothering you, Friedland?'

'The passage of the years. The loss of time, the proximity of death and hell. You wouldn't know, you're only twenty.'

'So does hell exist?' asked Finckenstein. 'What does ontology say?'

'It has to exist,' said Kalm. 'But it could be empty.'

'And what happens there? Fire that hurts but does not consume, like in Dante?'

'Dante isn't depicting hell,' said Kalm. 'Dante's depicting the truth of our existence. We really visit hell at night during those moments of truth we call nightmares. Whatever hell may be, sleep is the gateway through which it forces its entry. Everyone knows hell, because everyone is there every night. Eternal punishment is simply a dream from which there is no awakening.'

'Well then,' I said. 'I'm off to sleep.'

Outside the tram had already arrived. I got in and it departed immediately, as if it had been waiting for me. I sat down.

'Excuse me,' said a thin voice. A man in rags with a straggly beard and two overflowing plastic bags was crouching in front of me. 'Will you give?'

'Sorry?'

'Money,' he said. 'As to the lowliest of my brothers. So to me, said the Lord.'

He held out a chapped palm. Naturally I reached into my jacket pocket, but at that same moment he knelt, then lay down on his back.

Baffled, I leaned forward. He smiled and rolled slowly, almost pleasurably, to and fro – from his left shoulder over onto his right, and then back again. I looked around. There were only a handful of people in the car, and they were all staring somewhere else.

But it was my duty. Christianity demanded it. I stood up and bent over him.

'Do you need help?'

He put a hand around my ankle. His grip was astonishingly strong. The tram stopped, the doors opened, two women hastily got out, the car was now almost empty. He looked at me. His eyes were clear, sharp, and alert, not confused – more curious. A trickle of blood ran out of his nose and disappeared into the grey mat of his beard. The doors closed, the tram set off again. I tried to free my leg from his grip. But he didn't let go.

No other fellow traveller looked my way. We were in the second car, and the driver seemed impossibly far away. The man's free hand grabbed my other leg and hung on so tight that I could feel the fingernails. The tram stopped, the doors opened, more people got out, the tram waited for a few moments, then the doors closed, and on we went. I couldn't get away, the man was stronger than he looked. He bared his teeth, looked questioningly into my face, and closed his eyes. I yanked on my right foot, but I couldn't get free. He was breathing fast, and his beard quivered. He drew a sharp intake of breath, then spat. I felt something warm and soft run down my cheek. He hissed.

I kicked. He tried to straighten up, but I kicked again and he sank into the floor. My toes hurt. I grabbed one of the straps so as not to lose my balance and kicked a third time. One of his hands let go, but not the other one, a plastic bag fell over, and dozens of balls of paper rolled out: pages from newspapers, pages from books, pages from glossy magazines and advertising brochures. The other bag emitted a whimpering sound: something inside seemed to move. The tram stopped, the doors opened, I stepped on his wrist, he groaned, and then finally his left hand let go too. I leapt out and began to run.

I ran and ran. Only when I couldn't keep going did I stop, panting, and check my watch. Ten minutes after midnight. My birthday was over.

'It wasn't him,' said Ivan. 'Definitely not.'

'Who knows.'

'It was *not* the devil! Even if that would suit you. You people are always looking for something to reinforce your faith. But it wasn't him.'

We were sitting in the room that had once been Arthur's library. The spines of books marched across the walls in rows, and the peaceful sound of a lawn mower could be heard outdoors.

'Faith isn't that important,' I said.

'Oh.'

'The priest has the power to bind and to release. Regardless of what he himself thinks. He does not have to believe in the Sacrament for the Sacrament to exercise its power.'

'And you believe that?'

'I don't have to believe it, it's true regardless.'

Next year Ivan would be going to study at Oxford. Everyone knew that great things were in store for him, and nobody doubted that in ten years he'd be a famous painter. I had always felt insecure around him, always inferior, but Catholicism suddenly gave me a position, an attitude and an argument for everything.

Ivan was getting ready to answer when the door flew open and in he came for the second time. Although I was prepared for it, the magic trick worked, and it took me a moment to get a grip on it.

'Please do not ever put this book in front of me again.' Eric threw an edition of *My Name Is No One* onto the table. 'I won't read it.'

'But it's interesting,' said Ivan. 'I'd really like to know what you . . .'

'Not interesting to me. For all I care, he can die. I don't care what he writes.'

'Eric doesn't mean it that way,' said Ivan. 'It's just that he's theatrical sometimes.'

'And you?' Eric said to me. 'Are you serious about all that? Praying, church, the seminary? Are you really serious? We're Jews, you know, can you even do that?'

'We're not Jews,' said Ivan.

'But our grandfather – '

'All the same,' said Ivan. 'Unfortunately we're neither one thing nor the other. You know that.'

'And Martin's only doing it because he can't find a girlfriend.'

I concentrated on breathing in and out calmly. I absolutely must not blush.

'I'm appalled by the banality of your mind,' said Ivan. 'Martin is a serious person. I know it's impossible for you to imagine, but he has faith and he wants to serve. You'll never understand.'

Eric stared at me. 'Seriously? The virgin, water into wine, the Resurrection? Really?'

'It's a process.' I cleared my throat. 'In matters of faith one is always a traveller. One never . . .'

'You just don't want to work!'

I stood up. How did he always manage to make me furious so quickly? How did everything he said ring true, and yet ring true in such a fake way?

'Whenever all the praying gets to be too much for you, you'll come crawling,' said Eric. 'Then you'll beg me to give you a job.'

'And what will you do then? When I come crawling?'

'Then I'll give you a job, what else? You're my brother.' He laughed and went out without saying goodbye.

'He's been nervous lately,' said Ivan. 'He's not sleeping enough. Don't take him seriously.' He opened *My Name Is No One*, thumbed a few pages absentmindedly, and closed it again. 'I also believed once that I'd encountered the devil. It was in the department store, I was ten. There was a woman at a bargain counter, she didn't look in any way unusual, but I knew: if I stay here a few seconds longer, something dreadful is going to happen. Mama didn't find me until an hour later, I was hiding behind a fridge in the electronics department, she was out of her mind with worry. I still believe I did the right thing. If she'd seen me . . .' He looked thoughtfully out the window. A gardener was trimming the hedge outside, the shears glinted in the sunlight. 'But it's all crazy. I was ten.' He looked at the table-tennis table, then at me, as if he'd forgotten for a moment that I was there. 'And otherwise? Goals, plans? That's what birthdays are for. Resolutions?'

'I'm training for the championships.'

'The cube again?'

'The cube.'

'Good luck. But more important . . .'

'Yes?'

'Nothing.'

'Say it!'

'Well, somebody's got to. As long as there's time to do something to stop it. You should . . .'

'Yes?'

'Never mind.'

'Say it!'

'Go on a diet, my pious brother! There's still time, but later it'll just get harder. You really need to lose weight.'

Is *My Name Is No One* a merry experiment and thus the pure product of a playful spirit, or is it a malevolent attack on the soul of every person who reads it? No one knows for sure, maybe both are true.

The opening sets up an old-fashioned novella about a young man embarking on his life. All we know about his name is its first initial: F. The sentences are well constructed, the narrative has a powerful flow, the reader would be enjoying the text were it not for a persistent feeling of somehow being mocked. F is put to the test, he defends himself, fights, learns, wins, learns more, loses and develops as he moves on, all in the grand old manner. But there is a sense that no sentence means merely what it says, that the story is observing its own progress, and that in truth the protagonist is not the central figure: the central figure is the reader, who is all too complicit in the unfolding of events.

Slowly but surely the little discrepancies accumulate. F is home, looking out at the rain, puts on a jacket and cap, takes his umbrella, leaves the house, wanders through the streets, where it isn't raining, puts on a jacket and cap, takes his umbrella, and leaves the house, as if he hadn't just done that already. Shortly after that a distant relative appears, who has already been registered in a subordinate clause as having died ten years ago, an innocent visit to the fair by a grandfather and his grandson turns into a labyrinthine nightmare, and a piece of clumsiness on F's part with major consequences is wound backward until it clearly never happened. Of course this all leads to the construction of theories. Very slowly there comes a dawning sense of comprehension, then the realization of being on the brink, and then the story breaks off – just like that, without warning, right in the middle of a sentence.

The reader keeps trying to make sense of it all. Perhaps the hero died. Perhaps the inconsistencies are harbingers of the end, the first defective spots, so to speak, before the entire warp and woof unravels. For what, the author seems to be asking, is death, if not an abrupt break in the middle of a sentence which the reader cannot elide, a soundless apocalypse in which it isn't humanity that disappears from the world, but the world itself that disappears, an end of all things that has no end?

The second half is about something else. Namely that you, yes, you, and this is no rhetorical trope, you don't exist. You think you're reading this? Of course you do. But nobody's reading this.

The world is not the way it seems. There are no colours, there are wavelengths, there are no sounds, there are vibrations in the air, and actually there is no air, there are chains of atoms in space, and 'atoms' is just an expression for linkages of energy that lack either a form or a fixed location, and what is 'energy' anyway? A number that remains constant throughout all changes, an abstract sum that remains inalterable, not substance, not ratio: pure mathematics. The more attentively one looks, the emptier it all is, and the more unreal that emptiness is. For space itself is no more than a function, a model of our minds.

And the mind that creates these models? Don't forget: nobody inhabits the brain. No invisible being wafts through the nerve endings, peers through the eyes, listens from within the ears, and speaks through your mouth. The eyes are not windows. There are nerve impulses, but no one reads them, counts them, translates them, and ruminates about them. Hunt for as long as you want, there's nobody home. The world is contained within you, and you're not there. 'You', seen from inside, are cobbled together on a makeshift basis: a field of vision amounting to no more than a few millimetres, and already dissolving into nothing at the outer edges, containing blind spots, and filled with mere habit and a memory that retains very little, most of it invented. Consciousness is a mere flicker, a dream that nobody is dreaming.

There are fifty pages of this stuff, and it more or less works, you're more or less convinced. It's just that there's a creeping sort of feeling that this too is an ironic demonstration of – well, what? You're already on the final chapter. It's short and it's merciless, and there can be no doubt – it's all about Arthur himself.

F appears again and a human being is dismembered in the course of a few pages: gifted, gutless, vacillating, egocentric to the point of sheer meanness, self-loathing, already bored by love, incapable of engaging seriously with anything, using everything including art as a mere excuse for doing nothing, unwilling to take an interest in anyone else, incapable of taking responsibility, too cowardly, incapable of facing his own failures, a weak, dishonest, superfluous man, good for nothing except empty mind games, bogus art lacking all substance and the silent evasion of every unpleasant situation, a man who has finally reached the point of such aversion to his own self that he has to assert that there is no such thing as a self.

But even this third part is not as clear as it seems. Is this self-loathing really genuine? Given the representations above, there is no 'I', and this entire exploration of consciousness is meaningless. Which part supersedes which other part? The author gives no indication.

Ivan, Eric and I had each received a copy through the mail, wrapped in brown paper, minus dedication or sender's details. The book was not reviewed anywhere, and I didn't see it in any shop. It was an entire year before I saw it on the street. I was on my way home from school, and for a moment I thought what I was seeing was pure fantasy. But there it really was, in the hands of an old man on a bench who was holding it and smiling as he read it, obviously captivated by the question of the reality of his own existence. I bent over and looked at the plain blue cover, the man looked up uneasily, and I hurried away. Two weeks later I saw the book again, this time in the subway, a man with a leather briefcase and a raggedy hat was reading it. When I saw it again the next week, it was all over the newspapers, and the first people had already killed themselves over it.

It was a dreamy soul with metaphysical tendencies, a medical student in Minden, who having read it set up a lunatic experiment to test his own existence. No one understood the details, but it had something to do with the log he kept of his every flicker of aware-ness, with controlled needle jabs that he administered alternately to himself and to a pathetic guinea pig, and with the jump that he made, with absolute premeditation and equally absolute precise execution, from a railway bridge. In the following week a young woman jumped from the television tower in Munich clutching a copy of *My Name Is No One*, which unleashed yet another flood of newspaper articles, which in turn resulted in a greengrocer in Fulda taking poison along with his wife. Between the two corpses lay a copy of Arthur's book.

That marked the end of the wave of suicides, although the wave of articles, commentaries and rebuttals kept going, not least including the incident of the well-known radio talk-show host who voluntarily checked into a locked psychiatric ward after declaring on the air that he was convinced of his own nonexistence. Given that he wound up by reading out a rather long excerpt from *My Name Is No One*, this provoked a debate in parliamentary committee about whether the index of dangerous films, video games and books should not be administered more severely. This provoked mocking responses from several MPs, and a pronouncement from a bishop, which in turn engendered a further wave of commentary, in which there was much speculation about who this Arthur Friedland person was, who kept in the background, didn't defend his book, didn't step forward, and didn't allow himself to be photographed.

When the subject had been so exhaustively explored that there wasn't a human being in the country who wasn't bored by it, Arthur was famous. His second book, the novel *The Hour of the Hunter*, a superficially conventional thriller about a deeply melancholic detective who, despite his vast intelligence and desperate efforts, is unable to solve an apparently simple case, spent several weeks on the lower ranks of the best-seller lists.

Shortly thereafter, *The Mouth of the River* appeared, a novel about a man whose fate branches out again and again, depending on different decisions or the whims of Fortune. Each time the two alternatives are explored, the two paths that life can take from the same event. Death is an ever-more-frequent visitor, between a successful existence and its horrifying end, there is often no more than a moment of inattention or some tiny incident – more and more paths lead to sickness, accident and death, while very few lead to old age.

This book moved me in some extraordinary fashion, and it provokes my anxiety to this day. In part because it shows how immense the consequences of every decision and every move are – every second can bring destruction, and if you really think things through to their conclusion, how is it possible to live at all? But also in part because I could never rid myself of the suspicion that it had more to do with me than Arthur's other books did: with a summer afternoon long ago when I was almost killed by a car, now little more than a distant memory, a brief anecdote, at best an echo in a bad dream after a heavy dinner.

There is a creak of wood, a figure pushes its way in and goes down on its knees. I put the cube to one side. I just completed it in twenty-eight seconds; my best time is nineteen, but that was long ago.

'In the name of the Father, the Son and the Holy Ghost,' I say crossly.

'For ever and ever, amen,' a hoarse male voice responds.

'I'm listening.'

He's silent, breathing heavily, searching for words. I look at the cube again, but it's not okay, twisting the rows might make a noise and he'd notice it.

'Unchastity. I pleasure myself. I do it all the time.'

I sigh.

'Even just now. On the street. No one saw. I have a wife and a girlfriend. They both know about each other, but neither of them knows about my second girlfriend, although she knows about them. Then I have a third girlfriend that none of them knows about. And she doesn't know about any of them, she thinks I live alone.'

I rub my eyes. I'm tired, and it's so hot.

'Things went wrong when Klara made fun of my wife on Facebook. She didn't think of the fact that Pia's her friend and can read it.'

'Her friend?'

'Facebook friend. I told all of them that I'm stopping, things are going to be different now. But it's so hard! How do you do it? No woman ever! I get shaky after just two hours.'

'We're speaking about you.'

'And besides I've taken money.'

'Ah.'

'Not that much. A thousand euros. From the company cash register.'

'What is your profession?'

'I'm an accountant. My girlfriend works in my office.'

'Which one?'

'Which office?'

'Which girlfriend!'

'Well, Klara. The one my wife knows about.'

'Why an accountant?'

'Excuse me?'

'Why would anyone be an accountant? I've always wondered.'

He says nothing. But why can't I ask questions, where is it written that I'm not allowed to learn anything in the confessional?

'I like crossword puzzles,' he says. 'When everything is neatly filled in. All of it is right. I like that. You look at all the receipts, at first it's all pure chaos, but then you begin to fill in the answers. One thing here, another thing there, this space and that space, and at a certain point it all comes together. In life it's the only place you'll find order. Do you need an accountant?'

'No, no. Thank you.'

'The money wasn't from a client. You mustn't think that. It was from the office supply for petty expenses. A friend of mine has a furniture business, I told him I need to buy new swivel chairs, but you need to fill out the invoice a little higher, around three thousand euros, and then – '

'You just said one thousand!'

' – he delivered the chairs and I paid and we split the difference

62

between us. Unfortunately he then wanted to write off the money I got as a special expense on his tax return, and because he's our client, I had to tell him that this wasn't possible. I tried a couple of bookkeeping tricks – '

'Let's talk about the women.'

'It's terrible, Father! They keep calling.'

'Who?'

'All of them except my wife. She never calls. Why would she? And I visit one of them every day, I've got things well organized, but it takes too long, I still have to . . . just like before. How do you stand it, Father? I once managed for a whole week. I stayed at home, played with the children, and helped my wife in the kitchen. In the evenings we watched funny animals on YouTube. There are so many of them. Thousands. Thousands of funny animals.'

'What do they do?'

'Eat, roll around, make noises. On the third day I thought things weren't really so bad. On the fifth, I thought I'd have to kill myself. Then I went to her.'

'To which one?'

'I can't remember. Is it important?'

'No.'

'So what should I do?'

'Exactly that. Stay at home. Help with the cooking. Watch animal videos.'

'But that's terrible.'

'Of course it's terrible. That's life.'

'Why are you saying such a thing to me?'

'Because I'm not your therapist. Nor am I your friend. Look truth squarely in the face. You'll never be happy. But that's not important. You can live that way.' I wait for a moment, then make the sign of the cross. 'I absolve you of your sins. In the name of the

Father, the Son and the Holy Spirit. Be true to your wife for as long as you can. Try it for two weeks. Two weeks have to be possible. And give the money back. That is your penance.'

'How do I enter it on the books?'

'You'll find a way.'

'That's easy to say! How do you picture that? I can't just pay twelve thousand euros back to the office!'

'Twelve?'

'I'd rather stay at home for three weeks. Three, yes?'

'Give the money back!'

He's silent. 'The absolution still holds, yes? I mean, independent of the penance? It's not a . . . condition?'

'The Sacrament is fulfilled. But not paying the money back would be a new sin.'

'Then I'll come back.'

'It doesn't work that way!'

'Of course I could do it as a tax refund. But if there's an audit, what do I do? I can't re-credit it.'

He waits. I don't respond.

'Goodbye, Father.'

The wood creaks, his footsteps recede. I would have liked to get a look at his face, but the sanctity of the confessional forbids it, and I stick to the rules. The Protestants have a God who wants to know what's going on in your soul, but I'm a Catholic, and my God is only interested in what I actually do. I pick up the cube, and just as I'm wondering whether to use the classic approach or to start with a block of four, the wood creaks again.

'I drink.'

I put down the cube.

'I drink all the time. I can't stop.'

I envy alcoholics. People make movies about them, the best actors star in them, articles and novels get written about them. But people who eat a lot? Thin people say it's all a question of will-power, but maybe they're just thin because they're less hungry. Earlier, I bought two chocolate bars from the machine on the corner. Not to eat, just to have on hand. What a stupid idea.

'It's all I want any more. Just drink. My wife's left me, I lost my job, nothing matters. I just want to drink.'

'I can only absolve you if you sincerely want to change.'

My telephone vibrates. I fumble it out and see Eric's office number on the screen. That's odd, because Eric never calls me. But I can't answer it now.

'I don't know, I don't know, I don't know.'

'You don't know if you want to stop drinking?'

'I would love to not want to drink, but I want to drink.'

Is that a clever distinction or an absurdity? The telephone stops vibrating.

'Are you eating, Father?'

'No! Try not to drink for two days. That's a start. Then come back!'

'Two days? I can't.'

'Then I cannot absolve you.' The first bite was wonderful. The breaking chocolate, the fine prickling taste of the cocoa. But already you can taste that it's too fat and far too sweet. That's the way it is with most things, something Jesus overlooked. Buddha was more alert. Nothing is ever truly sufficient. Everything falls short, and yet you can't get free.

'You're eating!'

'Come back in two days.'

'Stop eating!'

'I'm not eating.'

'In the confessional!'

'In two days. If you haven't had a drink. Then you should come back.'

65

The wood creaks, he leaves. I crumple the empty foil and think about the second bar. It's still in my pocket, and that's where it will stay.

I pull it out of my pocket.

But I haven't unwrapped it. And even if it were already unwrapped, I wouldn't have bitten into it. Everything is within my power. The mystery that is free will: I can bite into it or I can leave it be. It's up to me. All I have to do for it not to happen is not to do it.

The second bar doesn't taste good. I chew quickly and angrily. The second one never tastes good. The telephone vibrates. Eric's office again. It must be important.

'I envy you,' said Ivan.

'That's going overboard.'

We were sitting on a bench in the covered walk of the Eisenbrunn monastery. Trees swayed in the soft wind, birds sang, cooking smells were coming from the kitchen, and now and then a monk in his habit went past, head bowed. You could think you were in a different century.

I was happy to see Ivan. After a week of gruelling spiritual exercises I was tired of the pious faces. My brother had surfaced unannounced, as was his way. The porter had wanted to shoo him off, but then finally let him in. Ivan was not someone it was easy to shoo.

'They even confiscated your cube?'

'Part of the exercises,' I said. I missed it to begin with, but in the meantime I had begun to wonder if what I had regarded as my favourite activity was merely an addiction.

'You met Lindemann?' I asked.

'It was totally unproductive. Not an interesting man.'

'But did he remember? Could he explain to you – '

'I told you, he's not interesting.'

'But – '

'Martin, there's nothing to tell! I wish I were like you. You know what you want. I'm not even suited to be an artist.'

'Rubbish.'

'It's not modesty, and it's not a crisis. I've realized I'm not cut out to be a painter.'

Three monks swathed in their habits came along the colonnade. The one on the left drank, the one in the middle watched sports programmes for hours every evening on the old black-and-white TV, the one on the right had recently been given a warning about his collection of pornographic videos. But to Ivan, who didn't know them, they must look like Illuminati.

'If need be, I can become a professor of art. Or a curator. If I kept on painting . . . I'd be average. At best, average. At best.'

'Would that be so terrible? Most people are average. By definition.'

'Exactly. But then think of Velázquez and the way he uses the white of the actual canvas as if it were a colour. Or of Rubens and his skin tones. Or of Pollock's sheer strength, his courage to paint like a lunatic. I can't do that. I can only be me. And it's not enough.'

'You're right,' I said thoughtfully. 'How can anyone live with the fact that they're not Rubens? How does anyone come to terms with it? To begin with, everyone thinks they're the exception to everything. But hardly anyone is an exception.'

'By definition.'

'Are you still looking for a topic for your dissertation?'

'Not a bad idea.' He scraped the toe of one shoe in the gravel, looked up, and smiled. 'Not a bad idea at all. We don't talk often enough. Have you received minor orders yet?'

'Not yet.'

'I mean it, I envy you. Leaving the world behind. Stepping away from it all. Simply no longer being part of it.'

'It would be nice.' Rays of sunshine came through the crowns of the tall trees, flecks of light danced on the pebbles. 'But one is always part of it. Just differently. There's no way out.'

'Pray for me.' Ivan stood up. 'I fly to England tomorrow, maybe we'll see each other at Christmas. Pray for me, Brother Martin. I am one of the people who need prayers.'

I looked after him. The gate to the monastery hummed as it opened. Things looked medieval here, but there was electric current everywhere, and security cameras, and more and more monks could be seen talking into tiny mobile phones. Here, as everywhere, the world was changing unavoidably. I slowly got to my feet. The bells would start ringing at any moment for evening services.

For the first two days I thought the boredom would kill me, but then it got better, and along the way I managed to kneel in church for hours and listen to the rise and fall of the Gregorian chants. And hunger no longer plagued me constantly, so I could forget the pain in my knees, look up at the high windows, and be convinced that I was where I ought to be according to fate and providence.

It was just that I didn't feel God.

I waited, prayed, waited and prayed. But I did not feel Him.

I got along well with the other seminarians. One of them was called Arthur like my father and could do all kinds of card tricks I'd never seen before. Another was called Paul and had had conversations with the Virgin Mary. He asserted that she'd worn a raincoat and an odd hat, but there was no doubt that it had been the Holy Virgin. One of them was named Lothar and wept so noisily every night that we could hardly sleep, and even my old friend Kalm was here, surrounded by the gentle radiance of his own piety.

'I wish I were like you,' said Kalm at supper. There were mashed potatoes with fish. The potatoes were tasteless and the fish over-cooked, but I still would have liked more.

'Nonsense.'

'You'll be able to help people. You'll go far. To Rome. And who knows how high you'll go.'

After supper, we reassembled in the chapel. We knelt, the monks sang, their voices flowed together into a single resounding voice, and the candles filled the nave of the church with dancing shadows.

I demand it, I said. I've earned it. Give me a sign.

Nothing happened.

I stood up. Curious glances were cast at me, but nobody got involved. After all, these were spiritual exercises, some people had visions, others heard voices, it was expected, part and parcel of the whole thing.

Now, I said. Now would be the moment. Speak to me the way you spoke to Moses out of the burning bush, to Saul on the road to Damascus, to Daniel in front of the king of Babylon, to Joshua when he stopped the sun in its course, to the Apostles of the risen Christ, so that they could spread the truth. The world has barely aged a single day since then, the same sun moves through the heavens, and just as they stood before you, I am standing before you now and I ask for a word.

Nothing happened.

It really isn't my fault, I said. I'm trying. I look up and You're not there, I look around and You're not there, I don't see You, I don't hear You. Just one little sign. No one else would have to see it. I wouldn't make it all into a big fuss, no one would find out about it. Or better still, don't give a sign, just let me believe. That would be enough. Who needs signs? Let me believe, then it'll all happen without anything having to happen at all.

I waited and looked into the flickering candlelight. Had it

happened? Perhaps I already believed without knowing it. Did you have to be aware of your own belief? I listened to myself.

But nothing had changed. I was standing in front of an altar in a stone building on a small planet that was one of a hundred billion billion. Galaxies expanding unbearably whirled in black nothingness, shot through with radiance, as space itself slowly dissolved into cold. I knelt again on the flat, friendly prayer cushion and folded my hands.

The next morning I was summoned to see the abbot. Fat, intelligent and intimidating, Father Freudenthal sat at his desk in the purple robes of the Augustinian canons. He waved at me to come in, and worriedly I sat down.

It had not passed unnoticed, he said softly, yesterday at evening prayers.

'I'm sorry.'

Young people such as myself were rare. Such enthusiasm. Such seriousness of mind.

I realized that I was smiling modestly. A hypocrite, I thought in amazement. I had never intended it or practised, but clearly I was a hypocrite!

Sometimes we think, said Father Freudenthal, that such young men don't exist any more. But they do! He was very moved.

I nodded my head.

'A request.' He opened the drawer and took out a copy of *My Name Is No One*. 'Our monastery library collects signed copies. Could you ask your father to inscribe this one?'

Hesitantly I reached out and took the book. Arthur never signed them, nobody knew what his signature looked like.

'That's no problem,' I said slowly. 'I'm sure he'll be glad to.'

I've been waiting for forty-five minutes. I have no idea why I'm here, but the air-conditioning is working, so I'm not complaining.

The heat presses against the windows, the outside air is saturated with sunlight; involuntarily I wonder if the panes are going to hold. I take sips of coffee from my paper cup. In front of me there's an empty glass plate; I ate the cookies that were on it long ago. Nobody refills it.

Office noises echo from the next room: voices, phones ringing, the humming of printers and Xerox machines. A secretary is sitting at a desk. Her skirt is very short, and I can see her legs quite clearly: tanned, muscular, smooth-skinned and supple. When her eyes meet mine, she might as well be looking at a table, or a refrigerator or a pile of boxes. I'm glad of my priest's clothes. If I were in street clothes, a look like that would be unbearable.

I concentrate on the cube. I have to get better at using the Petrus method. Competition is fierce, the young people are fast, and the conventional way is too slow for the world championships. Recently cubes in many competitions have started being smeared with Vaseline, to speed up the twisting. When I first started and the cube was new, the routine was to begin with one layer, which got completed, broken up, and then restored, but that's no good any more. Today two layers get worked on simultaneously, then the rest gets constructed from there, without ever having to break up anything already completed. It goes quicker, but you have to concentrate like crazy, none of it is merely mechanical, none of it runs of its own accord. You have to locate the first corner intuitively, and if you're not quick enough, you lose seconds that you can't make up.

A hand touches my shoulder. Another secretary, a little older. 'Your brother can see you now.'

Eric's office looks the way I'd imagined it: pristine desk, ostentatiously big window, pretentious view out onto roofs, TV antennas and spires. My brother sits motionless, staring at an enormous screen, and pretends not to see me.

'Eric?'

He doesn't answer. His finger clicks on the mouse, then he reaches slowly for a water glass, lifts it to his mouth, drinks, sighs quietly, and sets it down again.

How long is this supposed to go on? I pull up one of the leather chairs, let myself sink into it, and am immediately enveloped in its softness.

Eric turns his head, looks at me, and says nothing.

'So?' I say.

He's silent.

'What's up?' I say.

'Can I do something for you?'

I rub my eyes. Whenever we see each other, no matter what the circumstances, no matter when, no matter where, he always finds a way to make me furious. 'You called me!'

'I know.' He looks me up and down expressionlessly. 'We spoke.'

'No we didn't! That was your secretary. She told me I had to come.'

'I know.'

'So what's it about?'

He reaches for some piece of paper, looks at it, grins for a moment, reaches for another one, looks serious again, sets both of them aside, picks up his phone, and looks at it. 'How are you?'

'Good. The state championships are in six months. I can't win, but I can still participate.'

He stares at me.

'The cube.'

He stares at me.

'Rubik's Cube!'

'It still exists?'

I decide not to go there. 'And how are you?'

'Interesting developments in the housing market in Eastern

Europe. We're hedging with sources of alternative energy. Have you eaten already?'

I hesitate. I think of my breakfast, the chocolate bars in the confessional, the curry sausage I ate along the way, and the dry cookies outside. 'No.'

'So come on!' He jumps to his feet and walks out without waiting for me to follow.

I want to heave myself out of the chair, but the arms aren't firm and I sink back in. The older secretary is watching me through the open door. It takes me three attempts to get up: I smile at her as if I'd done it on purpose, master clown and king of slapstick, and go down the corridor to the elevator where my brother is waiting.

'Finally!' he calls.

There are two men with ties in the elevator, and the mirror on the wall multiplies us into an army.

'Are there statistical investigations?' asks Eric. 'Into horoscopes and people's lives? Do things come out the way astrologers predict? It should be possible to clarify that statistically. Do you know anything about it?'

'How should I know anything about it?'

'But you make horoscopes!'

'No!'

'No?'

'Horoscopes are sheer nonsense!'

'You don't make horoscopes?'

'Is that supposed to be a joke?'

He pulls out his phone, taps on it, and puts it back in his pocket. The elevator stops, we get out. I can hardly keep pace with him. We cross the lobby, the glass doors open, I collide against a wall of pure heat. He crosses the street, just like that, looking neither right nor left. A car honks, he pays no attention. Luckily the restaurant is right on the opposite side. I couldn't go any farther in this temperature.

It is an elegant place: linen cloths on the tables, lamps shaped like glass drops, waiters in black shirts, and, thank God, air-conditioning. Eric heads for a small table, jammed in between two other small tables in front of a leather banquette along the wall. Not a good idea, but how can I explain this to him? The waiter has already pulled out the table, Eric steps to one side, so there's no option but for me to sit on the banquette between two men in suits who glower at me, their disapproval of my bulk only partially tempered by respect for the cloth. The waiter pushes the table back into position, Eric sits down opposite me and says, 'The usual.' The waiter hurries off before I can contradict him. Where does Eric get the idea he can order for me?

He looks at his phone, taps it, puts it away, and stares at the wall behind my head. Then he picks up the phone again.

'How's the economy doing?' I ask.

'What?' He's tapping away, not looking up.

'How's the economy? Do you have a prognosis?'

'Prognosis?' He taps. 'No.'

As always, people all around the room are looking at me surreptitiously. I'm used to it. If they were to see me at the head of a procession, they would think nothing of it, and nor would they regard it as odd if I were discussing questions of morality on TV. But seeing me just sitting there in a restaurant like this with a glass of water in front of me, facing a businessman staring fixedly at a phone, strikes them as curious. Many of them feel comforted by the fact that people like us still exist – that we still walk the earth, saying Mass, praying, and behaving as if man had a soul and there was hope. I feel it myself when I see priests I don't know.

The waiter brings the food. The portions are even smaller than I had feared. A minuscule heap of tangled threads of pasta and mussels in the centre of a more or less empty plate.

Eric puts the phone away. 'If you send someone a message and he answers and you answer back and ask for a quick reply, and none comes, would you assume he didn't get the message or that she's simply not answering?'

'He or she?'

'What?'

'You said "he" and then you said "she".'

'And?'

'Nothing.'

'What does that have to do with my question?'

'Nothing, but – '

'What do you want to know?'

'Nothing!'

'It doesn't matter what kind of message. It's irrelevant.'

'And that's not what I asked.'

'Perhaps it's all part of what you do. Perhaps you have to be so curious.'

'But I'm not curious!'

He stares at his phone, taps on it, and ignores me. That's fine by me, because the dish is proving so complicated that I have to concentrate. It defies all reason that you're not allowed to cut noodles. A commandment that carries quasi-religious authority. Cutting noodles would be a gigantic misstep. Why? Nobody knows. And mussels? You have to pull open every shell and then extract the tiny, tasteless lump of stuff. It's hard enough with your fingers, even harder with a fork.

'Do you still conduct exorcisms?'

'Do we . . . ?'

'Demonic possession. Do you still do that? Do you have people for that?'

'I don't know. It's possible.'

He nods, as if my answer confirms a suspicion.

Eric hasn't yet touched his food. I open the last shell, sauce drips onto my sleeve, then I concentrate on the noodles, but it's not easy, the plate is full of broken mussel shells. My fingers smell of fish. And my neighbour on the banquette keeps jabbing me with his elbow, he's gesticulating wildly. He's facing a man with a bald head and glasses; the two of them are discussing the credit rating of a fixed-income fund.

'What's the classic school of thought?' asks Eric. 'Do you have to let a demon in if he comes? Does he need an invitation, or can he just take possession of someone?'

'Why do you want to know?'

'A book, just a book. I read this book. A strange book. Never mind.' He picks up his glass of water, looks at it, takes a sip, and puts it down.

'So, what did you want to talk to me about?'

He frowns and looks at his phone. I wait. He says nothing.

This is gradually becoming exhausting. I pull out my phone, tap in a message: *How are you, call me if you have time! Martin*, and I send it to Eric.

He's just put down his phone. It vibrates, he reaches out and looks at it and raises his eyebrows. I wait, but he doesn't say a word. He doesn't smile either. He rubs his brow, puts down the phone, picks it up, puts it down again, and says, 'This heat!'

I admit it wasn't the wittiest joke, but a brief smile would not have been amiss. Why does he find it so hard to be polite?

'How's Laura?' I ask. I barely know his wife. An actress, what else. Very good-looking. What else. 'And Marie?'

'She's doing well in school. Sometimes I worry about her.'

'Why?'

'Sometimes I worry about her. But she's doing well in school.'

'And your mother?'

'She's got this TV programme now. People call in, talk about their illnesses, and she comments.'

'I thought she was an eye doctor.'

'There was an audition, three hundred doctors, and she won it. She gets good ratings. And your mother?'

'Healthy. Thank God. Retirement suits her, she reads everything she always wanted to read.'

'Do you still live with her?'

I look at him to see what he's thinking. But why should I keep it a secret? The hours I spend with Mama are bright and peaceful, the best hours of the day. We eat cake, sitting facing each other, we don't talk much, we wait for evening to come. What's bad about that? 'I live at the presbytery, but I visit her often.'

'Every day?'

'Are you still eating your pasta?'

He looks at his untouched plate as if it's the first time he's seen it. But before he can answer, a man stops behind him, bares his teeth, and claps him on the shoulder. 'Friedland!'

Eric jumps up. 'Remling!' He pretends to box the man in the stomach, while the man holds Eric's upper arm tight. Both of them laugh awkwardly.

'Do they let just anyone in here?'

'As you can see!'

'Everything okay?'

'Obviously. And you?'

'Absolutely.'

'That last game! A disgrace!'

'Madness!'

'I wanted to shoot myself! This is my brother.'

Remling looks at me. A fleeting look of surprise passes over his face: the usual look people get when they find themselves unexpectedly face-to-face with a priest. He holds out his hand, I reach out too, and we shake hands.

Then the two of them stare blankly into nothing. Obviously neither of them can think of anything to say.

'So!' says Remling. 'Well then!'

'Absolutely!' cries Eric.

'Why don't we. Get together.'

'For sure!'

Remling nods to me and goes back to his table at the window.

'I hate him. Almost wrecked the Ostermann deal for me last year.' Eric sits down again and starts tapping at his phone. The waiter reappears behind him, bends over his shoulder, and whisks away my empty plate and Eric's untouched one so fast that I can't protest. 'So!' Eric puts the phone away, pushes his chair back, and gets to his feet. 'Nice to see you. I've got to run, you can't imagine everything that's going on. Of course I'm paying.'

'But why did you want to talk to me?'

Eric is already on his way to the exit. He doesn't turn around again, pushes the door open, and is already gone.

Shall I order something else? But it's expensive, the portions are small, and I can get a curry sausage right on the corner.

I stay for another few minutes. I will have to ask the waiter to pull the table out, then the man next to me will be forced to stand up, then they'll pull his table out too, which means in turn that the man sitting opposite will have to stand up too. Half the restaurant will be on its feet by the time I'm on mine.

I'm late. Mama will be waiting with the cake by two p.m., then I have to get to a meeting of the Catholic Youth, and in the evening I have to hold Mass again. What on earth did Eric want with me?

Thoughtfully I finish the water in my glass and smile amiably at everyone in the room. Blessings be upon you, whether you want them or not. That's my job. Day after day I bear witness to the fact that there is an order to things and reason rules in cosmic affairs. What is, must be. What must be, is. I am the legal representative of all that prevails, defender of the status quo, whatever that may be. That is my profession.

And the world really isn't that bad. Thanks be to God, though He doesn't exist, for things like restaurants and air-conditioning. I'm going to order dessert after all. I'm already signalling the waiter.

I was sitting in the seminary library with the cube hidden behind an edition of *Stages on Life's Way* when Kalm came in to tell me my father was on the phone.

To reach the public phone, you had to go down a flight of stairs, along a long corridor, then up a second flight of stairs. The whole way there I was worrying that Arthur might hang up again. I was panting when I reached the phone; the receiver was swinging on the cord.

'Do you have time?'

It really was his voice. I'd never been able to conjure it up in my memory, but now I recognized it as if not a day had gone by.

'Time for what?'

'I'm in the neighbourhood right now. Bad moment?'

'You mean – now?'

'I'm here.'

'Where?'

'Come out.'

'Now?'

'So it's really a bad moment?'

'No, no. You're here?'

'That's what I'm saying. In front of the building.'

'This building?'

Arthur laughed and hung up.

It was a year since his strangest story had appeared in his last

79

collection. It was called 'Family', and it was about his father, his grandfather and his great-grandfather, it was the story of our ancestors, generation by generation, all the way to some vaguely sketched version of the Middle Ages. Most of it is pure invention, for according to Arthur right at the beginning, the past is unknowable: *People think the dead are preserved somewhere. People think their traces are inscribed on the universe. But it's not true. What's gone is gone. What once was, is forgotten, and what has been forgotten never returns. I have no memory of my father.* Oddly, this made me feel robbed. They were my ancestors too.

I went out into the street and he was standing there. His hair as mussed up as always, his hands in his pockets, the same glasses on his nose. When he saw me he spread his arms wide, and for a moment I thought he was going to hug me, but it was a gesture of astonishment at my seminarian's garb. He suggested we go for a walk. My voice was suddenly so hoarse I couldn't answer.

We walked in silence. Streetlights flashed, cars honked, and I heard fragments of words as people passed. It felt as if all the noises were part of a secret conversation, as if the world were talking at me in hundreds of sounds, but I couldn't concentrate and didn't understand a thing.

'I'll be in the city for a while,' he said.

'Under a false name?'

'I'm only a well-known writer. Nobody knows well-known writers. I don't need a false name.'

'What have you been doing all these years?'

'Have you read my books?'

'Of course.'

'Then you know.'

'And apart from that?'

'Nothing. I haven't done anything apart from that. That's what it was all about.'

'Oh, that's what!'

'You're angry with me?'

I said nothing.

'That I wasn't there? That we didn't have sack races, or visits to the zoo, that I didn't come to parents' days, roll around on the carpet, and take you to the annual fair? You're angry about that?'

'What if the books aren't any good?'

He looked at me sideways.

'What then?' I asked. 'Everything sacrificed and then they're no good? What then?'

'There's no insurance against that.'

We went on in silence.

'Obligations,' he said after a while. 'We invent them when required. Nobody has them unless they decide they have them. But I love you a lot. All three of you.'

'And yet you didn't want to be with us.'

'I don't think you missed much. We'll talk about all of it. The hotel opposite the station, come this evening, Ivan will be there too.'

'And Eric?'

'He doesn't want to see me. Come for dinner at eight. I'm guessing you like to eat.'

I wanted to ask what gave him the right to say such a thing, but it had been his form of farewell. He waved, a taxi pulled up, he got in and shut the door behind him.

That evening we sat together for hours. Ivan talked about the moment when he realized he would never be a great painter, and Arthur described his idea to write a book that would be a message to a single human being, in which therefore all the artistry would serve as mere camouflage, so that nobody aside from this one person could decode it, and this very fact paradoxically would make the book a high literary achievement. Asked what the message would be, he said that would depend on the recipient. When asked who the recipient would be, he said that would depend on the message. Around midnight, Ivan talked about how his suspicion that he was homosexual was confirmed, without anxiety or distress, when he was nineteen, but how he had never been able to tell Eric, for fear it would make him lose faith in himself because they were so alike. At one a.m. I was on the verge of admitting that I didn't believe in God, but then didn't, and talked instead about Karl-Eugen Zimmerman, the thirteen-year-old who beat me by three seconds in every championship; I had no chance against him. At one thirty, Arthur said he had worked out how to live with guilt and regret the way other people live with a stiff foot or chronic back pain, around two a.m. I cried a little, at two thirty we said our goodbyes and promised to meet again the next evening.

When we reached the hotel the next day, Arthur had checked out. He had left neither an address nor a note. For a few weeks I kept expecting him on a daily basis to make contact and explain things. Then I gave up.

A windowless room in the cellar of the bishop's palace. It doesn't smell good and there is no air-conditioning. Linoleum on the floor, whitewashed walls, the ceiling covered with soundproof tiles, the regulation crucifix on the wall. A table for table tennis, a table for foosball, two ancient computers, two PlayStations, and a horde of adolescents who know that they just have to accept the presence of two priests and all this will be at their disposal. Even the drinks are free. There are many duties that come with my job. If I could be spared one of them, I would choose this one: the Catholic Youth meeting.

Next to me stands Father Tauler, a gaunt Jesuit. He rubs his eyes and sighs.

'It won't be long,' I say.

'An hour.'

'It goes by.'

'You think?'

'It has to.'

He sighs again. 'Besides, your friend Finckenstein is here.'

'Oh!'

'Upstairs in the palace. Just back from Rome.'

Father Tauler goes to one of the worn-out chairs and sits down. Immediately two girls come over to sit with him and start talking to him quietly. One of them is worked up, her eyes are glistening, the other one puts an arm around her shoulder from time to time.

Smiling uncertainly, I take the other chair. I'm sweating heavily, and I wish I could get a drink from the machine. But that's impossible. I cannot drink Coca-Cola out of a bottle here. I have to preserve a remaining scrap of dignity. If I were lean, it would be no problem. But not the way I am.

I sit and wait. Maybe nobody will want anything from me. Two boys are playing foosball, they bang the ball this way and that with angry gestures, behind them three girls are jumping around the table-tennis table, they're really good, I can hardly see the ball. The PlayStations squeak and whistle; there's a smell of sweat. A girl comes towards me and I flinch, but luckily she's heading over to the computers. The worst is when girls come to me because they're pregnant. I know what I have to say to them, the rules are strict, but in reality I don't know what to do. It's easier when it's about religious doubts. That doesn't take any reflection, I just talk about the Mysterium. Unfortunately religious doubts have gone out of fashion.

I close my eyes. On top of it all, Finckenstein! I'll have to say hello to him, he knows I'm here, otherwise it would look odd. And I shouldn't avoid him. One should never make room for envy.

I open my eyes. Someone has tapped me on the knee. A young man is sitting in front of me. I know him, he's often here, and his name is . . . I've forgotten. If I were better at names, I'd know. He already has beard stubble, he's wearing a blue baseball cap with the letters N and Y on it, and his right nostril is pierced by a thin ring. His T-shirt says *Bubbletea is not a drink I like.* His jeans are torn, but they're the kind you buy already torn. He has a pale face, which may explain why the beard stubble is so visible. He stares at me, his eyes slightly inflamed.

'Yes?' I say.

He clears his throat, then begins to speak. I bend forward. He's talking too softly and too fast, it's hard to understand him.

'Hold on. Please slow down.'

He looks at his sneakers, clears his throat again, starts all over again. Gradually I understand. There's been a fight, and a butterfly is also involved. *Butterfly*, he says over and over again and makes fluttering movements with his hand, like this and this and this: *butterfly*.

Butterfly . . . ? A suspicion dawns on me.

Yes, he says. A knife – a butterfly. This is how you open it, this is how you stab, it all went very fast.

'Just a moment. Say that again.'

Sighing and sweating, he does. Some of it I don't understand, but I get the gist. He and two friends named Ron and Carsten had a fight in a discotheque two nights ago with someone named Ron; the two of them both being called Ron was an accident and didn't mean anything. What makes things harder, however, is that the boy in front of me is also called Ron. So: he, Ron, and Carsten had this fight with Ron, for reasons nobody can remember, maybe it was about money, or maybe a girl, or maybe nothing at all, there are always fights happening over nothing, but if someone strikes a blow, the reason for it becomes immaterial, the only thing that matters is that a blow got struck.

'On your shirt there, what does that mean? *Bubbletea is not a drink I like*. What does it mean?'

He looks at me, baffled; apparently the question has never occurred to him.

'Doesn't matter,' I said. 'Go on.'

He coughs and rubs his eyes. So, he, Ron, and Carsten had run into Ron #3 on the street, Ron being the Ron who'd attacked Ron in the disco.

'What a strange coincidence!'

Not really, he said; in the afternoons they were often on that street, and Ron #3 was on that street almost every afternoon, but they hadn't seen this coming, nor obviously had Ron #3, otherwise it would have really been too dumb of him to cross their path on this street when he was alone. So he got himself beaten up. Not totally brutally, but good and proper.

'That's bad,' I said.

Yes, but not the worst, because the butterfly hadn't come into it yet. A man who was full of himself had weighed in, and . . .

Father Tauler stands up, goes to the drink machine, gets a bottle of Coca-Cola, opens it, goes back to the two girls, and drinks. I watch him enviously.

'What? I'm sorry, I was distracted – what?'

Ron asks if I haven't been listening to him.

'Please tell me again.'

Well, so this guy. So he got all full of himself! Although none of it had anything to do with him, absolutely none of it! Such a snot-nose. Didn't fit into the neighbourhood at all, no idea where he came from! He just got all full of himself!

'And then?'

Well, the knife. The butterfly. Just like that, push hard, click, stab, all in a flash. Then they'd run away, except Ron stayed lying there.

'Ron?'

Well, not the one who'd done the stabbing, the other one! Number 3! He rubs his face.

The slogan on his T-shirt really bothers me. Why does anyone make these things? 'Did someone call the police?'

Probably, he says. Someone always calls the police.

'Was the man wounded?'

He looks at me as if I'm mentally defective. Obviously, he says slowly. Of course. How on earth would he not be? Ron *stabbed him*. With the *butterfly*! How could anyone not be wounded, I ask you? He looks over at the Ping-Pong table, then at the PlayStation, then leans forward and asks if I have a solution.

'Absolution?'

Yes, absolution. If he can get it from me. And should the police surface at his place, if I can corroborate that it wasn't him that did the stabbing, that it was Ron. The other Ron. His friend.

'How could I corroborate that?'

I feel dizzy, and this time it's not because of the heat. Is this really happening? No one has ever come to me in the confessional and admitted to an act of violence, that sort of thing just doesn't happen, never mind if thriller writers and scriptwriters think it's an everyday occurrence. I could call the police. But I'm not allowed to do that. Or do I have to anyway? Is what is going on here a confession at all? We're not in the confessional, not even in a church. Am I obligated in any way to call the police? It's all very complicated, and it's so hot.

As if he'd read my thoughts, he begins to cry. Tears stream down his stubbled baby cheeks. Please, he says, please, Mister Priest!

On the other hand, I think, let's accept this is a confession. I can decide, and I'm making it into one. In this case I may not go to the police. Canon law forbids it, and the law of the state protects me. That seems to settle the matter. And absolution? Well, why not! There is no God, obliged to forgive the boy just because I've made the sign of the cross. They're words. They change nothing.

Ron wipes his tears away. Everything happened so quickly, he says, there was nothing he could do about it. And why did the snotnose have to get so full of himself?

I know I'm going to reproach myself, or rather I know I'll have to forget it all, in order not to reproach myself. But since I've begun the gesture, I can't break it off: I make the sign of the cross over him, from top to bottom and then right to left, and he starts to cry again, this time because he's so moved, perhaps he really does believe he's been spared the fires of hell, and I fend him off and say that he has to go to the police and tell them everything, and he says yes of course, of course he'll do that, and I know he's lying, and he knows that I know.

Thank you, he says again, thank you, Mister Priest!

'But go to the police. Tell them what – '

Of course! To the police. And then he wants to start all over again and tell me the whole dismal story a second time, but I've had enough. I jump to my feet.

Ron looks up at me – liberated on the one hand because he thinks I've taken the sin from him, and worried on the other, because he's confided it to me. I look into his face, into his vague eyes, there's fear in them, but also a mild flash of viciousness as he asks himself if I'm not someone who needs silencing.

I smile at him, he doesn't smile back. 'That's all,' I say, and have no idea what I mean. I hold out my arm to him, he stands up, and we shake hands. His is soft and damp and he lets go again imme-diately. I have the sense that everything would be clearer, better, more right somehow, if only I could understand the slogan on his shirt. I turn away deliberately and indicate to Father Tauler that I have to go. He raises his eyebrows in surprise; I point to my watch and then the ceiling – the universally recognized gesture that means I'm being called upstairs.

'Mister Priest?' A young girl wearing a cross on a chain positions herself in front of me. 'I have a question.'

'Talk to Father Tauler.'

Disappointed, she moves out of the way. I reach the door and the stairwell. I pant my way up, and, bathed in sweat, step into the marble coolness of the entrance hall.

'Friedland!'

He's standing right there. At this exact moment. He's thin and tall, his black robe is elegantly cut, his hair beautifully barbered, and his glasses by Armani. Of course he's not sweating.

'Hello, Finckenstein.'

'It's hot here.'

'You must be used to it by now.'

'Yes, summers in Rome are bad.' He crosses his arms, leans against the stone balusters, and eyes me with a vaguely amused expression.

'I've just heard someone's confession. Imagine, he's . . . I mean, what do you do if someone . . . what happens to the secrets of the confession if . . . doesn't matter. Not now. Doesn't matter.'

'Do you still play with your cube?'

'I'm practising for the championship.'

'You mean there are still Rubik championships? Do you have some time, shall we go and get something to eat?'

I hesitate. I really don't want to hear about his career, and his life in air-conditioned rooms, and his rise and success. 'Love to.'

'Then come on. An early dinner, something light, it's hard to get anything done in this weather.' He goes up the marble stairs, and I follow him hesitantly.

'Have you seen Kalm recently?' I ask.

'Still the same. He'll soon be a bishop, God willing.'

'He'll be willing.'

'I think so too. He'll be willing.'

'Do you believe in God?'

He stops. 'Martin, I'm the deputy editor in chief of Vatican Radio!'

'And?'

'You're asking the deputy editor in chief of Vatican Radio if he believes in God?'

'Yes.'

'Seriously?'

'No. But if I were asking seriously, what would you say?'

'I'd say it's not the right question.'

'Why?'

'God is a self-fulfilling concept, a *causa sui*, because He's conceivable. I can conceive of Him, and because He's conceivable, He must exist, anything else would be a contradiction, so I also know that He exists even if I don't believe in Him. And that's why I believe in Him. And don't forget, we act out His existence through the exercise of human love. We do our work. He becomes real through us, but we can only allow Him to become real because He must exist. How can one love human beings if one doesn't see them as God's creation, merely some chance form of life: successful zoological specimens, mammals with lousy digestions and back pains? How is one supposed to feel empathy for them? How is one supposed to love the world if it has not been willed into being by Him who is the very essence of Benevolent Will?'

I think about Ron again, it's more important, I ought to talk about it. But something holds me back, it feels as if I've brushed against something greater and more malevolent than I can grasp right now; maybe it would be better to forget about it.

'And what does "believe" mean anyway? The concept is logically hazy, Martin. When you're sure of a proposition, then you know it. When you think that something might be so, but at the same time you know it maybe isn't so, then you call that belief. It's a speculation about probability. Belief means assuming that something is probable, although it might be otherwise. Lack of belief means assuming that something probably isn't so, even when it absolutely could be so. Is the difference really that big? It's all a matter of nuance. What's important is that we do our work.'

We climb step by step. Our tread echoes through the stairwell.

'Did you mean it when you asked?'

'I was just curious.'

'And what do you believe?'

'I believe I should be in Rome too.'

'Yes, that's an injustice. But you didn't answer my question.'

We reach the second floor. The statue of a saint with virtuously steepled fingers fixes his eyes on us.

'What question?'

'The question of what you yourself believe.'

I stop, support myself on the banisters, and wait for my heart rate to drop. 'I believe we should eat soon.'

Family

People think the dead are preserved somewhere. People think their traces are inscribed on the universe. But it's not true. What's gone is gone. What once was is forgotten, and what has been forgotten never returns. I have no memory of my father.

He wrote poems. I haven't read any of them. He wrote them on scraps of paper, he wrote them at the bottom of menus, and on envelopes, casually, for pleasure. Some he took with him, others he left lying, he kept thinking up new ones, and he knew it was all just a beginning.

It was at the university that he first learned he was a Jew; until then he had thought that kind of thing was as meaningless as a horoscope sign. His mother was Jewish, although she was a non-believer. Her grandfather had been a long-bearded trader from Bukovina.

He never went to lectures. A girl he had met through mutual friends said she was prepared to marry him. One afternoon there was a crowd. Men waved flags and their fists, he wanted to get a closer look, but a fellow student pulled on his sleeve and said it would be a better idea to disappear. He thought this was ridiculous. His father had been killed in the war, he was the son of a hero, what could happen?

When I was born, he was working in a factory, he had been expelled from university. The factory made things out of metal; what they were used for, he had no idea. One time two workers took him aside: they knew he was a saboteur, they said, but there was no need for alarm, they would cover for him. When he replied in astonishment that he'd always worked the hardest he could in the factory, they laughed and said they didn't believe a word, nobody could be that clumsy. On the way home that day, he composed a poem in his head about the droning propellers of a plane whose pilot has nodded off for a moment and is dreaming of an ant climbing a stalk that's trembling in the wind, which still carries the distant echo of the droning of a plane. Not bad, he thought, it has a rhythm and a simplicity; if things keep on this way, I'll soon be able to have something printed. When he got home an official letter was waiting for him, asking him coolly to present himself at the railway station with a change of clothes and a blanket.

Better for you to head for Switzerland, he said to my mother, I'll follow as soon as I can. There's an official there who was an admirer of my grandfather's, he saw him playing Laertes. He'll help you.

At first she didn't want to go, but he talked her into it. It couldn't be all that bad. He'd always had luck until now.

I don't know what he looked like. There is no photo of his face.

My father's father wasn't even twenty. He survived the first year of the war, thousands of hours in churned-up mud, barbed wire, grenades, the whistling in the air, the flying shrapnel. When he got leave from the front and saw his wife and tiny son, they seemed like strangers to him. He survived for another year. During that time he became so accustomed to the idea of his own death that he no longer believed it could actually happen. But then a bullet hit him, boots trampled on him, and out of sheer force of habit he wondered how he would get out of it this time. He suffocated in the filth and never came back.

My father's grandfather lived for the theatre and never got cast in the right roles. Never Hamlet, but Laertes, never Mark Antony, but Cicero, never Romeo, but Mercutio. He never stopped telling his two sons and his two daughters about the sacrifices that must be made for art, but none of the children had any talent. As the years passed, he hoped for King Lear and Prospero. His older son died of the Spanish flu, his younger son married a Jewish girl, which he didn't like, but he didn't have the strength to fight it. The older daughter married a teacher, the younger daughter stayed resentfully at home and cooked for him and his wife.

He saw his first film. Pale figures rushed around on a white screen. He didn't understand what everyone was laughing at, all he saw was ghosts, and the thought that they would now be able to watch people throwing cakes at one another's faces long after they were actually dead struck him as horrifying. A little man with a moustache, a huge fat man and a clown with his mouth turned down grotesquely – it's the end of the world, he thought. It may still seem to exist, but it's all an illusion, like these images.

From that day forward he never got out of bed again. Even the outbreak of war left him indifferent. When his son came in uniform to say goodbye, he managed to look as dignified as the situation demanded. After all, he wasn't an actor for nothing.

My father's great-grandfather was a doctor, though not a good one. He had only studied medicine because his own father had been a doctor. He had a small practice, a lot of patients died on him, except for those his wife could handle; she was more intelligent than he was. She often knew which cures worked. Then she died on him

95

too. To have someone to look after the children, he married again. The new wife made him sad, and even more patients died.

Whenever he had the opportunity, he told people that when he was a young man, he'd met Napoleon. Actually all he'd seen was a coat billowing out over the rump of a horse, and a hand in a white glove. When he was finally able to settle down again, it occurred to him that perhaps the great commander had killed fewer people than he himself, the bad doctor, had. Then his second wife died too. His final years were completely happy.

The doctor's father, also a doctor, had the gift of being able to calm the sick while he talked to them. Mostly he could guess what they were suffering from. He busied himself with Mesmer's experiments and learned how to put a suffering patient into a magnetized sleep. When his son also became a doctor, he was delighted. His daughter would also have liked to study, she was intelligent and gifted, but he had to forbid it. To even things out, he found her a good husband, who worked hard and didn't hit her. At the age of sixty, he went to bed, breathed out, and never came back.

A bullet cost his father a hand. He was dark-skinned, no one knew why, his mother had brought him up in poverty somewhere, all on her own. He became a soldier, because the recruiters thought a black man would be stronger than a white man. He marched a lot, was sometimes promoted, sired three children along the way, all of them white. Finally a bullet struck him in the back, he choked on his own blood, and never came back.

His father had gone to England, having signed on as a cabin boy for the crossing. He saved a little, and tried his hand at being a trader but didn't have much luck. Once he fell into conversation with a young Frenchman who was visiting the stock exchange in

London in order to write about it. The man was puny and thin, but sly, with eyes that captured everything like lightning and an intellect more powerful than any he'd ever encountered before. If you were like that, he thought, you could do anything, things wouldn't be so hard and the world so full of resistance. As they said goodbye, he asked the stranger his name. Arouet, he replied, and immediately went on his way, because the man had bored him.

He never got over this encounter. He was tired. He still managed to open a little shop near Fleet Street that sold pitchers, keys, and odds and ends, and marry a woman he didn't like, and father a child; it seemed to him that the strength for this had not been his but had come from the son, who was striving so uncompromisingly to arrive in the world. When the boy was born, he had dark skin, but he himself was white as snow, and so was his wife, which meant she'd cheated on him. He screamed, she cried, he roared, she swore, he called out to God, she did too, and with the last of his strength he pushed her away. His stomach was already hurting badly as he did this, a month later he was dead and never came back.

His father went to sea. The sadness of his forefathers was deep in him. In Hamburg harbour he lay with a woman whose name he didn't know, nor she his; he really didn't like any women, but this one looked like a man, which helped. He signed on as a ship's cook on a boat headed for India, but it sank three weeks out from port. Fish stranger than any he could have imagined ate his flesh, his bones turned to coral, his hair to sea grass, his eyes to pearls.

His father was dark-skinned. He was the son of a landowner and a maid who came from Trinidad and was as black as night. Nobody paid attention to him as he was growing up, which was perhaps his good fortune, but when he was fifteen his father gave him some money and he left. He didn't know where he was going, one place seemed just like another, and he had no plans. Time, he thought as he leaned his head against the window of the stagecoach, was strictly an illusion. Others before him had crossed these hills, others would cross them after him, but they remained the same hills and the ground was the same ground. And fundamentally the horses were the same horses, where was the difference? As for people, he thought, the differences really aren't that great either. Might it be possible that we're always the same, in ever-changing dreams? Only the names deceive us. Set them aside and you see it right away.

He had himself set down in a small village. The inhabitants found it amazing that he was black, they'd never seen such a thing before. At first he worked as a farrier, then as a horse doctor; he had an instinct for their bodies and what hurt them. A blessing hung over him. The animals trusted him and people didn't hate him. He married and had seven children; some died at birth, others survived, and to his surprise they were all white. God sends us on mysterious paths, he said to his wife, and we must walk those paths without complaint.

And so he grew old. He was content, the only one in the line of his ancestors ever to be so. One rainy afternoon he sank to his knees in front of the house, looked around with curiosity, closed his eyes, laid his head back as if to listen to the earth beneath him, and never came back.

His father, the landowner, was an alchemist who never succeeded in transforming dross into gold, but this was in no way surprising, since no other alchemist ever did either. He lived in a draughty manor house, sired more than a dozen children with the maids, among them a black girl from Trinidad who could both mesmerize and heal. He never married. He also spent a lot of time contemplating whether he should be Catholic or Protestant. The black girl, on the other hand, thought often of the place from which she came: she remembered its warmth, she remembered rain that was as light as air, she remembered the power of the sun, and she remembered the fragrance of its plants. She tended her dark son, she kissed and hugged him whenever she could, which was not often, for her work was hard, and when he finally set off on his own road, she knew that he would not come back.

Meanwhile the landowner was plagued by trouble with his teeth. One after the other, they fell out, and sometimes the pain drove him to the brink of madness. One clammy morning an abscess in the jaw made him so ill that he had to go to bed. Someone he no longer recognized squashed herbs against his face, and they had a stinging smell. Half an hour later he died of blood poisoning and never came back.

His father was made big by the biggest of all wars. At Lüttich he lost three fingers, outside Antwerp an ear, at Prague a hand, but alas not the one already missing the fingers. But he knew how to plunder, he knew where gold was to be found, and when he'd accrued enough he left service with the Swedish king and bought a manor. He married, sired three children, and shortly thereafter fell victim to a band of marauders. It was a long-drawn-out event, because they had all sorts of things they wanted to try out on him; meanwhile his wife and children hid themselves in the cellar. When the intruders left, he was still alive, but his family could barely recognize him any more; it took him two days to die. He did come back. Even today, there are nightly sightings of what must be his ghost, wandering through the house and looking exhausted.

His mother was an unusual woman. She had vivid dreams, and sometimes she felt she could see the future, or things that were happening far, far away. If she had been a man, many avenues would have been open to her, and she would have had a destiny.

One night she dreamed about a one-eyed, one-legged old man, hidden in a shed. He felt his body grow stiff, he felt a cold hand on his neck, and he laughed as if nothing that interesting had ever happened to him. But before he died, she woke up.

She was interested in many things. She secretly dissected corpses, of which there was an ample supply, given that the war had lasted so long that there were old people who had never known peace. She focused on muscles, fibres, nerves; in between times she gave her husband five children, of whom three survived birth, but then a roof tile fell on her head. It wasn't part of God's plan, no destiny had willed it, it was just that the roofer was incompetent, and she never came back.

Her father had originally been a highwayman. His mother had abandoned him and he was brought up by a farming couple who needed a cheap labourer. They gave him the minimum to eat, and he left as soon as he could.

He hadn't imagined the forest could go on for ever. It had no governing law, and whoever needed to get through it was protected neither by God nor any ruling prince. For a time he robbed travellers and slept in holes in the ground, but one day, unexpectedly, he found himself face-to-face with a witch: a hideous creature that was all hair and warts, one-third woman, one-third man and one-third tusked hog. She was eating a small, bloody creature, a fawn perhaps, maybe even a human child, he didn't dare to look. The witch raised her head. Her eyes were poison green, and the pupils a mere dot. He grasped that she had seen into the very heart of his being and that she wouldn't forget him. He ran and he ran. His breath rattled, branches struck him in the face, first night came and then day. Utterly exhausted, he finally reached a walled city.

Once there he allowed himself to settle down, and he worked as a guardian of houses, properties and fields. He had nine children, three of whom – all girls – survived. He made friends and earned money and lived as if he'd forgotten the threat over his head. He taught his daughters as if they were sons, and was proud of them. They married and gave him grandchildren. The family was solidly Catholic because the town was solidly Catholic. Every Sunday he went to church and paid the priest for the salvation of his soul. People said there was going to be war, but he didn't believe it. And one night the witch appeared before him. He saw her quite clearly, although the room was pitch black and she herself was darker than the darkness. They found him the next morning. He never came back.

His father was a tutor in the household of Count Schulenburg. The count had a daughter. There were secret letters, oaths and plans to flee overseas, to a country that had just apparently been discovered, but might also be no more than a fairy tale, how could one possibly know? Their fate seemed to the two of them to be so weighty that it must be written down somewhere in a book.

But when the girl became pregnant, two men trapped the tutor on the street and beat him to death with iron bars. She gave birth in secret, the child was given away, and she was forced to marry a local minor nobleman who never knew he wasn't the first.

After some years, she withdrew from worldly life into the convent at Passau, where she wrote a commentary on Aristotle's book on clouds. God, she explained, was not outside the world, He *was* the world, which was thus without either beginning or end. As a consequence one could describe God as neither good nor bad – He was the sum of all things and thus there was neither chance nor stroke of fate, for the world was not a theatre. She would be renowned until today, if the manuscript had not been devoured by termites.

*

The father of the luckless tutor was a priest. That wasn't so bad. Luther hadn't yet nailed up his Ninety-Five Theses and the Holy Mother Church wasn't in an uproar. He had numerous children. He gave last rites to victims of the plague, then he opened their veins, which only brought on death quicker.

It was a quiet time for the Black Death. Bubonic plague was on the wane, the worst outbreaks were occurring farther south, but then he got infected anyway from the blood of the sick. It was not unexpected – almost no one who was involved with victims of the plague survived. He prepared to die with something close to relief. At his bedside there suddenly appeared an old, old man, one-eyed and one-legged, and weather-beaten, who placed a heavy hand on his shoulder and whispered incomprehensible things in his ear. It was as if he had lost the power of human speech. Muttering and hopping, he went on his way.

The father of the priest was a farmer, prosperous, with a lot of land. He was a man with a happy disposition, without ever knowing why. He liked playing with his children. Many of them died, and when he stood at their tiny graves, he thought it would be sensible not to give one's heart too soon.

He never left his property. He paid his taxes to the authorities without complaint. Sometimes people came by who were from other places and wanted to go who knows where, but they seemed to him to be as unreal as ghosts. One time an old man appeared who had only one eye and only one leg, and who insisted the two of them were related. He stayed for several weeks, eating copiously and frightening the servants at night with his screams. Then he hobbled away on his crutches.

One night the farmer was overcome by a feeling that he'd been cursed by someone, so that he was too afraid to look anyone in the eye, not his wife, not his servants, not his children. For a time he was plagued by lust, but he knew he must resist, in order not to end up in hell. He failed to resist. Then he resisted for a time. Then he failed to resist again. When he was dying, he wept a lot, for fear of hell. His oldest son, who had just been ordained as a priest, would dearly have liked to know how his father's soul had fared, but his father never came back, and no one knew.

His father too was a farmer. He never left his landholding. Occasionally people passed by who came from other places and were heading for still other places. He wanted none of it.

His father too was a farmer. He never left his landholding. Occasionally people passed by who came from other places and were heading for still other places. He wanted none of it.

His father too was a farmer. He never left his landholding. Occasionally people passed by who came from other places and were heading for still other places. He wanted none of it.

His father too was a farmer. He never left his landholding, and he didn't understand why people got on the road, as if trees, hills and lakes weren't the same everywhere. He tilled his fields, made sure he never saw his sisters, died young, and never came back.

His father too was a farmer. He never left his landholding and had many children. Two of them came into the world in one go – they were girls, and they resembled each other so exactly that they seemed to be one and the same person. The work of the devil, he cried. Even the priest said there was no good explanation for it, and his wife called on the grace of God. But he couldn't bring himself to drown them. So the girls grew up and married farmers in the village nearby. He gave them generous dowries. Their children looked nothing like one another.

His father was a traveller, a magus, a puller of teeth and a con man. He had fled the plague, and in Cologne he had taken flight before a huge crowd and soared three times around the as-yet-unfinished cathedral. Later people told all kinds of stories about how he'd faked it, but in reality flying isn't hard, provided you are devoid of either scruples or fears, and you're crazy besides. Somewhere near Ulm he was accused by a merchant of having stolen money, which was true, but he also knew you just had to be able to run faster than the idiots on your tail, and nobody would be able to threaten you. In a village under particularly high trees he fathered a child. He never saw it, but then he'd never known his own father either.

And so his days passed. Some said he had been killed in Palestine, others that he had ended on the gallows. Only a handful later asserted that he was still alive, for you could kill almost anyone, but not someone like him.

His father was the son of a mercenary who had overcome an unwilling woman by the side of the road as they campaigned. As he held her, she understood that God would not help her, because hell was no future thing, hell was now and hell was here. Suddenly the mercenary realized that things were wrong, and he let her go, but it was already too late, and he ran away and forgot. She abandoned the child in the stable as soon as it was born, and she forgot it too.

But the boy survived. He survived the miasma of the plague that swept through the land, he survived pain, he survived typhus, he did not want to die, even when nothing held out the promise of life, and there was almost nothing to eat; he survived even when there was nothing but vomit and flies, he survived, and if he hadn't,

I would not exist and nor would my sons. There would be others in our place, others who regarded their existence as inevitable.

He grew up, became a blacksmith, found a wife, started a little business that was soon destroyed by fire, then became a groom. He sired eight children, three of whom survived. Soon thereafter he was run over by a wagon, lost a leg, but didn't die, although the gangrene also affected his brain. He dreamed that the devil came to him, and he asked the devil for a long life; the devil went back to hell, and soon after that the fever broke.

One morning, weeks or perhaps years later, he woke up with confused memories of cards, wine and open knives. He didn't retain many memories of the night before, the world seemed somehow smaller, something was missing, and as he reached up past his nose, following the path of the pain, he realized that an eye was missing. At first for a brief moment he was shocked, but then he laughed. What a good accident it was that that was all that happened to him, and nothing worse, for men had two eyes. Only one heart, one stomach, but two eyes! Life was hard, but sometimes fate was kind.

Duties

I've already been hearing the sobbing for some time. At first it was a sound in my dream, but now the dream is over and the sobbing is coming from the woman next to me. Eyes closed, I know that the voice is Laura's, or, rather, that suddenly it's been hers all along. She's crying so hard that the mattress is shaking. I lie there motionless. How long can I pretend I'm asleep? I would love to give up and sink back into unconsciousness, but I can't. The day has begun. I open my eyes.

The morning sun pushes through the slats of the blinds and draws fine lines in both carpet and wall. The pattern on the carpet is symmetrical, but if you look at it for a long time, it captures your attention, gripping it until you can't shake free. Laura is lying next to me in perfect peace, breathing silently, sound asleep. I push back the blanket and get up.

As I'm groping my way down the hall, the memory of the dream returns. No doubt about it, it was my grandmother. She looked tired, worn out, and somehow not complete, as if only a portion of her soul had managed to force its way through to me. She stood in front of me, bent over, leaning on a walking stick, with two ball-point pens sticking out of her bun. She opened and closed her mouth and made signs with her hands; she was determined to tell me something. She looked unutterably weary, lips pursed, eyes pleading, until in the next moment some change in the dream washed her away and I was somewhere else, surrounded by other things. I will never know what she wanted to tell me.

I shave, get into the shower, and turn on the hot tap. The water is warm, then hot, then very hot, which is how I like it. I tip my head back and let the water beat down on me, listen to the noise, feel the pain, and forget absolutely everything for a moment.

It doesn't last long. Already the memory comes crashing back like a wave. Perhaps I can hold out for another couple of months, maybe even three, but not longer.

I turn off the water, get out of the shower, and push my face into the terrycloth of the bath towel. As always, my memory reacts to the smell, calling up images: Mama taking me to bed wrapped in a towel, Papa's tall figure outlined by the ceiling light, his tousled hair in silhouette, Ivan already asleep in the other bed, our sandbox where I always knocked over the towers he built, a meadow, a worm he found that I split in half, and he cried and cried. Or was it the other way around? I put on my bathrobe. Now I need my medication.

In my study everything is normal. This calms me. The desk with its big screen, the Paul Klee on one wall and the Eulenboeck on the other, the empty files. I have never worked here. Even the drawers are empty and not one of the reference books has ever been opened. But when I sit here and pretend to be lost in thought, no one comes in, and that counts for something in and of itself.

Two Throprens, a Torbit, a Prevoxal and a Valium – I can't begin the day with too much, because I have to be able to up the dose if something unforeseen occurs. I swallow them all in one gulp; it's unpleasant and I have to use all my willpower to conquer the gag reflex. Why I always take them without water, I have no idea.

Already I can feel them working. It's probably my imagination, nothing could work that fast, but is that important? Indifference settles over me like cotton wool. Life goes on. One day you'll lose it all, the name Eric Friedland will be abhorred, those who still trust you will curse you, your family will fall apart, and they'll lock you up. But not today.

I'll never be able to tell anyone how much I hate this Paul Klee. Lopsided diamonds, red on a black background, and next to them a windblown, truly pitiful little matchstick man. Even I could have painted it. I know I'm not supposed to even think such a sentence, it is utterly forbidden, but I can't help it, even I could have painted it, it would have taken me less than five minutes! Instead of which I paid seven hundred and fifty thousand euros for it, but a man in my position must possess a very expensive painting: Janke has a Kandinsky, Nettelback of BMW has a Monet – maybe it's a Manet, what do I know? – and old Rebke, my golf partner, has a Richard Serra on the lawn, huge, rusty, and always in the way at garden parties. So I asked Ivan two years ago to get me a picture too, it just had to be something that was a sure thing.

He immediately pretended he didn't understand me. He likes doing that – it amuses him. What did I mean, 'sure thing'?

'Sure thing,' I said, 'means that it impresses everyone. That no expert has something against the artist. Like with Picasso. Or Leonardo. One of those guys.'

He laughed at me. He likes doing that too. Picasso? There were hundreds of experts who didn't take Picasso seriously, and if you chose one of his wrong periods, you'd be criticized willy-nilly. Almost no one had a good word to say about his late work, for example! But Paul Klee, you could get one of his, no one had anything against Paul Klee.

'And Leonardo?'

'No Leonardos on the market. Take Klee.'

Then he attended the auction for me. At half a million he called me to ask if he should keep bidding. I would like to have yelled at him. But what if he thought I couldn't even afford a matchstick man? For a while it hung in the salon, then Laura suddenly didn't like it any more. So since then it's been hanging over my desk, staring at me in a pushy way and doing damage in my dreams. I can't sell it, too many people have seen it in the salon where I have of course pointed it out to them, look at my Klee, what do you think of my Klee, yes of course it's genuine! As soon as the investigators start work, one of their first questions will be where the Klee is. Art is a trap, nothing more, cleverly dreamed up by people like my brother!

Still in my bathrobe I go along the hall and down the stairs to the media room. There's a screen and a video beamer. The black cubes of the speakers are powerful enough to service a football stadium. A soft leather couch sits in front of it.

The remote is lying on the table. Without thinking about it I sit down, reach for it, and press a couple of buttons. The screen hums into life: the early-morning TV programming – a nature film. A dragonfly lands on a stalk. Its legs are no bigger than a hair, its wings tremble, and its antennae touch the rough green. Interesting, but it reminds me about the camera.

There's one hidden in one of the appliances. It would be strange if there weren't one, because they're so easy to conceal, I would never find it among all the lenses. I push another button, the meadow disappears, to be replaced by some undersecretary standing behind a lectern and talking so fast that you'd think everything must hang on his finishing as fast as possible.

'No,' I say. 'No, no, no, no. No!'

Luckily that helps. He slows down.

But unfortunately he's noticed me. Without stopping talking, he casts a swift glance in my direction. He did it very unobtrusively, but it didn't escape me.

I hold my breath. I must not make a wrong move now. Without question it's crazy, I know it, the broadcast with the undersecretary is a recording, nobody gives press conferences this early in the morning.

But I also know that he looked at me.

'Totally calm. Always keep calm.'

With cold terror I realize that I said it out loud. I can't make this kind of mistake. And the undersecretary, whose name I suddenly recall – he's called Obermann, Bernd Richard Obermann, and he's responsible for power or education or something – heard it, for a mocking smile appears for a moment on his face. I don't let anything show; I don't lose my cool so easily. Keep calm, I say to myself again, but this time silently and without moving my lips, behave as if everything's fine! Somehow I have to manage to look away from the screen. I concentrate on the edge of my field of vision, and then somewhat blurrily I see something on the carpet, a disturbance in the symmetry: a red wine stain. Damn it, this carpet cost thirty-five thousand euros!

My fury helps me to look away from the screen. Out of the corner of my eye I register that Undersecretary Obermann has disappeared. Some harmless man is now talking into the microphone and has no interest in me. Quickly I lift the remote, the picture flames up for a moment and is gone.

That was a close-run thing. I stand up, notice someone in the doorway, and jump back.

'Did I frighten you?'

'No, of course not. No, no. No!' I look at my daughter, my daughter looks at me, and to say something I ask, 'Do you have a test to take today?'

'Yes, in maths.'

I congratulate myself, now I'm behaving like a father who has a grip on things and takes part, while all I know is that children are always having to take tests for school. Something mean is always in the offing, and every day is certain to bring its own unpleasantness.

'Do you know anything about this red wine stain?'

She shakes her head.

'If it was you, it's okay to tell me. You won't be punished.'

'I don't drink wine!'

She said it charmingly. I would love to kiss her now on both cheeks, but I think about the camera and leave things be. 'And?' I ask instead. 'Learned it all? Well prepared?'

She shrugs her shoulders as if she doesn't believe I'd be interested. This upsets me. Because even though it really doesn't interest me, I do my best to act like it matters.

I notice a tiny spider – a little dot working its way up the wall by the door. What does it live off, what does it eat, what does it drink, or don't spiders drink? I would like to ask Marie, she's bound to learn things like that in school, but instead I ask, 'What's up for today? Have you got as far as differential calculus?'

'What's that?'

'You don't know?'

'I'm ten, Papa.'

She has an answer for everything. Meanwhile the spider has worked its way over to the other side of the door; how did it get there so fast?

'What?' she asks.

'"Excuse me". You must say "Excuse me", not "What".'

'Excuse me?'

'What?'

'What sort of spider, Papa?'

Did I talk out loud? For heaven's sake!

'You said –'

'No!'

114

'But you did – '

'I didn't say a word!'

That came out too loud. I don't want to frighten my daughter, and I mustn't forget the camera. Stricken, I run my hand over Marie's head. She smiles at me, then turns around and leaves, the way children always do, with a hop, a skip, and a jump.

'Hurry up!' I call after her. 'You're late, school's about to start!' I have no idea when school starts. But it's bound to be true.

What will she think of me when I'm in prison? On the way to the dressing room upstairs I ask myself yet again why I don't pluck up the courage to cut things short. So many have managed it: guns, pills, a leap from a high window. Why not me?

I'm actually too strong. Being strong isn't just an advantage. You can tolerate more, you can get into even deeper trouble, and it's harder to give up. The washed-out, the empty and the spineless, who have nothing to lose if they lose themselves, can all just hang themselves somewhere. But there's something inside me that won't allow that.

I like being in my dressing room, there are very rarely problems in here. Seventeen black bespoke suits hang in a row, thirty-nine white shirts are stacked on the shelves, and the tie rack holds twenty-five flawless ties in the selfsame shade of red. Sometimes people give me other ties, mostly with sophisticated patterns, and I throw them away. I have one black one, for funerals. On the floor there are twenty-one pairs of well-polished shoes.

It's weekends that are hard. On your free days you can't wear a suit, nor can you keep wearing the same check shirt. It would be sensible and rational, so of course if you did it people would think you were weird. So I have a wardrobe for weekends, days off and holidays. In it are all kinds of colourful shirts: solid colours, check, stripes, even one with dots. Laura doesn't like it, but I claim it's my favourite. People ought to have a favourite shirt, it's expected, it's appealing. The wardrobe also houses jeans, corduroys, leather belts, every kind of jacket, sports shoes, hiking shoes, fishing boots, though I've never been fishing and have no intention of ever changing that.

Luckily today is a weekday, so I'm done in five minutes. Black suit, white shirt, red tie. Everything feels better when you're dressed in a suit. I nod into the mirror on the wall, my reflection nods back without hesitation. The world is functioning.

As I step into the hall, Laura is standing there.

'Did you sleep well?' I ask. I ask her this every morning, although I have no idea what it's supposed to mean. Either you're asleep or you're awake, but I know from television that people ask one another these questions.

She takes a step back, in order to leave room for the answer.

How beautiful she still is! I nod and say, 'Aha!' and 'Oh,' while she talks about a journey and a magician and a rose bed. Thousands upon thousands of roses, a whole wide sea. Can you really dream any such thing? Perhaps it's all invention, the way I invent almost everything I tell people.

'Are you listening to me?' she asks.

'Of course. Bed of roses.'

As she talks on, I stealthily log on to my phone: 8 August 2008, two thousand seven hundred and thirty unopened emails. And even as I'm looking at the screen, in come another two.

'Is that more interesting than what I'm talking about?'

'Darling!' I hastily stow the gadget. 'Princess! It couldn't be less interesting! Do please go on.'

This is in fact true, I haven't read a single email for weeks, but because it's the truth she takes it as a lie and sticks her lower lip out in a sulk.

'Laura! Please go on! Please!'

Obviously I'm not managing to hit the right tone today, for her brow furrows reproachfully. 'Marie needs tutoring in maths. You have to find a teacher. Mr Lakebrink says it's urgent.'

This is all going too fast for me. First roses just now, and here we are already with Lakebrink. 'Is that her teacher?'

Her frown deepens.

'Lakebrink,' I say. 'I know. That Lakebrink. That man.'

She takes another step back.

'Okay, so who is he?'

'Eric, what's the matter with you?'

'Shall we just fly off somewhere?' I ask hastily. 'Next weekend, just you and me . . .' Now I have to think of a really hot place, and quick. Where have we been recently? 'To Sicily?' It was Sicily, or I'm pretty sure it was. Or just possibly it was Greece. Damp and hot as hell, absurdly high prices, impudently whispering servers, mangy cats staring down from sharp rocks like gargoyles, but Laura was in heaven.

She opens her arms, lays her head on my chest, and hugs me. Her hair smells sweet – a little like sage, a little like lemon, in fact she always smells good. She murmurs that I'm wonderful, generous, one of a kind; I can't hear her that well, because her face is buried in my jacket, and I stroke her back.

'The headmaster,' she says.

'What?'

'Mr Lakebrink is the headmaster of Marie's school. You talked to him last week. At the parents' meeting.'

I nod, as if I'd always known that. Of course I'll have to come up with a convincing reason why we can't go to Sicily. She's going to be so disappointed that I have to come up with an even bigger promise, to sweeten her up, and then I'll have to break that one too. All of it because of this parents' meeting, that I can actually remember all too well: low ceiling, some kind of artificial flooring, harsh lights and a poster with a slogan about getting yourself inoculated against something as soon as possible.

'Just one more thing, Eric!' She strokes my cheek. Her emotion makes me recall just how much I desired her even recently. 'The day before yesterday, you told Marie the most important thing is never to stand out. Never to arouse other people's jealousy.'

'So?'

'She took it very much to heart.'

'Okay, and?'

'But yesterday you told her that one should never make compromises. Keep fighting, keep trying to be the best you can. Never duck a fight.'

'And?'

'Now she's confused.'

'Why?'

'Because it's a contradiction!'

'Sicily!' I cry.

Her face lights up at once.

We embrace again, and I am overcome by a sense of déjà vu so powerful that it makes me dizzy. I remember that I stood here once before and held her in my arms and had exactly this conversation with her, in a dream or in another life or even in this life, two or three days ago. And soon we'll be standing here once again, and then probably Mr Lakebrink will appear again, and the axe will fall, and the police will storm in, and the loop will finally stop replaying itself. I give her a horribly damp kiss on the forehead, head quickly for the stairs, and say 'I love you' without turning around. Why, when it's true, does it feel like a lie?

'Love you back,' she calls, and although it sounds fake, I know it's true.

Being distracted, I take the first step of the stairs with my left foot. Such a thing should never happen; in this house of all places I cannot afford to be careless. From the beginning, even the very first time we looked at it, I didn't feel good here.

Do not think about the attic, not right now. I have to pretend I've forgotten it's even there. Everything about it is repellent: the slope of the roof meets the floor at a particularly hideous angle, mud-brown rectangles are printed on the wallpaper, because of the blobs of dirt in the glass shade the old lamp casts a most horrible pentangle on the floorboards, and behind the narrow table, put there by someone, who knows who, many years ago, is an awkward gap. You only have to spend a few minutes up in it to know someone died there.

There's nothing too unusual about that. In an old house someone will have croaked in almost every room. But what happened in this attic was a particularly hard way to die. It was long and drawn out, and it was extremely painful. Ghosts appeared and demons made themselves visible, attracted by the death throes. But how could I have explained all that to Laura? Seven and a half million. She fell in love with the house at first sight. Moorish tiles on the terrace, five bathrooms, a media room. What was I supposed to do?

So one night I went up there. It's possible: people can confront fear, until it submits and retreats. I lasted almost three hours. The table, the shadows, the lamp, me. And someone else.

Then I ran. Down the stairs, across the hall, into the garden. A half-moon in the night sky was surrounded by shimmering clouds. I must have lain in the grass for a good hour, and when I slipped back into bed, Laura woke up and told me about her dream, some brightly coloured bird, a friendly postman and a locomotive. And I stared up at the ceiling and thought about how there will be that room up there for as long as we live. Even when we no longer live here, when other people have replaced us for the longest time, it will still be there.

I open the front door. My God, it's hot. The car is waiting, with the engine running, Knut sitting sullenly at the wheel. He hates waiting. I have no idea how someone like him became a chauffeur. Besides which I'm baffled about why he's called Knut. He's Greek and looks it: stubble, black hair, brown skin. On a long journey once he told me the story of his name, but I didn't listen, and if I asked again now, he'd be offended. I get in. Knut drives off without so much as a hello.

I close my eyes. Already I hear him honking the horn.

He yells, 'Idiot!' and honks again. 'Did you see that, boss?'

I open my eyes. The street is completely empty.

'Smack at us from the left!' he yells.

'Unbelievable.'

'Idiot!'

While he bangs on the steering wheel, curses, and points this way and that, I ask myself for the thousandth time how I can get rid of him. Unfortunately he knows too much about me; I'm sure that the day after he was fired, he would be writing anonymous letters to Laura, to the police, to anyone that occurred to him, what do I know? The only possibility would be a discreet assassination. But if I really did want to kill someone, he'd be the only person I'd know to ask for help. He's one tricky customer. I pull out the telephone and look at the market. Prices of raw commodities have fallen, the euro hasn't recovered against the dollar, and the IT papers, which were overvalued, are exactly where they were yesterday. I don't get it.

'Hot!' cries Knut. 'So hot, so hot!'

I was convinced that IT stocks would fall. On the other hand I've seen the opposite coming – not out of some insight into the market, but because in the meantime I've accustomed myself to the knowledge that everything that happens is the opposite of what I expect. But what should I follow: my insight, or the knowledge that I'm always wrong?

'March, April!' cries Knut. 'Always rain. May – rain. Always! – and now this!'

But losses don't frighten me any more. If the market had developed the way I said it would, nothing would have changed. Rising share prices won't save me any more. It would take a miracle.

The phone vibrates, the screen says, *Are you coming today?*

Of course, I type.

As I'm hitting the Send button, I'm thinking about what excuse I could use in case she writes back that I should come at once. I have no time. Adolf Kluessen has checked in; he's my most important client. But she's usually working during the day, and if she writes that I shouldn't come until the evening, she'll feel guilty and that's helpful, it's something I can build on.

I stare at the phone. The screen with the grey face stares back. No answer.

And still no answer.

I close my eyes and count slowly to ten – Knut talks and I pay no attention. When I reach seven I lose patience, open my eyes, and look at the screen.

No answer.

Okay, forget it. I don't need her, I get on better without her! And perhaps this is her revenge for last Sunday.

We met outside the entrance, it was an art movie house, they were showing Orson Welles's last film, she absolutely wanted to see it, I wasn't interested, but so what, no other film would have interested me either. The lobby stank of frying fat, and as we queued for tickets we ran out of things to say. We were just taking our seats when a man jumped up in the row right in front of me and yelled my name.

It was such a shock that I didn't recognize him right away. The first things to organize themselves were his features: mouth, nose, eyes. Then the ears resumed their usual places, and the entity became Dr Uebelkron, the husband of Laura's best friend, who was a fixture at all of our garden parties.

I hugged him like a long-lost brother. Then I hit him on the shoulder a couple of times and began to ask him questions like how his wife was doing, and his daughter, and his mother, and what were we all supposed to be making of this heat wave. The film had already started. People around us were shushing and clearly even Dr Uebelkron wanted to leave things be, but I kept on talking, asking questions, didn't give him time to answer, and kept manipulating his shoulder mercilessly. When I finally let go of him, he sank into his seat exhausted, without managing to ask who the woman with me was. I checked the time, waited exactly four minutes, pulled out my phone, cried, 'Oh no', 'Oh God', and 'Coming right away,' leapt up, and ran out. It wasn't until I was sitting in the taxi that I realized Sibylle was still in the cinema.

The phone vibrates. *Good. Come!*

When?

Three seconds later: *Now!*

Can't, I type. *Important client.* It's habit, so it feels like an excuse, but it's the truth. I hit the Send button and wait.

Nothing.

So what's going on, why isn't she answering? Mobilizing my entire willpower I put the phone away. We're here.

As always I get out on the street and leave Knut to drive into the underground garage. I can't go down there, it's simply not possible. Quickly through the blazing heat, the glass doors are opening already, and I'm in the lobby. The elevator takes me to the twelfth floor. I hurry through the open-plan office, full of identical faces in front of identical screens. Some of them I know, some I don't, I'm glad that none of them speaks to me. Recently I've been forgetting too many names.

My secretaries greet me silently. One of them is beautiful, the other capable, they hate each other, and they're not that fond of me either. I've slept with the beautiful one, her name is Elsa, six or seven times. I would have got rid of her a long time ago, except she could blackmail me. The other one, Kathi, I only slept with once, under the influence of new medication that made me do all sorts of things I don't want to think about any more.

'Mr Kluessen is waiting,' says Kathi.

'Fine.' I go into my office, sit down behind the desk, fold my hands, and slowly count to ten. Then I finally pull the phone out of my pocket. No answer. Why is she doing this to me?

I administer Adolf Albert Kluessen's entire estate, and I've lost everything. All the statements and accounts he's received in the last two years were faked. The man is old and not very clever, and even if I'm no longer in any condition to win back his money, I can still manage to invent impressive balances and report gains I would have made, had I foreseen the movements of the market. I also add all sorts of curves to the figures, drawn in red, blue and yellow, which increase trust. But every conversation with him has its dangers.

I stand up and go to the window. The view is spectacular; it's hard to accustom yourself to the sheer extent of it, and the brightness. As ever, when the world, uninvited, threatens me with its sparkle and brilliance, I have to think of Ivan, and a long-gone afternoon in Arthur's library. We were twenty-two, it was shortly before Christmas, Ivan had come from Oxford, I had come from the sanatorium.

'Tell!' he said.

I had almost no memory of the last months. Everything had been eggshell coloured, the walls, the floor, the ceilings, the staff's coats. At night you didn't know whether the voices you were hearing came from the other patients or out of your own head.

'You have to play along,' said Ivan. 'That's the whole trick. You have to lie. You think people see through you, but nobody sees through anyone. People are impossible to read. You think other people get what's going on inside you, but that's wrong.'

'I don't know what you're talking about.'

'That's the right answer. Watch, bend the rules. People are almost never spontaneous; mostly they're machines. What they do, they do out of habit. You have to undo the rules, and then you have to follow them as if your life depended on it. Because it does. Your life depends on it.'

I stared at the table. Very old wood, a family heirloom, it once belonged to our great-grandfather, who had supposedly been an actor. The black grain made an unbelievably beautiful pattern. It surprised me that I should even notice such a thing, but then I realized I wasn't the one who had noticed. It was Ivan.

'Truth!' he said. 'That's all well and good. But sometimes none of it gets you anywhere. Always ask what people are expecting of you. Say what people say. Do what people do. Ask yourself who exactly you'd like to be. Then ask yourself what that person you'd like to be would do. Then do it.'

'If the cell hadn't split back then,' I said, 'there would only have been one of us.'

'Concentrate!'

'But who would it have been? Me, or some third person we don't know? Who?'

'The trick is to sort things out with yourself. That's the hardest thing. Don't expect help from anyone. And don't imagine you can go into therapy. All it'll teach you is to accept yourself. You get good at excuses.'

I should have told him he was right, I think now, I should never have gone into therapy. I would like to talk to him, even today, I need to see him, I need his advice. Maybe I could borrow money from him and disappear. A fake passport, a plane to Argentina, just me. It would still be possible.

I pick up the phone and unfortunately hear Elsa's voice, not Kathi's: 'I need to speak to my brother. Call him, ask him to come here.'

'Which brother?'

I rub my eyes. 'What do you mean, which?'

She says nothing.

'So call him! Tell him it's really important. And will you finally get Kluessen in here!'

I hang up, cross my arms, and try to look as if I were sunk in thought. Suddenly it occurs to me that I didn't see Kluessen outside in the waiting room. The couch was empty. But didn't she tell me he'd arrived? If he was already here and not in the waiting room, would that mean . . . ? Worried, I look around.

'Hello, Adolf!'

He's sitting there, staring at me. He must have been there the whole time. I smile and try to look as if it had all been a joke.

Adolf Albert Kluessen, a substantial old man in his mid-seventies, well dressed, accustomed to being obeyed, skin wrinkled by the sun, bushy eyebrows, looks at me as if he'd swallowed a frog, as if he'd lost his key today, along with his passport and his briefcase, and was being held up to ridicule for all of it, as if he'd been robbed and then his sports car had had its paint scratched. There are dark patches of sweat under the arms of his polo shirt, but that's a result of the heat and doesn't mean a thing. Adolf Albert Kluessen, son of the department store owner Adolf Ariman Kluessen, grandson of the founder of the department store Adolf Adomeit Kluessen, scion of a family whose eldest son has borne the name Adolf for so long that no one could rally themselves to give up the tradition, go figure, looks at me as if the whole world were despicable. And with all of that, he doesn't even know he's bankrupt.

'Adolf, how nice to see you!'

His hand feels as knotty as wood. I hope mine isn't damp with nerves. Nonetheless, I have control of my voice, it isn't trembling, and my eyes are clear. He says something about me not answering his emails, and I cry that it's a scandal and I'll fire my secretary. I quickly lay three printed sheets in front of him: figures that mean nothing, and include the most famous risk-free stocks: Apple, Berkshire Hathaway, Google and Mercedes-Benz, lots of pie charts, everything as lit up as can be.

But today it's not working. He blinks, then sets the sheets of paper aside, leans forward, and says he has something really basic he needs to get off his chest.

'Something basic!' I get to my feet, walk around my desk, and sit on the edge. Always make sure you're a little higher than your counterpart – an old negotiating trick.

He's no longer the youngest of men, he says. He doesn't want to risk things any more.

'Risk?' I fold my hands. 'On my father's life!' Folding your hands is helpful, it looks sincere. By contrast, what looks totally false is laying your hand on your heart. 'We've never taken risks!'

Warren Buffett, says Kluessen, has advised never to invest in anything you don't understand.

'But I understand it. It's my profession, Adolf.' I stand up and go to the window, so that he can't see my face.

A few years ago everything was still in good order. The investments were lucrative, the results satisfactory. Then there was a bottleneck in liquidity and it occurred to me that nothing was stopping me from simply asserting that I'd made gains. If you report losses, investors pull their money out. Declare profits and everything stays the same – you can continue, you balance out the loss, no one is hurt, it's only numbers on a piece of paper. So that's what I did, and after a few months the money was there again.

But a year later I was in the same situation. At the worst moment my second-most-important client wanted to withdraw twenty-nine million euros. I had positions I couldn't liquidate without losses, so I reported fake gains, which brought me new investors, and I used their money to cover the payments. I was sure that the stock exchange would quickly recover its equilibrium and everything would go back to normal.

But the market kept dropping. More investors wanted to take their money out, and if I hadn't made more raids on capital, the whole thing would have blown up. When the market really did recover, too much was already missing.

But I still had hope. I was considered to be successful, investors flocked to me, and I used their money to pay previous investors their gains: ten, twelve, sometimes even fifteen per cent, so much that almost nobody had the idea of withdrawing their capital. For a long time I thought a way out would suddenly present itself. Then, one night two years ago when I was forced to run the numbers in my head, and run them, and run them, I knew it wasn't ever going to happen.

Argentina or Venezuela. Ecuador. Liberia. Ivory Coast. New passport, new name, a new life. I should have done it. Marie might have been enchanted. Laura could have given parties somewhere else. The weather is inarguably better anywhere than here.

But then the moment was lost. I had been too slow, too undecided. It takes a lot of money to vanish in comfort. Now I am totally wiped out. All the capital is gone, all my credit is used up.

'Do you know the Bhagavad Gita?' I ask.

Kluessen stares at me. He hadn't reckoned on this.

'The god Krishna says to the commander Arjuna: You will never be able to explain why things are as they are. You will never be able to sort out the complications. But here you stand, mighty warrior. Don't ask why, stand up and give battle.'

I once heard this on the car radio. The quote pleased me so much that I asked Elsa to look it up.

'Yes, but where?' she asked.

'In the Bhagavad Gita.'

'How do I find it?'

'When you read it.'

'The whole thing?'

'Only until you hit the right sentence.'

'And if it's right at the end?'

She didn't find it, so I'm quoting from memory. Kluessen isn't going to be looking things up.

He's silent. Then he says: Whatever. He wants to reassign his portfolio.

'Adolf!' I clap him so hard on the shoulder that the old man's body shakes. For a moment I lose the thread: it's to do with his eyebrows. With brows that bushy, it's no wonder that someone might get confused. 'Together we've earned a great deal of money. And it's going to grow! Base prices are all on the uptick. Anyone who bails out now is going to regret it.'

Whatever, is his response once again, and he massages his shoulders. His wife, his son and he have reached an agreement to redistribute the assets. His son thinks the entire system is heading for collapse. Everyone is piled with debt. Capital is far too cheap. It's not going to come out well.

'Redistribute assets? You don't even know what that *means*!' No, this time I've gone too far. 'I mean, of course you do, but this doesn't sound like you, these are not your words, this isn't the Adolf I know.'

He says his son has just got his MBA and –

'Adolf! University is one thing, but reality . . . !' What is all this, what is his son doing, mixing himself up in it? I say nothing for a moment, then draw back and cut loose. It doesn't matter what I say, Kluessen understands almost nothing and notices even less. What counts is that there is the sound of a human voice, with no interruption and no hesitation, what counts is that he hears my voice and grasps that there is something more powerful at work here than he can summon up, with an intellect that dwarfs his own.

Soon I'll have to talk this way in front of the court. My lawyer will advise me to make no statement, that's what lawyers always do. They worry about contradictions, they don't trust anyone to cope with the prosecutor, they think no one can talk with conviction about anything. It's possible that I will even have to part company with my lawyer, which in the middle of a trial will have a devastating impact. Perhaps it's better if I conduct my own defence. But people who defend themselves are regarded as idiots, any respectable defendant must have an expensive defence counsel, a pompous, grandstanding gentleman. There's no way around it. But I'll keep control of my own testimony.

'What do you mean?' asks Kluessen.

'Excuse me?'

'What testimony? Where?'

He looks at me, I look at him. It can't be that I spoke out loud, it must be a misunderstanding. So I make a dismissive gesture and keep talking: about derivatives and secondary derivatives, under-valued real estate funds, dispersed risk and statistical arbitrage. I quote the professional magazine *Econometrica*, of which I possess a single copy, mention game theory and the Nash equilibrium, and don't omit a hint that I have connections to people in key positions who give me inside information – borderline illegal, but extremely profitable.

Finally I stop. One must always give one's opponent the chance to collect his thoughts. He has to come to his senses and be able to grasp that he's lost. I fold my hands, bend forward, and look him in the eye. He pulls out a handkerchief and does a thorough job of cleaning his nose.

'Handshake, Adolf!' I hold out my hand. 'A man and his word. We'll carry on together. Yes?'

He says he's confused.

'Handshake!'

He says he's confused.

With my left arm I reach for his right arm and try to take his hand in mine. He resists. I pull, he keeps on resisting, and he's surprisingly strong.

He needs to think, he says. He will talk to his son, and write me a letter.

'Just think about it!' I say hoarsely. 'As long as you want! Thinking is always important.'

Now we do actually shake hands, but not to seal our professional partnership, just to say goodbye. I squeeze so hard that all the suntan fades from his wrinkled face. I know I've lost. He will demand his money back. And he knows that I know. What he doesn't know is that I no longer have his money.

For a moment I fantasize about killing him quickly. I could strangle him or break his skull with something hard. But then what? How do I get rid of the body? Besides which it's likely that there's a camera in here. Wearily I collapse into my chair and prop my head in my hands.

When I look up, Kluessen has left. In his place there is a tall man standing in the room. He's leaning against the wall and watching me. I close my eyes, then open them again. He's still there. He has a hideous gap in his front teeth.

Not good, I think.

'No,' says the man. 'Not good at all.'

I close my eyes.

'Won't help,' says the man.

And yes, I can still see him.

'Don't get mixed up in it,' says the man. 'Just walk right past. When you see them, don't get mixed up in it. Leave it be. Don't speak to the three of them, keep on going.'

I feel dizzy. Mixed up in it? Keep on going? I can't ask him what he's talking about, right now I have to deal with Kluessen. I can drag things out for a week or two, tangle him up in some complicated exchange of letters, be unreachable, and generally bring things to a standstill with a series of excuses and questions. But at some point he'll press charges, then the prosecutors will weigh in with their interrogations, but the time will tick by and until then I can stay living in my house and drive to work every morning. Autumn will come, the leaves will fall, and with any luck I won't be arrested before the first snowstorm.

The man is no longer there. I hold up my hand in front of my eyes. The sunlight in the window is so harsh that it seems to destroy the tint of the glass. I pick up the receiver and ask Elsa for a glass of water. It's already here and I drink it. As I set it down, I see a priest I know. He's even fatter than he was the last time. When did my brother come in? And the glass in my hand, who brought it so quickly?

'Can I do something for you?' I ask cautiously. Perfectly possible I'm just imagining him. I mustn't give myself away.

He hems and haws, murmurs something, obviously doesn't want to say anything specific.

I take a sheet of paper and pretend to read. My hands are shaking. The thing with Kluessen really got to me.

He asks something.

So – it's not a fantasy. Ghosts never ask questions. But his black outfit unsettles me, it makes me think of exorcisms. Then he says something about a cube and at first I think he's talking about some dice game, but then it becomes clear that he means his hobby, and in order to avoid having to listen to the whole nonsense, I ask if he's already eaten, get up, and leave the office. Outside I stop by Elsa's desk, bend over, smell her perfume, force myself not to lay hands on her, and ask what in the world my brother's doing here.

That was her task, she says. To call my brother! And ask him to come at once. That's what I told her.

'Oh,' I say. 'Right. Got it. I know.' I have no idea what she's talking about. Why should I have set this up?

I walk quickly to the elevator. The phone vibrates in my pocket. I extract it. *So now what, do you want to come or not?*

Now? I write back. I wait. My brother is nowhere to be seen. Why is everyone always so ponderous? Wretched, life-sapping inertia! And why isn't she answering?

Here he comes. The elevator doors open, we step in, and once again I'm thinking of *The Exorcist.* You mustn't underestimate priests. I ask about horoscopes. I've always wanted to know: it has to be possible to test them statistically. All you need is a hundred people who've died on the same day, either there will be significant similarities in their horoscopes or there won't! Why doesn't somebody do it?

He gapes at me like an idiot. Evidently I've offended him. Turning wine into blood is perfectly fine, but horoscopes are beneath his dignity. I pull out my phone. No answer. We've already reached the main floor.

We go through the lobby, the glass doors open. Dear God, it's hot. My phone vibrates. *Can you do it at five?*

Why not now??? I text. A car horn blasts next to me, I realize I'm in the middle of the street – the restaurant is right over there, I go there every day. The décor is horrible, the waiters are arrogant, and I don't like the food. But so what – I'm rarely hungry anyway, because of the medication I'm on.

The waiter pushes the table aside so that my fat brother can force his way onto the banquette. I order for the two of us, what I always order, spaghetti with shellfish. I don't like mussels, but it's an appropriate dish, not too much, not too heavy, not too few calories, not too cheap. My phone vibrates. *Good, that's fine. Now.*

Martin asks me about the economy and my forecasts. I answer something or other. Why are we sitting here, what does he want? *I can't right now*, I text. How does she think I live, does she believe I can just drop everything from one minute to the next, just because she feels lonely? *Late afternoon, okay?*

I wait. No answer. My brother asks things, I answer without even listening to myself. I look at the phone, put it aside, pick it up again, put it aside, pick it up. Why isn't she answering?

'When you send someone a message,' I ask, 'and he answers, and you answer back and ask for a quick answer and none comes, would you assume he didn't get the message or that he's simply not answering?'

'He or she?'

'What?'

He looks at me slyly. 'You said "he" and then you said "she".'

Nuts. I know what I said. A laughably obvious trick. 'And?'

'Nothing,' he says furtively.

What is he trying to get out of me, how has he managed to get me to talk about personal things? These priests are slick. 'What do you want to know?'

'Nothing!'

His mouth is smeared with sauce. There are plates between us, his is almost empty, mine is untouched. When were they brought? 'It doesn't matter what kind of message,' I say. 'It's irrelevant.'

He murmurs something, trying to talk his way out of it.

Why isn't she answering? 'Perhaps it's all part of what you do. Perhaps you have to be that inquisitive.'

My telephone vibrates. *Okay, then later.*

When? I write, and ask myself for the thousandth time how many servers this message will pass through and how many strangers can read it. Any one of them could blackmail me. Why does she force me into such careless behaviour? 'Do you still do exorcisms? Demonic possession. Do you still deal with that? Do you have people who do it?'

He gapes at me.

'What is the classic school of thought? Do you have to let a demon in when he comes? Does he need an invitation, or can he just take possession of someone?'

'Why do you want to know?'

Always a question to counter a question. Why can't he just tell a person what they want to know? Because I'm afraid of ghosts, every day, all the time – is that what I should answer? 'A book, just a book. I read this book. A strange book. Never mind.'

The phone vibrates. *Already booked. Flight and hotel, leaving Saturday, back Sunday night, so looking forward. :-)*

It takes me a moment to realize it's from Laura. Since when does she book her own flights?

Wonderful! I write back. I will really need a good excuse.

I've barely hit the Send button when the phone vibrates again. *How are you, call me if you have time! Martin.*

Good. Stay calm. Always calm. I look up, there he is, sitting in front of me. Martin. My brother. I look at the phone, the message is still there. I look at his face. I look at the phone. Is it my imagination after all? Am I sitting here alone? His plate is empty, mine is full, which argues against that.

But why should it argue against it? I don't know any more, I've lost my train of thought. Anyone who can imagine a brother can also imagine an empty plate. Don't panic. The main thing is to stay calm. Carefully, making sure not to hit any wrong button, I erase the message. Then I put away the phone and say, 'This heat!' just in order to have something to say.

He asks about Laura and Marie, I answer him. I talk about my mother's new TV broadcast, then ask after his mother. Obviously he spends all his time with her, poor bastard, it's tragic. For all that, I like his mother, at least more than I do my own. Just as I'm about to ask him if it's really necessary, all this visiting business, and if something shouldn't be done about it, someone slaps me on the shoulder. Lothar Remling. The phone vibrates but I can't look now. I jump up. Shoulder slapping. Punch in the upper arm. Football talk. Then he takes himself off. I can't stand the guy, he almost wrecked the Ostermann deal for me a couple of years ago. Finally I can look. Three messages.

I can't take it any more.

Come later, come now, doesn't matter.

Come now or don't come at all.

I stand up, say something about an urgent appointment, and run.

The heat seems to have got even worse, it's not far to go, she lives only ten blocks away. But I quickly register that today it would have been smarter to take the car.

I stop, pull out the phone. The free signal: once, twice, three times, four. Has she stopped answering when I call? Are we that far along?

Sibylle picks up. 'What is it, Eric?'

'I have to see you.'

'But I wrote you that you can come right now.'

'But right now I can't!'

I think she's already disconnected, but she's still there. 'Eric, it's unendurable. First the thing in the movie house, and now – '

'Don't say any more! Not on the phone.'

'But – '

'Do you know how many people could hear us?'

'You called *me*!'

'Because I have to see you.'

'And I said come.'

'But I can't right now.'

'Then don't come.'

I feel dizzy. Did she really say I shouldn't come? 'Are you at home?'

She says nothing.

'Why aren't you saying anything?'

I listen, and only after a while do I realize she's disconnected.

I have to sit down. Next to the street there's an asphalt playground, surrounded by a wire fence, with a bench at its edge.

I sit there for some time with closed eyes. I hear the noise of the traffic: honking, engine sounds, a pneumatic drill. The sun is burning. My heartbeat steadies.

When I open my eyes, two children are sitting next to me. A boy with a baseball cap and a girl with long black hair that has a blue bow in it. She's about six years old, he's about ten.

'What are you doing here?' he asks.

'I'm sitting,' I say. 'What are you doing?'

'I'm sitting too.'

We look at the girl.

'Me too,' she says.

'Do you live around here?' I ask.

'A long way away,' she says. 'And you?'

'Also a long way away,' I say.

'How old are you?' asks the boy.

'Thirty-seven.'

'That's old,' says the girl.

'Yes,' I say. 'That's old.'

'Are you going to die soon?'

'No.'

'But you'll die sometime.'

'No!'

We say nothing for a bit.

'Are you here to play?'

'Yes, but it's too hot,' says the boy.

'You can't do anything when it's this hot,' says the girl.

'Do you have children?' he asks.

'A daughter. She's about the same age as you.'

'Is she here too?'

'In school. She's in school. Why aren't you in school?'

'We're playing truant.'

'You shouldn't do that.'

'Why not?'

I think. Absolutely no good reason presents itself to me. 'Because it's not okay,' I say hesitantly. 'You have to learn.'

'You don't learn much,' she says.

'If you don't go for a day, you don't miss anything at all,' he says.

'So you're going back tomorrow?'

'Perhaps,' he says.

'Yes,' she says.

'Perhaps,' he says again.

'So what are your names?'

The girl shakes her head. 'We're not allowed to tell strangers our names.'

'I think you're not supposed to talk to strangers at all.'

'Yes we can. Talking's okay. But not telling anyone our names.'

'That's strange,' I say.

'Yes,' he says. 'It's strange.'

'Is she your sister?' I ask.

'He's my brother,' she says.

'Do you go to the same school?'

The two of them look questioningly at each other. He shrugs.

I absolutely know that I'm in a hurry, that I should be moving on, that I have to get to Sibylle's and then the conference. But instead of getting to my feet, I close my eyes again.

'Were you ever in a plane?'

'Yes. Why?'

'Why can it fly?'

'Because it has wings.'

'But a plane's so heavy. Why can it fly?'

'The lift.'

'What's that?'

'I don't know.'

'But why does it fly?'

'The lift.'

'What is that?'

'I don't know.'

'You don't know?'

'No.'

'But you went to school.'

'Yes.'

'But why does it fly?'

The darkness behind my eyelids is lit by sunlight. Glowing orange with yellow circles in it that wander and rise and fall. Even the noise of the pneumatic drill suddenly sounds peaceful.

'Leave the three of them,' says the boy. 'Don't butt in, just keep going.'

'What?' I blink in the sun. 'What did you say?'

'I said we have to go now.'

I stand up quickly. 'Me too.'

'Josi,' says the boy. 'My name's Josi. That's Ella.'

'And what is your name?' asks the girl.

'Hans.' I'm touched by the fact that they've given away their names, but that's no reason to be careless.

'Bye, Hans!'

I leave and feel so light that I could just float up off the ground. Perhaps it's the sun, perhaps it's hunger. I should have eaten my pasta with mussels. In order not to faint, I stop at a fast-food stand.

There's a long line. Three teenagers are standing ahead of me, arguing with the vendor. One of them is wearing a T-shirt that says *Morning Tower*, the second has one that says *Bubbletea is not a drink I like*, the third sports a huge bright red Y. Dumb, says one of them to the vendor, absolute bullshit, to which the vendor says they should go the hell away, to which one of them replies that the vendor is the one who should go the hell away, to which the vendor says no, he'd rather *they* went the hell away, to which another of them says no, you do it, and it goes on like that for a while. I'm about to give up and move on, but then they run off, swearing, and disappear down the next subway entrance and I can buy my hot dog. It tastes quite good. My phone rings. It's Ivan. Reluctantly I press Receive.

'I thought I should give you a call,' he says.

'Why?'

'Just a feeling. Everything okay?'

'Of course.'

'So why do I have this feeling?'

'Maybe because today I hoped you and I . . . Ah!' Now I get it. I stand still in surprise. Cars hoot, a policeman yells at me, once again I've got myself into the street without even noticing.

'Why are you laughing?'

'I told my secretary to call you, but she . . . just think: she called Martin!'

'Martin!'

'We went to lunch. The whole time I was wondering why.'

'How's business?'

'Good. Like always. How's art?'

'I have to keep an eye on the auction houses. You can't lose control over prices. Besides . . .'

'Have you spoken to Mother recently?'

'Yes, right, I have to give her a call soon. She left me three messages. But something's up with you. I can tell. You can deny it, but – '

'Have to go now!'

'Eric, you can tell me every – '

'Everything's fine, honestly, got to go now.'

'But how – '

I press the Disconnect button. It's a strange experience talking to Ivan, almost like talking to myself, and suddenly I'm clear again about why I've been avoiding him for some time. It's hard to keep secrets from him, he sees through me, just as I see through him, and he cannot find out just yet how bad things are with me and with business, it would be too painful, a great defeat, and besides I couldn't be sure he'd keep it to himself. The old rule: a secret only stays a secret if absolutely nobody knows about it. If you stick to that, it's not as hard to keep them as people think. You can know someone almost as well as you know yourself and still not read their thoughts. I cannot ask Ivan for money. I cannot ask him to help me disappear. He is too upright a person, and he wouldn't understand.

I wish he weren't homosexual. When I found out, it made me totally crazy for weeks. Someone who's so like me – what does that say about me, what does it mean? Nothing, I know that, nothing, nothing, it means absolutely nothing, but I've never been able to forgive him.

I send a message to Knut – the address, and instructions to set

140

off at once. Then I open Sibylle's front door, run up three flights of stairs, want to wait outside her apartment door to get my breath back, but am too impatient for that, and knock. I could also ring the bell, but after she snubbed me like that, I need to make a more impressive entrance.

She opens the door. I'm immediately struck by how good she looks. She isn't as beautiful as Laura, but she's more exciting: the long hair, the delicate neck, the bare arms with their colourful bangles. She was my therapist, but she stopped treating me six months ago because, she said, it would be a breach of professional ethics. It doesn't matter anyway, the therapy was totally pointless, I told her nothing but lies.

'Is the bell broken?'

I walk across the hall and into the living room. There I catch my breath, search for words, and fail to find any.

'Poor guy. Come here.'

I clench my fists, inhale, open my mouth, but can't say a word.

'Poor guy,' she says again, and already we're on the carpet. I want to protest and get the two of us to pull ourselves together, for that's what matters most, knowing how to pull yourself together, but it doesn't help, because I suddenly realize that I don't want us to pull ourselves together, what I want is what is going on right here, in her and over her and on her, and why not, because without this, what else is there in the world?

'But –'

'It's all right,' she whispers in my ear. 'It's all right.'

It's hot, she has no air-conditioning, she thinks it makes you sick. It seems to me as if I were on my feet and taking a step back so as to watch the two of us: a trifle strange, the whole thing, more foolish than awkward, and I wonder if people who love to discourse on human dignity have ever actually observed this with a sober eye. But at the same time I'm still the man on the carpet and

I feel that the moment is about to arrive when I am no longer divided but a single entity, and only for a few fractions of a second do I form the thought that I'm setting myself up for blackmail if there's a camera in this room, and then I have an image of Laura, whom I'm deceiving again and to whom I'm doing an injustice with my continual lies, but a moment later the image is gone again and all I know is that every person must do what will save him, and everything is finally what it is, and nothing else, and every-thing is good.

We lie on our backs, her head on my chest. I don't want to be anywhere else, nothing is bothering me. It won't last very long.

'How is she?' asks Sibylle.

I have to think to figure out who she means. I cradle her head, and stroke her silky hair. Very soon everything that is bearing down on me will become real again.

'Perhaps I could help her.'

I pull my hand away.

'I mean, I could recommend a colleague. Ancillary talk therapy. When she's recovered, we can all get on with our lives. She with hers. And the two of us with ours. Together.'

At the beginning I didn't have any specific plan, it was one of many tales that I spun, but later it turned out to be helpful: no one leaves a wife who has cancer, no one can demand it of anyone else. And sometimes I feel this version is actually true, as if it were play-ing out in a parallel universe exactly as I've told it to Sibylle. I could talk about it with a therapist, but Sibylle doesn't want to treat me any more and I wouldn't want to try it with anyone else, I've got enough problems already.

'I have to leave right away,' I say.

How peculiar that I spend all day thinking about her and yet want only to disappear as soon as I'm with her. Gently I push her head to one side, stand up, and start gathering my clothes together.

'You're always in a hurry.' She laughs sadly. 'You leave me sitting in the cinema and then you write such messages! My therapist asked why I do it to myself. Because you're good-looking? I said he's not that good-looking, but then she wanted to see a photo and I couldn't lie about it. Or is it because of this?' She points at the carpet. 'Yes, it's good, it's really good, but it's also a kind of transference. My therapist thinks I show reactions that are triggered quite automatically by the collision of regression and aggression. What can I do?'

I clear my throat in an empathetic sort of way, climb into my trousers, button my shirt, tie my tie without using a mirror, and manage to look as though I know what she's talking about.

'Don't worry,' she says. 'You'll make it. You're stronger than you think.'

'I know.'

She smiles, as if she'd made some enigmatic joke. I smile too and go out of the room. I rush down the stairs and run along the street. There's an office building on the other side, I take the back entrance, ride up to the second floor, go into Starbucks, and get a soy milk cappuccino with extra froth, so that Knut will see I really have been in the building. Then I ride down again and leave by the other exit. I see Knut immediately.

He's having an argument with a street sweeper and it looks serious. The man has lifted his broom to use as a weapon, Knut is making fists, and both are emitting an uninterrupted torrent of insults. It's the heat, everyone is on edge today. Interested, I listen.

'Pig!' roars Knut.

'Son of a bitch!' roars the street sweeper.

'Shithead!'

'Son of a pig!'

'Pig, pig, pig!'

I'm enjoying this, but I don't have time. So I swallow a

mouthful of coffee, put the container on the ground, and approach Knut.

'Lousy, old, greasy, fat pig!' screams Knut. 'Baldy! Pig shit!'

I push him at the driver's door, then get into the backseat.

It's blissfully cool in the car. As Knut starts to drive, still cursing quietly, my phone vibrates. I see the number and take the call, apprehensively.

'Mother?'

'Be quiet and listen. I – '

'How's the practice?'

'Far too successful. The whole country wants to have me as their doctor. All because of the broadcast. I – '

'It's a very interesting programme.' I've only seen it once. 'We never miss a follow-up.'

'I'm an eye doctor. I understand absolutely nothing about all these illnesses. All I do is tell people they should go and see their doctor.'

'I didn't notice.'

'I wanted to propose an investment to you.'

'A . . . aha.'

'It's about some property. My – below our house. Someone wants to buy it, to build on. We have to beat them to it. It would ruin the view.'

'Ah.'

'It would be a good investment.'

'I don't know.'

'What is that supposed to mean?'

I try to think about the previous minutes on the carpet. About Sibylle's breath next to my ear, about her body in my arms, her hair, her smell. But none of it helps. I have to be back with her again immediately, naked on the carpet again immediately, and probably not even that would suffice.

144

'Why don't you say something?' Mother asks. 'Why is it impossible to have a normal conversation with you?'

'I can't hear you any more!' I call. 'Bad connection!'

'I hear you perfectly well.'

'What are you saying?' I hit the Disconnect button.

'Bad connection,' I say to Knut. 'It's become impossible to have a telephone call these days.'

'They should all be locked up!'

'Why?'

'They're all nuts!'

'Who?'

'All locked up, I said. Nuts, all of them!'

The phone vibrates. I put my thumb on the Disconnect button, but then I answer anyway.

'Do you hear me better now?' she asks. 'It's become impossible to have a telephone call these days.'

'The connection was fine. I hung up.'

'You didn't.'

'Yes I did.'

'You wouldn't just simply hang up if you were talking to your mother. You wouldn't do it.'

'Buy the property yourself. You're making enough money with the programme.'

'But it's a good investment.'

'How can it be a good investment? You say I'm not allowed to *build* anything.'

'Do you want to ruin my view? What do you want to build?'

'I don't want to build. I don't want to have it at all!'

'Don't you scream at me! When your mother asks you –'

I hit the Disconnect button. A few seconds later the phone vibrates again. I ignore it. Then I think for a while, stare at the phone, rub my eyes, and call back.

'You hung up!' she said. 'I know. Don't lie!'

'I have no intention of lying.'

'I wouldn't believe that either.'

'So.'

'Don't ever do that again!'

'I'll do what I want. I'm an adult.'

She gives a mocking laugh, and I hit the Disconnect button with a shaking hand.

I wait, but she doesn't call again. To be on the safe side, I switch the gadget off. I remember that Sibylle recently said something astonishingly astute about my mother, which was all the more surprising because she knows nothing about my mother; it was so obviously accurate that I must have had to suppress it immediately, for all I remember about it is that it was so to the point.

Knut begins to tell a story about a Marine, an ancient monkey and a gardener from Thailand, and it also features a watering can, a plane and, if I'm getting it right, a professor of numismatics. I nod from time to time and become convinced the whole thing would make no sense whatever even if I were paying attention. When we get there, it's ten past four. The conference has already begun.

I get out of the car, walk through the heat into the cool of the lobby, and enter the elevator. Perhaps they've actually been waiting for me.

The elevator is already starting its ascent. It stops at the fourth floor, no one gets in. It's just going up again when my knees give way and my head slams against the wall.

I hear something. It's all dark around me. What I'm hearing is sobbing. I manage to straighten up a little. Slowly the shadow dissolves. I grope my head: no blood. Now I can see the dirty green threads in the carpeting. The person sobbing in here is me. I don't know what it is, but something terrible has happened. Something that should never have been allowed to happen. Something that will never come good again.

I stand up. I'm not the only thing swaying, the elevator cabin is swaying too: seventh floor, eighth floor, ninth floor. Nothing like this has ever happened to me before. I wipe away my tears and check my watch: fourteen minutes past four. Note the day, note the time: 8 August 2008, fourteen minutes past four. You'll find out what this means soon enough. The cabin stops, the doors open. At the last moment before they close again, I leap out.

I have to stay leaning against the wall for a bit, then I walk through the office in a daze. Everything seems different from the way it was before, every desk, every face, every object. I enter the conference room and murmur my excuses, because of course they have started without me. I take off my jacket, throw it over an empty chair, sit down, and manage to look as if everything is in order. At this I am an expert.

The sight of my colleagues depresses me even more than usual: all that lethargy, all that mediocrity. Possibly it is also to do with the fact that I only hire mediocre people. The last thing I need is someone who sees through me. Lehmann and Schröter are here, Kelling, whose daughter is my godchild, Pöhlke, whom I'd fire in a moment if only he gave me an excuse, because I just don't like him. Maria Gudschmid is here, and so is the guy whose name I can never remember. And Felsner. I like him, but I don't know why. When I came in, Lehmann had just been speaking. Now they're all still, looking at me and waiting.

I take a breath. I'm hoarse and I feel as if I might burst into tears again, but I still have to say something. So I stammer out a few phrases about pleasurable working conditions and the good things we make, and I quote the Bhagavad Gita: Here you stand, Arjuna, so do not ask, stand up and fight, for God hates the lukewarm. Not a bad address, I think. They don't know that they will soon be unemployed; some will be suspected of having collaborated, but the truth will come out: they are not criminals, they are merely incompetent.

The bit about God and the lukewarm, says Maria Gudschmid, isn't in the Bhagavad Gita, it's from the Bible.

The danger, says Kelling, that Triple A bonds could lose a significant portion of their value, can be discounted in practical terms. Triple As are and will remain classical value investments and thus risk free.

A problem arises, says Pöhlke, that it's a known fact that investment banks invested in the very positions they were actively offering for sale to smaller firms. They thus set the value themselves of what they were selling; in other words, they unilaterally decided how much their customers owed them.

At some point, Felsner says, there will be a class-action suit against this system. But at the moment the only thing to do is wait. There has been an announcement that Krishna's next avatar will appear before this epoch of ours is over.

Which doesn't mean that it's certain that the avatar will have to be human, says Maria Gudschmid.

If for example anyone is holding significant insurance paper, says Lehmann, it would be impossible to calculate the extent of exposure in the event of a collapse of the large derivative conglomerates. There is, he says, no tool to work out a reasonable rate of risk.

'Kluessen wants to withdraw his money,' I say.

At a stroke the room falls silent.

But hopefully it's not yet a sure thing, says Felsner. And there are certainly things we can still do.

Not a good moment to lose our most important account, in Maria's view.

In an emergency there are tricks, says Lehmann. If for example the value of a set of assets cannot be reliably established because of

148

a legally suspect asymmetry in the market, the trustee has the right to freeze those assets on a temporary basis. Even against the wishes of the owner.

Pure theory, says Schörter. No court would accept such an argument.

To get back to the problem with the investment banks, says Pöhlke. His proposal: short a few of them, without great investment.

Only to him that dares, says Lehmann, will Krishna give.

Quite a few dare, is Pöhlke's infuriated retort, and Krishna does not give. The god has freedom of action, because he is freedom itself.

Which is why bad people sometimes get the lot, says Kelling, while good people get nothing. The risk potential in the lower reaches of the mortgage pool is not good, and –

'Thank you!' I stand up. Until now I've kept a straight face, I've stayed sitting with my back straight and haven't given anything away. Now I've had enough.

'Just one more question,' calls Schröter.

The door closes behind me.

On the way to the elevator I wonder about how to establish that I really did hear what I think I heard. But if I ask someone, he could lie, and even a recording can be manipulated.

'Now it's happened,' says the man next to me in the elevator. 'Now it's all coming to an end.'

He's wearing a hat and his teeth are hideous. I've seen him already today, but I can't remember where. He doesn't look right at me but talks to my reflection in the mirror on the back wall of the elevator, so that it is not he but his reflection that stares at me fixedly. Apart from us there are two other men standing there with briefcases, but they are looking straight ahead and paying no attention to us.

149

'What did you say?' I ask.

'Nothing,' he says.

I turn away.

'Sometimes every path is the wrong one,' he says.

I stare at him.

'The truth will set you free,' he says. 'Nice if it were so. But sometimes there is absolutely nothing that can set you free any more. Neither lies nor the truth.' He straightens his hat with an affected gesture. 'At bottom there is no longer any difference between the two, Ivan.'

'Excuse me?'

He frowns.

'What did you just say? About lies and truth? Did you call me Ivan?'

Now the two men with the briefcases are watching us, concerned. Yes, that's how it goes, that's how they shatter your nerves. And then all of a sudden, you grab someone and yell and start hitting them and then they can put you away. But I'm not going to make it that easy for them.

'Apologies,' I say. 'I must have misheard.'

'You think?' asks the man with the hat.

The elevator stops, one of the briefcase men gets out and a woman in a black jacket gets in. They've practised really well, everything looks natural. You could watch for hours and never have any suspicion.

'You're not going to hold out very much longer,' he says.

I don't react.

'Keep running. Look good in your suit. Keep running for as long as you can. You look the worse for wear.'

I don't react.

'You have to know, today is not a day like any other. Sometimes it's easier. Death brings us closer.'

The elevator stops, the doors open, I get out without turning around. I go out to the street, the heat has abated a bit, it will soon be evening. Knut is sitting in the car with the engine running. Did I tell him to wait for me? I get in.

'Question,' he says.

'Not now.'

'Municipal bonds – should you, shouldn't you, how does it look?'

How cool and quiet it is in the car. A good make of car, clean, tank full, with a chauffeur at the wheel, all give me more peace than the finest of religions.

'To be specific,' says Knut. 'My aunt. Dead. Bad thing. I told you about it. The building site. The crane.'

'Yes, I know.' As always, I haven't a clue.

'But it was also her fault. She shouldn't have hidden where she did. Nobody made her do that, did they?'

'No.'

'In any case, none of us would have thought she had a hundred thousand euros. We just didn't know. Particularly not after the thing with the innkeeper and the burglars. And also because she was always so stingy. Nothing ever at Christmas. Nor to the children. So now, what do we do? There's this old guy next door, his son is with the bank. I don't like him. He doesn't like me either. Particularly not after the whole thing with his dog. He stated that the beast was never in our garden, but I have two witnesses. So – municipal bonds. His son's idea. Mitznik.'

'What?'

'That's what the old guy is called. And he stutters! Municipal bonds. Mitznik's his name. So what now, boss, are they okay? Municipal bonds?'

'Yes, pretty much.'

'But do they pay anything?'

For no apparent reason he brakes sharply; luckily my seat belt is fastened. He hits the horn and then drives on. 'I want to make some money! If there's nothing in it, I'm out!'

'The more reliable an investment is, the less it pays. The highest wins you can make are in a casino, because the odds there are so terrible. Investing is gambling with good odds.'

'Can I give it to you, boss?'

'Me?'

'Will you invest it for me, boss?'

'We don't accept such small investments.'

'But for me? As a favour? For a friend?'

Did he really call me a friend? The manoeuvre is transparent, but it moves me. 'A hundred thousand?'

'Maybe even a bit more.'

Well, it would be enough to pay the rent on the office space for a while. Later that would make him one joint plaintiff among many, that's no longer the point.

I shake my head.

'Boss!'

'It wouldn't be right. Believe me.'

'Why?' He coughs, then he emits a series of high, sharp sounds. They could be sounds of rage, or they could be sobs.

'You just have to believe me. It's better this way.'

He brakes, opens the window, and screams at someone. I can't understand it all, but the words *animal*, *pig-ignorant* and *child abuser* emerge, along with something about strangulation. He's already driving on.

'Well, okay,' I say.

'Really?'

'For you, I'll make an exception.'

'Boss!'

'It's fine!'

'Boss?'

'Please, it's fine.'

But he brakes again, turns around, and reaches for my hand. At first I manage to avoid it, but then he gets hold of my shirt cuff. 'I'd die for you.'

'That's really not necessary.'

'I'd kill for you.'

'Excuse me?'

'I mean it. Just give me a name.'

'Please – '

'I'll kill him.'

'Keep driving!'

'It's not a joke.'

How can I avoid thinking about Kluessen? A car accident, a suddenly induced and mysterious heart ailment . . . Luckily Knut lets it go and keeps driving. I close my eyes and manage to black out his ongoing monologue. It occurs to me that my phone is still switched off. This explains why no one from the office has called me to ask where on earth I've got to.

We've already reached home. If you drive early, you avoid the rush hour. I evade Knut's last effusions of thanks, get out, and stride along the gravel path through the garden like the very image of a man accustomed to overcoming obstacles. I unlock the front door, go in, and call, 'I'm home!'

No answer.

There was no anticipation that I would be back so early. The house is silent, as if I'd caught it getting up to something. So this is what it's like when I'm not here. I call out again. My voice sounds lost in the large hall.

Then I hear something.

Not a knocking, more a scraping noise. It sounds like heavy metal objects being shoved around. I cock my ears, but it's already stopped. Just as I decide I must have made a mistake, it starts again.

It's coming from below me, in the cellar. Should I call someone, a plumber or the fire department? But if someone came and there was nothing to hear, what would that make me look like? I go into the kitchen and wash my hands. And there it goes again. The window shakes, the glasses in the cupboard clink gently. I dry my hands. Now all is quiet.

And then I hear it again.

Under no circumstances am I going to go down to the cellar on my own.

I listen. It's stopped.

It starts again.

I cross the hall and undo the heavy bolt on the cellar door. I've never been down there – why would I? It's where we store our wine bottles, but that's not my job, Laura's the one who takes care of all that.

A flight of stairs leads down; two naked bulbs cast a rather spotted light on the treads. Three old posters are glued up on the brick wall: Yoda, Darth Vader and some naked woman – I've never seen any of them before. At the bottom is a metal door. I open it, grope for the light switch, and locate it. The air is musty. A bulb crackles as it comes on.

A long space, a low ceiling, a large wine rack against the wall, half empty. That's my wine collection, that's what I spent all that money on? In one corner there's a tin bucket lying on its side, in the opposite wall I see another door. The noise has ceased. I move slowly through the room and push the lever of the door handle down. I feel a rush of cold air: another flight of steps. I feel for the switch: the light goes on.

This bulb is dirty and flickers badly. It must already be old. The treads are narrow. I put out my right foot and take a cautious step onto the top one, pause for a moment to collect myself, and then go slowly down.

There it is again. A dull thump, a dragging noise, a sort of squeal, of the kind made by the pistons of a large machine. But I cannot turn around. Succumb to your anxieties too often and you become small and pathetic. This is my house. Perhaps this is the critical test, perhaps now everything will change.

Silence falls.

I reach the bottom without a sound to be heard, except for my own breathing and the beating of my heart. It's cold. How deep is it down here? Another door, which I open; another light switch.

I hear it again. This room is surprisingly large, at least fifteen by thirty metres. Stone walls, the floor hard earth, two bulbs in the ceiling, only one of which is working. I see a crumpled cloth, and next to it a curved metal rod, one end rounded like the head of a walking stick, the other filed to a sharp point. Two doors: I try one, it's locked. I rattle it, but it doesn't budge. But the other one opens and on the other side is yet another set of steps. No light switch.

I stare down into the darkness, and try to count the treads. I can't make out more than nine.

Enough! I'm not going any further!

I go further, one step after the other, my left hand flat against the wall, my right hand clutching the phone with its feeble glow. When did the noise stop? I haven't even noticed. Another two steps. And another. And yet another. Now I've reached the floor.

In front of me is a door, which I try to open, but it's locked tight. I can feel the relief. There's nothing more here, I can go back. I try it once again, and it opens without the slightest resistance.

I grope my way forward. Under me is a step made of steel, and the wall next to me is curved. After a moment I get it: a spiral staircase. The shaft goes straight down vertically. I search my pockets and find a ballpoint pen made of plastic. I hold it out with my arm and let it drop.

I wait. No sound of an impact. Probably the pen was too small and too light. I search my pockets again and find a wallet, a metal lighter, a key ring and coins. I only have the lighter so as to be able to offer it to smokers. I snap it open. The flame, much brighter than the phone, lets me see the steps better. I hold it out over the shaft and it flickers. So air is streaming up from down there. I hesitate, then let it fall. The flame dwindles and is swallowed up in the darkness. No sound of an impact.

But I hear something else. I listen, wait, listen, the vibrations are getting stronger: something is hitting the steps. It takes me a few seconds to realize that someone is coming up the stairs. Towards me.

Then it goes dark.

And slowly the light returns. We're sitting at dinner: Laura, Marie, Laura's father, Laura's mother, Laura's sister and brother-in-law and two children, all around the table, which has been set.

'It's supposed to stay this hot all week,' says Laura.

'Every summer worse than the one before,' says her sister. 'Nobody knows where you can even take the children.'

'A house in Scandinavia,' says my father-in-law. 'Or on the North Sea.' He looks at me. 'Like your brother's. Everyone could use one.'

'We could visit him,' I am obliged to say. I would like to eat, because I'm really hungry, but my hands are shaking too badly.

Now my father-in-law is talking about politics. I nod at regular intervals, as does everyone else. He's an architect, and in the seventies he built one of the ugliest concrete buildings in the country, which earned him the National Medal. He gestures deliberately and makes long pauses before he says anything he thinks is important. That's how you have to do it, that's how you have to be, that's how you have to present yourself, and then you'll be respected. I admire him, I always wanted to be like him; and who knows, maybe in reality he's a little like me.

The trembling has eased up. Very carefully I push food into my mouth. Luckily nobody's watching me.

Or? Now everyone's looking at me. What is it, what did I get wrong, what did I mess up? Apparently Laura has said something about a trip to Sicily. They're all smiling and being pleased and saying how wonderful.

'Do please excuse me,' I say. 'Urgent call. Be right back.'

'You work too much,' says Laura.

'Everyone has to indulge themselves a little,' says my father-in-law. He pauses for thought, and then goes on in a tone that suggests he's imparting hidden wisdom to us: 'A man must know how to live.'

I ask myself if he's ever in his entire life uttered one single phrase that isn't a thousand times well-worn cliché. I envy him greatly.

On my way to my study I pass the open door to the salon. Ligurna, our Lithuanian maid, greets me looking tragic. I nod to her and hurry on past. A year ago in a moment of weakness I slept with her. Unfortunately it happened not in the kitchen or on my desk but in the master bedroom in our marriage bed. Afterwards Ligurna searched carpet and bedside table like a skilled detective for hairs, eyelashes, any other traces: nonetheless I was afraid for weeks that she could have overlooked something. Since then I've only spoken to her when it's unavoidable. I can't throw her out, she could blackmail me.

I sit behind the desk, swallow two tranquillizers without water, look at the Paul Klee, look at the Eulenboeck on the opposite wall: a canvas covered with a collage of newspaper cuttings, with a crushed Coca-Cola can and a teddy bear glued in the middle. You have to go right up close to realize that it's all trompe l'œil. The bear and the can aren't real, nor are the bits of newspaper; it's all painted in oils. If you examine the cuttings with a magnifying glass, you see they're all art criticism about collages.

The painting is from Eulenboeck's later period, his most valuable. I got to know the old poseur, he was very condescending, very white-haired, and never stopped making really stupid jokes about Ivan and me and how uncannily alike we were. Obviously he thought he knew me well, because he knew Ivan well. It cost one hundred and seventy thousand, supposedly a discounted price for a friend. But all the same it's got that teddy bear. He gives me joy. I know it's all a parody of something and nothing in it means what it's supposed to mean, but I don't care. On the short list of things that aren't horrible in my life, that bear is right up there.

What luck that these days you can order every medication on the Internet. How would someone like me have coped fifteen years ago? I cross my arms and lean back. I would like to work in order to relax a bit, but I have nothing to do. Without hope, there's leisure.

There's a knock. Laura looks in. 'Do you have a moment?'

'Unfortunately not.'

She sits down, crosses her legs, and looks first at the Paul Klee, then at me.

'Is it about Marie?'

'It's about me.'

'You?'

'Imagine, Eric. It's about me.'

This I needed. Is she going to tell me another dream? Or has someone offered her a role? That would be truly bad news.

'I've had an offer. A role.'

'But that's wonderful!'

'Nothing big, but at least it's a start. It's not easy going back again after fifteen years.'

'You're even more beautiful than you were then!'

Not bad. It didn't take me half a second to come up with that, the sentence is all prepared and always at hand. Of course she isn't more beautiful than she used to be, why should she be, but she's slimmer and the exercise has paid off, and fine mature lines around her eyes look good on her. She could certainly have a career in movies. I have to stop it.

'I've been thinking.'

'Yes?'

'I must concentrate on myself.'

She stops, evidently to give me the chance to reply. But what do I say?

'It's only for a while, Eric. To begin with. We're not separating yet. Everything will sort itself out.'

She looks at me. I look at her.

'Eric, what is it?'

She pushes her hair off her face and waits. Apparently it's up to me to say something, but what does she want to hear, what's she talking about?

'I would move out, but it's impractical. I have to look after Marie, and I also need Ligurna. It's better if you look and find somewhere else. Then you wouldn't have such a long journey to the office.'

'To the office?'

'Besides which the house is close to school. I won't be able to be home much while they're shooting. Of course you can see Marie whenever you want.'

I nod, because now I understand what she's saying, even if it makes no sense. The words have a meaning, apparently the sentences do too, but when you put them together, they're so empty that she could be talking pure nonsense.

'Eric, I can't get caught up in your games right now.'

I nod as if I understand. Luckily I don't have to say anything at first, for she stands up and keeps talking. Through a fog I hear her voice speaking about long, lonely hours and how I'm perpetually busy and how money and cold rationality don't take precedence over everything else. After a while she stops, sits down again, and waits. I look at her helplessly.

'Don't try that with me,' she says. 'Your tricks. Your negotiating tricks. All your tricks. I know you. It doesn't work with me.'

I open my mouth, take a breath, shut it again.

She talks on. Her arms are so fine, her hands delicate and elegant, again and again the desk lamp catches the diamond ring on her middle finger so that it flashes sparks. Now she's saying I mustn't think that it has anything to do with another man, there is no other man, if I thought any such thing I'd be wrong, because there most certainly isn't another man and I shouldn't think anything else.

I concentrate on continuing to look at her attentively, and not letting myself get distressed by the fact that the colour has drained out of everything and my face feels as if it's made of cotton wool.

'Answer me, Eric! Stop it! Say something!'

But when I try to search for a reply, everything just retreats still further. I'm back in the cellar, way down, even deeper than I was, and something is coming up the stairs, someone is speaking. Words put themselves together, it's dark, and there's a hundredweight pressing down on me. The voice seems somehow not unfamiliar, and from somewhere a crack of light comes in. The window by the desk. I feel as if much time has passed, but Laura is still sitting there talking.

'To begin with everything can go on like normal,' she says. 'We can behave as if nothing had happened. We'd fly to Sicily. Next week we'll go together to the party at the Lohnenkovens'. In the meantime you can look for an apartment. We don't have to make it hard for ourselves.'

I clear my throat. Did I really pass out here at my desk in front of her eyes, without noticing? Who the hell are the Lohnenkovens?

'I'm not talking about a divorce just yet. It doesn't have to go that far. But if it does, we have to be sensible. Of course you have good lawyers. That's the same for me. I spoke to Papa. He's behind me.'

I nod. But who are they, who are the Lohnenkovens?

'Okay.' She gets to her feet, pushes her hair back off her face, and leaves.

I open the drawer and pick three, four, five pills out of the plastic packet. As I leave the room, my legs seem to belong to someone else, as if I were a marionette, being manipulated by a not-very-skilled puppet master.

In the dining room, they're all still sitting at the table.

'All done, your call?' My father-in-law smiles at me.

Next to him, Laura smiles too. Her mother smiles, her sister smiles, her daughters smile, only Marie yawns. I have no idea what call he's talking about.

'Laura,' I say slowly, 'did we just . . . have you . . .' It could be the effect of the pills. They're strong, and I took a lot of them. I could have imagined the whole thing.

Or? I took the pills precisely because of Laura. If she hadn't come to me, I wouldn't have swallowed so many. So the pills can't be the reason that I'm imagining Laura said things that made me take the pills. Or?

'Bad news?' My father-in-law is still smiling.

'You should lie down,' says Laura.

'Yes,' says my mother-in-law. 'You're pale. Better go to bed.'

I wait, but no one says anything more. They all smile. I leave the room unsteadily.

Right foot down the first step. I avoid looking in the direction of the cellar door, because I know that if the bolt isn't fully closed or the door is actually open, my heart will stop. I go through the hall and open the front door.

It's dark, but the air is still very hot. To my right, pressed against the wall, crouches a shaggy-coated creature that stares at me. Its smell is acrid and biting. As I stop, it bounds away on cloven feet and disappears into the blackness of the hedge.

I haul up the garage door. Knut is already off duty, I have to drive myself. Perhaps I shouldn't be doing this, given the state I'm in, but I'll manage it somehow. The engine rumbles into life and the car rolls onto the street. I see my house in the rearview mirror. A pale glow of light is emanating from the attic. Who could be up there?

But I've already rounded the corner.

Please no accident now, not after all the pills. This time I'm not calling Sibylle, I want to surprise her.

And if she isn't alone?

The thought cuts through my daze. The car swerves into the middle of the street, horns blare, but I get it under control again. If there's a man with her, I'll have to kill him! I turn the steering wheel and a yellow plastic rubbish bin gets in my way. I dodge, but it hits the right side of the car so hard that the lid flies off and cardboard boxes go sailing all over the street. I brake, and the car stops. Pedestrians are staring at me. A car stops on the other side of the street; two men get out and come towards me.

I'm ready to step on the accelerator and run them over, but that's what they intend: I'm supposed to lose control of myself. I get out, fists clenched.

'Do you need help?' one of them asks.

'Are you hurt?' asks the other.

I start to run. I run through a narrow alley, jump over the fence surrounding a building site, clamber over an excavator shovel and another fence, and keep running until I lose my breath and look around with a pounding heart. No one seems to be following me. But how can I be sure? They're so cunning.

A pedestrian zone. I detour around two women, a policeman, and two youths, Adolf Kluessen and two more women. Kluessen? Yes, I saw him quite clearly, either it was Kluessen himself or they sent someone who looks just like him. For a moment Maria Gudschmid's face surfaces under a streetlight, but this at least means nothing, because all sorts of women look just like her. I leave the pedestrian zone, cross a street, walk up a narrow ramp, and reach the front door of Sibylle's building. It's locked. I press the buzzer.

'Yes?' It's her voice in the loudspeaker, and it comes so quickly that she must have been waiting at the door – but not for me, she didn't know I was coming, so who's she waiting for?

'It's me,' I say into the microphone.

'Who?'

If she doesn't let me in now, if she doesn't open the door at once, if she makes me stand out here on the street, it's over.

'Eric?'

I don't reply. The door opens with a hum.

Someone touches my arm. Behind me there's a thin man with a long nose and a narrow chin. In one hand he's holding the handlebars of a bicycle, and in the other he has a well-worn plastic shopping bag.

'You shouldn't have got involved,' he says. 'You should have left the three of them alone. It was none of your business.'

I slam the door behind me and run up the stairs. If she has a man with her, if there's a man, if she, if . . . her floor. She's standing in the doorway.

'So what's wrong?' she asks.

'The thing with the car should never have happened. Just left standing like that. What will people think!'

'What are you talking about?'

'I must report it stolen.'

I walk past her into the apartment. There's no one here. She's alone. I sink down onto the nearest chair and switch on my mobile phone. Nine calls, three from my office, six from home, three text messages. I switch it off again.

'What's happened, Eric?'

I want to answer that absolutely nothing has happened, that everything has simply become too much for me. I want to answer that I'm just stuck. But all I say is 'It's been a hard day.' And as I'm looking at her, I realize I don't even want to be here with her. I want to go home.

'I wanted to be with you,' I say.

She comes closer, I stand up and manage to do everything necessary. My hands go where they're supposed to, my movements are the right ones, and I even succeed in enjoying the fact that this is what she wants so much, and that she's soft and smells good and maybe even loves me a little.

'Me too,' she whispers, and I ask myself what I've gone and said again now.

Afterwards I lie there awake, listening to her breathing and looking up at the dark expanse of ceiling. I mustn't go to sleep, I have to be home before dawn comes and Laura wants to tell me her dream.

I get up silently and put on my clothes. Sibylle doesn't wake up. I slide out of the room on tiptoe.

Beauty

'Have you seen Carrière's new exhibition?'

'Yes, and I'm a bit stumped.'

'Oh?'

'People say he challenges our usual ways of seeing. He says it too. In every art magazine right now. But basically what it boils down to is him admitting that pictures are only pictures, not reality. He's as proud of this as a child who's just discovered there is no Easter Bunny.'

'That's mean.'

'But I really admire him.'

'Quite right, too.'

We both smile. The situation is complicated. In my profession it's not just a matter of selling paintings – you also have to sell them to the right people. Naturally I have to convince Eliza that her collection needs another Eulenboeck, but at the same time Eliza has to convince me that her collection is the right home for Eulenboeck. There won't be many more Eulenboecks coming onto the market, and meanwhile the museums have become interested in him, and granted, they pay less, but they can raise the reputation of an artist enormously, which in turn causes auction prices in the secondary market to soar. You have to be careful: if prices rise too precipitously, they soon collapse again, and the result is all the art magazines pronouncing that the market has delivered its verdict, and the name of the artist never recovers. So Eliza has to convince me that she won't dispose of the painting I'm going to sell her as soon as she can turn a profit on it; she has to convince me that she's a serious collector, just as I have to convince her that Eulenboeck's value will not decline in the long run.

But we don't talk about any of this. We each sit in front of a plate of salad, sip our mineral water, smile a lot, and talk about anything and everything except what it's actually all about. I'm a good artist's executor, she's a good collector, and we both know the game.

So we talk about the terraces in Venice. Eliza has an apartment in Venice with a view of the Grand Canal. I went to visit once and it never stopped raining; mist crawled over the water and the city seemed lethargic, dark and stagnant. We laugh about the parties at the Biennale, we both think that they're exhausting and loud and a big effort, but you still have to go, you have no choice. We agree that great beauty makes too many demands: you are helpless in front of it, it's as if you have to react in some way, do something, respond to it, but it remains mute, and rejects you with sovereign equanimity. This of course leads to Rilke. We talk about his time with Rodin, we talk briefly about Rodin himself, then, it's unavoidable, we talk about Nietzsche. We order coffee, neither of us has touched our salad, who has an appetite on a day as hot as this? And now, because time is running out, we get around to talking briefly about Eulenboeck.

Difficult, I say. There's a lot of interest.

She can well imagine, says Eliza, but if you're going to give a painting a home, it comes down to what neighbourhood it will find itself in, and what company it will be keeping. She already has a number of Eulenboecks. Back home in Ghent she has works by Richter, Demand and Dean, she has a few things by Kentridge and Wallinger, she has a Borremans, whose style is somewhat similar to Eulenboeck's, and she has a John Currin. In addition to which she was lucky enough to know the master personally – not as well as I did, of course, but well enough all the same to know that he was no friend of the museum world. His work, she feels, belongs at the heart of the here-and-now, not in the storage rooms of galleries.

I nod vaguely.

Oh this heat, she says.

She fans air towards her, and although the restaurant has soundless ventilators, the gesture doesn't look silly, coming from her. She has an effortless elegance. If women were my thing, I'd be in love with her.

Weather like this, she says, gives you a whole new respect for Moorish culture. How is it possible to build an Alhambra while exposed to such deadly heat?

In previous eras, I tell her, our species was more robust. Man's constitution is not fixed, it develops over time. The road marches of the Roman legions achieved distances our world could only attribute to Olympic athletes.

A thought, she observes, that would have pleased Nietzsche.

But one, I reply, that only a healthy person should even formulate. The moment a tooth hurts, you are infinitely grateful for modernity and its alienations.

We stand up and embrace quickly with air kisses on both cheeks. She leaves, I stay and pay the bill. We'll meet again, first at a dinner party, then perhaps a breakfast, then she'll visit me in Heinrich's studio, and then maybe the moment will come to actually talk about money.

I don't have far to go to get home, I live next to the restaurant. In the hallway of my apartment, as always, I pause in front of the little Tiepolo drawing, happy to be able to call such a piece of perfection mine. Then I listen to the messages on my answering machine.

There's only one. Weselbach, the auction house, informing me that a dealer from Paris has put up an Eulenboeck for auction the week after next. *Old Death in Flanders*, luckily a more or less minor work. No inquiries from potential buyers yet, but the dealer doesn't want to withdraw the painting.

Not good! No inquiries up-front means that the interest driving the auction will be limited, and I'll probably have to buy the picture myself to support Eulenboeck's value. The opening bid is set at four hundred and twenty thousand – a lot of money, and all I'll get for it is a painting I myself sold six years ago for two hundred and fifty. I've already had to buy three Eulenboecks this year, and it's only August. I have to do something.

I call Wexler, the new chief curator of the Clayland Museum in Montreal. Actually all I want to do is leave a message, but in spite of the time difference he answers right away. He says he's switched his office line over onto his mobile and no, he's not asleep, he's broken the habit.

We chat for a while – the weather, intercontinental travel, restaurants we like in Manhattan, Lima and Moscow. I wait for him to mention the Eulenboeck show he's mounting the year after next and which will be very important for me, but of course he wants me to ask about it first, so we spend fifteen minutes talking about skiing, Haneke's new movie and places to eat in Paris, Berlin and Buenos Aires. Finally he realizes that the cue isn't going to come from me, and brings the conversation around to it himself.

'Let's talk about it another time,' I reply.

He'll be coming to Europe in a couple of months, he says, disappointed. Perhaps we could meet. For breakfast or maybe lunch.

Wonderful, I say.

How nice, he says.

Terrific, I say.

Good, he says.

I hang up. And suddenly, for no reason, I feel I have to call Eric. I hunt through my address book, I can never remember numbers, not even my brother's.

'You?' His voice sounds even more tense than usual. 'What?'

'I thought I should give you a call.'

'Why?'

'Just a feeling. Everything okay?'

He hesitates for a moment. 'Of course.' It doesn't sound as if everything's okay, in fact it sounds as if he wants me to know he's lying.

'So why do I have this feeling?'

'Maybe because today I hoped you and I . . . Ah!'

I hear horns and car engines and then there's a sort of hiss: he's laughing.

'I told my secretary to call you, but she . . . just think: she called Martin!'

'Martin!'

'We went to lunch. The whole time I was wondering why.'

I ask about business, and as always his answers are vague. Something's not right, there's some question he'd like to ask me, but he can't get it out. Instead he focuses on my work, and although it doesn't interest him, I say that you have to keep an eye on the auction houses and control prices. Immediately he interrupts me to ask about our mother, that tiresome subject, but I keep on digging.

'Something's up with you. I can tell. You can deny it, but – '

'Have to go now!'

'Eric, you can tell me every – '

'Everything's fine, honestly, got to go now.'

He's already hung up. Talking with Eric is always strange, almost like talking to yourself, and suddenly I realize why I've been avoiding him for some time. It's hard to keep secrets from him, he sees through me, just as I see through him, and I can't be sure he'll keep them to himself. The old rule: a secret only stays a secret if absolutely nobody knows about it. If you stick to that, they're not so hard to keep as people think. You can know someone almost as well as you know yourself, and yet you still can't read their thoughts.

Talking to Eric has reminded me that I have to call our mother. She's left me three messages, so there's no help for it. Hesitating, I dial her number.

'So finally!' she cries.

'I was busy. Sorry.'

'You were busy?'

'Yes, a lot of work.'

'With your pictures.'

'Yes, with the pictures.'

'Eating out.'

'That's part of it. Meetings.'

'Meetings?'

'What's the subtext?'

'I'm glad you have such an interesting job. It obviously feeds you. Whichever way you look at it.'

'What did you want, anyway?'

'The land in front of my house. You know, the big piece that reaches from my fence to the end of the slope, with all the birch trees. It's for sale.'

'So.'

'Think about it, someone could build there. Because why else would anyone buy it! Whoever buys it is going to want to build on it.'

'Probably.'

'And my view? I mean, our view. You two will inherit the

house, so the view matters to you too. Even if you decide to sell. And you will sell, because I take it neither of you is going to want to live here.'

'But that's a long way off.'

'Oh, stop.'

'Stop what?'

'I wanted to propose that you buy the land before anyone else goes for it and starts building. That way you'll protect the value of our house. And it's a good investment.'

'How is it a good investment if I'm not supposed to build anything on it?'

'Don't act as if you understand something about business, you're . . . well, you're whatever you are.'

'I'm someone who knows that a piece of land you can't build on isn't a good investment.'

'You could grow crops on it.'

'What would I do with crops?'

'Rapeseed or something.'

'I don't even know what that is.'

'Cars can drive using it.'

'Talk to Eric. He has money, and he understands a lot more about investing.'

'But I asked *you*.'

'Talk to Eric, Mother. I've got stuff to do now.'

'Lunch?'

'Talk to Eric.'

She hangs up and I set off. Down the stairs, across the square in the heat of the sun, then into the subway. The escalator takes me into the cool twilight of the tunnels.

The train pulls in immediately, and the compartment is half empty. I sit down.

'Friedland!'

I look up. Next to me, hanging onto the strap, is the art critic of the *Evening News*.

'You, here?' he cries. 'You in the subway, of all people?'

I shrug.

'It's not possible!'

I smile. The main thing is not to have him sit down next to me.

He slaps me on the shoulder. 'Is this seat still free?'

His name was Willem and he was a Flemish student, eccentric, noisy, lovable, quick-tempered and unfortunately not very talented. As an admirer of Nicolas de Staël, he was an abstract painter, which I held against him, I called it cowardly and imitative, because I was a Realist, an admirer of Freud and Hockney, which he held against me, calling it cowardly and imitative. We fought a lot, we drank a lot, we did drugs in moderation, we wore silk shirts and let our hair grow down to our shoulders. For a short time we shared a studio in Oxford, which was actually nothing more than a room above a laundry. He painted by the north-facing window, I painted by the west-facing window, there was a fold-away bed that we used extensively, and we felt the future looking back at us, as if later art historians were observing us intently. When he broke off his studies, I told him he was lazy and didn't break off mine, and he told me I was petit bourgeois.

During our vacation we explored the damp green expanses of Wales, climbed hills in the twilight, sought out cliffs and steep ravines, and once we made love on a stone slab covered with runes, which was even more uncomfortable than we'd imagined. We argued, we threatened each other, we screamed, we drank our way to reconciliation and then drank ourselves back into new quarrels. We filled our sketch pads, we hiked at night, we waited in the clammy dawn hours for the sun to rise over the wan grey-green of the water.

At the end of the vacation, I went back to Oxford and he went to Brussels to convince his father to keep giving him money. It was 1990, Eastern Europe had freed itself, and because nobody wrote emails yet, we sent each other postcards almost every day. Even today I worry that all my effusions – of philosophizing, of romance and hopes and rage – may still be stored in a drawer somewhere. Later, I destroyed his mail because it would have seemed too theatrical to send it all back to him.

For when I went to Brussels during the next vacation, I realized that something had changed. We looked just the way we did before, we did the things we'd always done, we had the same conversations, but something was different. Perhaps it was only that we were so young and were afraid of missing something, but we'd started to bore each other. To balance things out, we talked even louder and fought even more. We stayed awake for three nights in a row in the rhythmic din and flickering light of one club after another, drunk with exhaustion and excitement, until all of them formed a single blur and all faces melted into a single face. At some point we stood in the museum arguing about Magritte, then we were lying in the grass again, then we were in his apartment, and suddenly we'd split up, neither of us knew how or even apparently why. Willem threw a bottle at me, I ducked, it smashed against the wall above my head; luckily it was empty. I ran down the stairs, I had left my suitcase standing there, he yelled after me, his voice echoing through the stairwell, then he yelled out the window that I should come back, that I should never show my face again, that I should come back, and only when I could no longer hear his voice did I ask the way to the station. A woman gave me worried directions, I was in fact very pale, and suddenly I saw the poster. It was the same photograph, and it was also the same words: *Lindemann will teach you to fear your dreams.*

At the end of the show, which I couldn't watch – I had wanted to rest on a park bench and had fallen asleep until the early evening – I was standing in front of the theatre. The people were just coming out. I looked for the canteen. Lindemann was sitting hunched over a table eating soup, and looked up in irritation when I sat down with him.

'My name is Ivan Friedland. Will you give me an interview? For the *Oxford Quarterly*?' I didn't know if there was an *Oxford Quarterly* or not, but this was in the days before the Internet, it was hard to check things out.

Physically he hadn't changed, the lenses in his eyeglasses reflected back the world, and the green handkerchief protruded from his breast pocket. As I began to ask him questions, I noticed how shy he was. Minus the spotlights and an audience, he came off as lost and insecure. He straightened his glasses, smiled in a stilted way, and kept touching the top of his skull as if to reassure himself that the few remaining hairs were still in place.

Hypnosis, he said, did not involve a single phenomenon but a cluster: the readiness to submit to an authority, a common vulnerability, a general openness to suggestion. Only occasionally were more mysterious operations of the conscious mind involved, but these had not yet been scientifically investigated because no one wanted to get involved in research of that kind. All of which led to the fact that a person could lose superficial control of their own will for short periods.

He was seized by a fit of coughing, and soup ran down his chin.

He used the word 'superficial', he then explained, because under normal circumstances nothing someone didn't wish to experience or do could be induced in them through a trance. Only rarely was anything spiritually profound stirred into life.

I asked what he meant by this, but he was already elsewhere in his thoughts and began to complain. He complained about the low fees, he complained about the arrogance of TV executives, he complained about a broadcast that had cut his appearance, he complained about the Stage Artists' Union, and in particular he complained about their pension fund. He complained about the endless train journeys, the delays, the sloppily organized timetables. He complained about bad hotels. He complained about good hotels, because they were too expensive. He complained about stupid people in the audiences, he complained about drunks in the audiences, and aggressive people in the audiences, and children in the audiences, and people who were hard of hearing in the audiences, and psychopaths. It was astonishing, according to him, how many psychopaths would crop up in a single hypnosis show. Then he went back to complaining about fees. I asked if there was anything else he would like to eat, the *Oxford Quarterly* was paying, and he ordered the schnitzel and French fries.

'To go back for a moment,' I said. 'The operations of the conscious mind.'

Right, he said. Mysterious operations, yes, that was what he had said. Mysterious to him too, even with everything he'd seen in his time. But of course he wasn't an intellectual and so he was unqualified to offer explanations. He had not chosen to embark on this particular profession, he'd actually studied something quite different.

'Such as? What did you study? What other things?'

The waitress brought the schnitzel. He asked if I'd enjoyed the show.

'Very impressive.'

'You don't have to lie.'

'Very impressive!'

Then he said, 'Not big enough,' and it took me a moment to realize he was talking about the schnitzel. Too expensive, given the size. But everything was expensive these days, the little man was always being ripped off.

I asked if the schnitzel tasted good, at least.

Too thick, he said. Schnitzels should be pounded thin, why did nobody understand this any more? He hesitated before asking where my tape recorder was.

'I have a good memory.'

Memory was an overvalued phenomenon, he said as he chewed. Simply astonishing how easy it was to seed it with false recollections, and how easy to erase other recollections without a trace. No tape recorder, really?

To change the subject, I offered him dessert, and he ordered Sachertorte. Then he cocked his head and inquired if the *Oxford Quarterly* was a student newspaper.

'It's widely read.'

'And what are you studying, young man?'

'Art history. But I'm a painter.'

He looked at the table. 'Have we met before?'

'I don't think so.'

'No?'

'I wouldn't know where.'

'Painter,' he repeated.

I nodded.

'Painter.' He smiled.

I asked him how great an influence a hypnotist could have on people. Could you cause someone to change his life? To do things he'd never have done without being hypnotized?

'Anyone can make someone change their life.'

'But you can't make people do things they don't want to do?'

He shrugged. Just between the two of us, what did 'want to' really amount to? Who knew what he actually wanted, who was that clear with himself? People wanted so much, and it changed all the time. Of course at the beginning you told the audience that nobody could be made to do anything he wasn't willing to do anyway, but the truth was that everyone was capable of everything. Humans had no boundaries, they were pure chaos, they had no fixed shape, and they had no limits. He looked around. Why in heaven's name was the Sachertorte taking so long, what were they doing, baking it?

I'm not just chaos without boundaries, I said.

He laughed.

The waitress brought the dessert, and I asked him to tell me some anecdotes. In such an illustrious career he must have had quite a few experiences.

Illustrious? Well. In olden times, in the heyday of the Varieties, of Houdini and Hanussen, a hypnotist could still be illustrious. But nowadays! A life lived for art did not easily reduce itself to anecdotes.

'Hypnosis is an art?'

Perhaps it was even more. Perhaps it already achieved what art could only aim at. All great literature, all music, all . . . he smiled. All painting was trying to be hypnotic, wasn't it? He pushed his plate away. He had to go to bed now, performances were a strain, they left you ready to collapse with exhaustion. He stood up and put his hand on my shoulder. 'Painter?'

'Excuse me?'

His expression had changed, there was nothing friendly in it any more. 'Painter? Really?'

'I don't understand.'

'Doesn't matter. Not important. But are you serious? *Painter?*'

I asked what he meant.

Nothing. He was tired. He had to lie down. He looked around as if he'd just thought of something, then he murmured something I couldn't make out. He looked small and puny, pale-faced, and his eyes were invisible behind the thick lenses. He raised a hand in farewell and walked with little steps towards the door.

It was only on the ferry across the English Channel that I realized I couldn't get his voice out of my head. *Painter, really?* Never had I encountered such disbelief, never such intense scepticism and mockery.

Shortly afterwards, back in Oxford, he appeared to me so clearly in a dream that even today I feel I actually met him three times. Once again it was in a theatre canteen, but in my dream this one was as big as a cathedral. Lindemann was standing on the table, and his smile was twisted into such a grimace that I could barely look at him.

'I forget nothing.' He sniggered. 'Not a single face and not a single person who was ever on the stage with me. Did you really think I wouldn't know any more? Poor child. And you think you've got it in you? Art. Painting. The creative power? Do you really believe that?'

I took a step back, half angry and half fearful, but I couldn't reply. His smile grew larger and larger until it filled my field of vision.

'You can do the essentials, but you're empty. Hollow.' He gave a sharp, high-pitched snigger. 'Go now. Go without peace. Go and create nothing. Go!'

When I came to, I was lying in half darkness in my bedroom and couldn't understand what had terrified me so much. I pushed back the covers. Underneath, rolled up into a human ball, glasses glinting, Lindemann was cowering. And as he sniggered, I woke a second time, in the same room, and pushed the covers back with a pounding heart, but this time I was alone and I really was awake.

He was right. I knew. I'd never be a painter.

Now I remember his name, it's Sebastian Zollner. I ask him where he's headed. Not that it interests me, but if you know someone tangentially and find yourself sitting next to them in the subway, you have to have something to chat about.

'To Malinovski. In his studio.'

'Who's Malinovski?'

'Yes, quite! Exactly! Who is he indeed! But *Circle* magazine is doing a story on him, and when it appears, *Art Monthly* will immediately do one too, and that same day my boss will call me in and ask why we've missed the boat again. So I'm taking the first step.'

'And if *Circle* magazine doesn't?'

'They'll certainly do something, because I will have done it already. And I'm going to write that it's a disgrace if someone like Malinovski doesn't get the attention he deserves. And that when it comes to us, sheer noise always triumphs over quality. That's what I'm going to say, not bad, huh? Noise over quality. Not bad! That'll make Humpner at *Art Monthly* really shit in his pants, and they'll follow up right away, and I'm already established as the man who discovered Malinovski. That's the advantage of writing for a daily paper instead of a magazine with a two-month lead time. You can figure out what they're planning, and you can beat them.'

'What kind of artist is he?'

'Who?'

'Malinovski.'

'No idea. That's why I'm going there. To find out.'

He sits there beside me, all bloated, unshaved, almost totally bald, his jacket so crumpled he looks as if he's slept in it. In the Middle Ages, a person's appearance mirrored their soul: evil people were ugly, good people beautiful. The nineteenth century taught us that this is nonsense. But all it takes is a little life experience and you realize it's not so wrong.

'Did you go to the Khevenhüller opening?' he asks.

I shake my head. And because I read the papers too, I know

with absolute certainty that now he's going to say that Khevenhüller has done nothing but repeat himself for a long time now.

'He doesn't do anything new any more. Always the same, rehash
after rehash. Between '90 and '98 he was original. He had something to say. Now it's older than old hat.'

The train stops, the doors open, and a group of Japanese tourists
pours in, about thirty of them, half of them wearing protective face
masks. Silently squeezed together they fill the entire carriage.

Zollner leans over to me. 'I wish I had your job.'

'You can have it,' I say in a drawl. 'You'd be good at it.'

He turns away again, so self-absorbed that he doesn't notice I'm
being dishonest. 'In fifteen years I'll be jobless. No more newspapers. Only on the net. And I'm not even fifty. Too young to
retire. Too old to change horses.'

I have an idea for an Eulenboeck painting. A portrait of Zollner,
from really close up, the way he's sitting next to me now, in the
greenish artificial light of the carriage, in front of a background
made up of the gaggle of Japanese, and the title *The Arbiter of Art*.
But of course it won't do, you've been dead too long, poor Heinrich, and nobody would believe it was genuine.

'All the young people! Fresh out of college, year by year,
more and more of them. They work as interns, fetch coffee, ask if
I want sugar, look over my shoulder, and brood about what it is I
can do that they can't. They all understand something about art,
Friedland! They're none of them stupid. They all want my job.
And where do I go then? To *Art Review Online*? I'd rather hang
myself.'

'Yes, well,' I say, embarrassed. He will remember this conversation, and he won't forgive me.

'But they don't have the feel for it. They don't know when it's
time to praise Malinovski and when the time for that is already
over. They allow themselves to be impressed, they like something

or they don't like something; that's their mistake. They don't know what's required of them.'

'Required?'

'No one can fool me. Nothing impresses me. To know whether someone's on the way up or on the way down takes experience, you have to have the instinct!' He rubs his face. 'But the pressure, you have no idea! Molkner, for example. First he praised Spengrich, whom it's impossible to like any more, then he made a point of recommending Hähnel, two days before *Lens on Culture* unearthed the fact that Hähnel is anti-democratic, and then he named photo-realism as the art form of the future. A pathetic attempt to position himself against Lümping and Karzel as the force of conservatism, but the idiot picked the exact moment when Karzel was using us in the *Evening News* to mount his attack on the New Realists. You remember, even Eulenboeck got handed his head on a platter. Totally lousy timing! And now? What do you think?'

'Yes?' I dimly remember Molkner: a little man, always sweating profusely, very nervous, balding, pointed beard.

'Now he's nothing but a sort of freelancer,' Zollner whispers, as if at all costs to conceal this from the Japanese. 'And Lanzberg, his former assistant and total piece of shit, is firmly ensconced as editor, overseeing the articles Molkner sends back from exhibition previews out in the sticks. Merciless! Believe me, this business is merciless.' He nods, listens to his own words, jumps up abruptly, and gives me another slap on the shoulder. 'Sorry, I'm in a lousy mood. My mother died.'

'How terrible!'

He pushes his way through the Japanese to the door. 'You'll believe anything!'

'So she didn't die?'

'Not today, at least.' He elbows aside a man with a face mask and leaps out. The doors close, the train moves on, for a moment I

183

can still see him waving, then we're travelling through the darkness again.

One of the Japanese sits down next to me and presses little buttons on his camera. This subway line is not a scenic route, the only thing up ahead is the industrial zone on the edge of town. The tour group is on the wrong train. Someone ought to tell them. I close my eyes and say nothing.

So I was never going to rank as a painter. This much I now knew. I worked the same way I had before, but there was no longer any point. I painted houses, I painted meadows, I painted mountains, I painted portraits that didn't look bad, they showed skill, but so what? I did abstract paintings that were harmoniously composed, with careful juxtapositions of colour, but so what?

What does it mean to be average – suddenly the question became a constant one. How do you live with that, why do you keep on going? What kind of people bet everything on a single card, dedicate their lives to the creative act, undertake the risk of the one big bet, and then fail year after year to produce anything of significance?

Of course, it is part of the nature of a bet that you can lose it. But when it actually happens to you, do you lie to yourself, or can you honestly come to terms with it? How do you proudly put together your little exhibitions, collect your scattered little reviews, and take it as a given that there's an entire realm of achievement way above you in which you will never take part? How do you deal with that?

'Write about being average.' It was Martin's idea back then, in the monastery garden at Eisenbrunn. And he was right: I could always become an art historian with an unusual field of research. So I wrote a letter to Heinrich Eulenboeck. I didn't lie, but I also didn't mention the title of my dissertation: *Mediocrity as an Aesthetic Phenomenon*. All I did was describe how I had come upon his

184

paintings by chance in an old catalogue: Flemish farmhouses, soft hills, welcoming riverbanks, friendly bales of hay, really well painted, with power and a certain soul. That, I'd thought, was what would have become of me. The stubborn expertise, the self-contained perfection. That would have been me.

He sent a delighted reply, and off I went. I was exhausted, because I had just ended a brief affair with a French choreographer, full of passion, fights, screaming and yelling, alcohol, a breakup, a reconciliation, another breakup, and a trip could not have come at a better time. A long stretch by train, then a long stretch with another train, then a crossing on the ferry, then a long stretch on a bus, until finally I was standing facing him in his bright studio. The sea shimmered in the windows with a cool, northerly light.

He was in his early sixties back then, more imposing than I had expected, an elegant gentleman with a white moustache, impeccable clothes and an ivory cane, witty, relaxed and cultivated. I had planned to leave again the next day, but I stayed. And I stayed the next day and the day after that, and then the whole week and the whole year, and the year after that. I stayed until he died.

The lights in the subway shrink, become a single patch, then disappear. Beauty has no need of art, it has no need of us, either, it has no need of witnesses, quite the opposite. Gaping observers detract from it, it blazes most brightly where no one can see it: broad landscapes devoid of houses, the changing shapes of clouds in the early evening, the washed-out greyish red of old brick walls, bare trees in winter mists, cathedrals, the reflection of the sun in a puddle of oil, the mirrored skyscrapers of Manhattan, the view through an aeroplane window right after it's climbed through the layer of clouds, old people's hands, the sea at any time of day, and empty subway stations like this one – the yellow light, the haphazard pattern of cigarette butts on the ground, the peeling advertisements, still fluttering in the slipstream of the train, although the train itself has just disappeared.

The escalator carries me upwards, the street organizes itself around me, the summer sky forms an arch high over my head. I look in all directions – not just out of caution, because this is a dangerous neighbourhood, but because we're put here on earth to see. The rubbish bins are casting their short midday shadows, a child whips past on a skateboard, arms outstretched, simultaneously swaying and in perpetual risk of falling. The same beam of sunlight flashes high up in a window and down here in the rearview mirror of a parked car. The dark rectangle of a drain cover, all geometrical, and way above it, as if set against it deliberately, the vague trail of a vanishing cloud. I open a door quickly, go inside, and shut it behind me. An ancient elevator carries me jerkily from floor to floor up to the top. Only on the third floor is there a seldom-used warehouse; the rest of the building is empty. The elevator grinds noisily to a halt, I get out and unlock a steel door. I'm immediately surrounded by the smell of acrylic, wood and lime, and the rich aroma of pigments. How good it is to be able to work. Sometimes I get the suspicion I'm actually a happy man.

No one knows about this studio, no one can connect me to it. It wasn't me who bought it, but a firm that belongs to another firm that is based in the Cayman Islands and in turn belongs to me. If anyone were to inspect the land registers, they wouldn't find my name. It would take a great deal of time and effort to keep digging until they found me. The property taxes, heating, water and electricity bills are handled automatically by a numbered account in Liechtenstein. Whistling to myself, I hang up my jacket, roll up my sleeves, and put on my overalls. A dozen paintings are leaning against the wall, covered by a cloth, and in front of them is one that's almost finished on the easel.

Luckily I have no need of glasses; my eyesight is as sharp as it ever was. Born to see, appointed to look. So I stand in front of the picture and contemplate it. A village square in a little French town. In the centre a gaudy sculpture, clearly by Niki de Saint Phalle: an outsized, brightly coloured female figure holding her arms in the air. The sky is cloudless. At the edge of the square, children with bicycles are clustered around a small boy who is holding his head in his hands and crying. A woman is looking out of a window. Her mouth is wide open – she's calling someone. A man in a parked car is looking up at her threateningly. There's a dark puddle at the edge of the square that may or may not be blood. A dachshund is drinking from it. Something terrible has happened and the people seem to be wanting to cover it up. If you were to look a little longer, hunt a little better for clues, you'd be able to figure it out, or at least you think so. But if you step back, the details disappear and all that remains is a colourful street scene: bright, cheerful, full of life. Large posters advertise beer, cheese spread and various brands of cigarettes in the style of the early seventies.

I work in silence, sometimes aware of my own whistling. Only a few details are still missing. The quiet of the studio surrounds me like a solid substance. The noise of the city doesn't penetrate up here, and even the heat is blocked. It can continue like that for long stretches. When I think back on the hours of work, I can barely remember them – it's as if they had been extinguished by my concentration.

Up here a couple of points of light to add, and down there a shadow to blur the features of the child. The number plate needs a fleck of rust. People need to be able to see the brushstrokes, thick, in the style of the Old Masters! And then the last point of light, an accent made up of white, ochre and orange. I step back, lift the palette, take a little bit of black, and with a quick stroke add the date and signature in the corner: *Heinrich Eulenboeck*, 1974.

*

When I was young, vain and lacking all experience, I thought the art world was corrupt. Today I know that's not true. The art world is full of lovable people, full of enthusiasts, full of longing and truth. It is art itself as a sacred principle that unfortunately doesn't exist.

It doesn't exist any more than God does, or the End of Days, or eternity, or the Heavenly Host. All that exists are works, different in style, in form and in essence, and the whispered hurricane of opinions about them. And the changing names of these artists that with the passage of time get attached to the selfsame objects. There are not a few Rembrandts that were once considered to be the apogee of painting and that we now know to have been painted by hands other than his. Does this lessen them?

'Of course not!' the laymen cry zealously, but it's not that simple. A picture is not that selfsame picture if it was made by someone else. A work is very closely linked with our image of who brought it into the world when, why, and driven by what impulse? A pupil who has acquired all his master's skills and now paints like him still remains a pupil, and if van Gogh's paintings had been made by an affluent gentleman a generation later, the same rank would not be accorded to them. Or would it?

Things really do get even more complicated. Who has heard of Emile Schuffenecker? And yet he painted numerous pictures for which we worship van Gogh. We've known this for some time, but has van Gogh's reputation suffered as a result? Lots of van Goghs are not by van Gogh, Rembrandt's paintings are not all by Rembrandt, and I'd be very surprised if every Picasso was a Picasso. I don't know if I'm a forger; it depends, like everything in life, on how you define it. Nonetheless Eulenboeck's most famous paintings, all the ones on which his reputation rests, were created by the same person, namely me. But I'm not proud of that. I haven't changed my opinion: I'm not a painter. That my paintings are hanging in museums says nothing against the museums and nothing in favour of my pictures.

All museums are full of fakes. So what? The provenance of each and every thing in this world is uncertain; there's no particular magic involved in art, and the works that are ranked as great have not been brushed by an angel's wings. Art objects are objects just like everything else: some are extraordinarily accomplished, but none of them springs from a higher universe. That some are linked with the name of this or that person, that some of them fetch high prices and others don't, that some are world-famous and most are not, is due to a number of different forces, but none of these is other-worldly. Nor do forgeries have to be successful to fulfil their purpose: perfect imitations can be unmasked while imperfect ones are hung on walls and admired. Forgers who are proud of their work overestimate the importance of well-grounded skill in exactly the same way as laypeople do: anyone who isn't totally inept and makes the effort can learn a craft. It's quite right that craft lost its importance within art, it makes sense that the idea behind a work became more important than the work itself; museums are sacred institutions that have outlived themselves, as the avant-garde has been saying for a long time now, with good reason.

But visitors to cities want somewhere to go when the afternoons are long, and without museums there would be a lot of blank pages in the travel guides. Because there have to be museums, they also have to exhibit things, and these things have to be objects, not ideas, just as collectors want to hang things, and pictures are better to hang on walls than ideas. Admittedly, an ironic free spirit once displayed a urinal in a museum to mock the institution and all its holy affectations and artistic pieties, but he also wanted money and honours and, above all, he wanted to be admired in the traditional way, and so a replica of the original still stands on its plinth, surrounded by holy affectations and artistic pieties. Although the theory that the museum has outlived itself is correct, the museum has in fact won, the urinal is exclaimed over, and as for the theory behind it, only students in their second semester still wonder about it.

I often think about the artists of the Middle Ages. They didn't sign things, they were craftsmen who belonged to guilds, they were spared the disease that we call ambition. Can it still be done that way, can you still do the work without taking yourself seriously – can you still paint without being 'a painter'? Anonymity is no help, it's merely a clever hiding place, another form of vanity. But painting in the name of someone else is a possibility; it works. And what amazes me all over again every day is: it makes me happy.

The idea came to me already on the third day. Heinrich was asleep next to me, the sea was casting its reflections on the ceiling, and I suddenly realized how I could make him a famous painter. What distinguished him, what he lacked, what I had to do were all quite clear to me. He would be good on television and in magazine photos, and he would give wonderful interviews. The only drawback was those farmhouses. It was going to take diplomacy.

A few weeks later I raised it for the first time. We had just been looking at his most recent work: a farmhouse with barn, a farmhouse with farmers mowing, a farmhouse with surly, arrayed farm family, plus cockerel, manure pile and clouds.

'Let's agree that it's possible to become famous by fulfilling all the requirements and doing what's opportune. Then what? You would be mocking a world that deserves it and simultaneously collecting what you're owed. What's bad about that?'

'That you're not owed it in such a case.' He stood before me, self-righteous as only a loser can be. His narrow face, the fine lines of his nose, the flashing eyes, the grey hair and the loden jacket with its silver buttons – it was all made to order for the magazines.

'It would be a victimless crime,' I said. 'Nobody loses anything.'

'You yourself would be the loser.'

'But what would you lose? Your soul?' I pointed at the farm-houses. 'Your art?'

'You'd lose both.'

And neither of them exists, I wanted to reply, but I kept quiet. So that's how it goes, I thought: with pride. When you're proud, you can tolerate being average. 'And if we – as a sort of experiment, if we try it – if we don't take either of those things too seriously? Either ourselves or art?'

We laughed, but we both knew, he just as much as I, that I was being serious.

'And what,' I asked a week later, 'what if we risk it? Paint a couple of pictures we know are likely to please the relevant people. And later we'll announce it was a joke.'

'It would be quite some joke,' he said thoughtfully.

I'd already finished the first three. A boulevard in Málaga, dis-figured with a Dalí sculpture, and painted in the wan naturalistic style of Zurbarán, a rain-soaked German pedestrian precinct in the heavily shaded manner of late Rembrandt, and *Tristia 3*, still one of his most famous works to this day – a surreally high-ceilinged museum gallery, with menacing sculptures made of grease and felt displayed in glass cases along the walls and in the centre, disturbed and unhappy, a little boy next to a severely ecstatic art teacher: pasty brushwork interspersed with holes and cracks that let the white canvas show right through.

'Heinrich Eulenboeck,' I explained as I showed him the paint-ings. 'A reclusive aristocrat, a proud outsider, who pursues the art of his time with contempt and has missed not one of its developments. In many paintings, with subtle mockery, there are references to the works of this or that contemporary artist whom he considers to be utterly worthless. He's seen everything, tallied everything, weighed it all, and finally found it wanting.'

'But I'm not an aristocrat. My father had a small factory in Ulm. I sold it when I was twenty.'

'Do you want to sign them yourself?'

He said nothing for a long time. 'You're probably better at that too.'

In fact his signature wasn't hard to imitate. I put it on all three paintings, then I took photos and sent them, along with an essay about the wilful outsider I'd discovered, to my former fellow student Barney Wesler, who was just in the throes of organizing a group exhibition in the Schirn Museum in Frankfurt: *Realism at the Millennium.* He immediately said he wanted to include them. Two days after the opening there were two long articles in the daily press ecstatically praising Eulenboeck's paintings: one of them was written by a well-known specialist on Max Ernst, and the other one was by me, and both of us talked of the biggest discovery of the year. Soon after that a young man appeared in Heinrich's studio who was a writer for *Texte zur Kunst.* His interview was published a month later under the title 'Art, for Me, Is a Cathedral', enhanced with a photograph of Heinrich looking incredibly aristocratic and condescending. Another interview appeared in *Stern.* Seven pages plus photos: Heinrich on the battlements of an ancient towered fortress, on board a yacht, at the wheel of a sports car, although he couldn't even drive, and in a library, with the stem of a Chinese pipe between his teeth. No sign of his paintings.

I've never seen anyone play a role better. 'Warhol? A commercial artist!' – 'Lichtenstein? The country or the charlatan?' – 'The only thing kitschier than a Balthus is a cat calendar.' – 'Klimt, the apotheosis of artistic handwork!' Such phrases pleased everyone.

He repeated them in dozens of newspaper interviews, he repeated them on television, he repeated them at the openings of his exhibitions, he repeated them at the launch of Leroy Hallowan's book *Eulenboeck, or The Great Negation*, and he repeated them, word for word, diligently and without variation, in Godard's short documentary *Moi, Eulenboeck, Maître*.

'And when do we break the whole thing up?' I asked.

'Maybe not yet.'

'Now would be a good moment.'

'Possible, but . . .'

I waited, but he didn't say anything more. We were sitting in a restaurant in Paris, and as I often had recently, I saw that his hand was shaking; the soup spoon was always empty by the time it reached his mouth. He'd obviously forgotten what we'd just been talking about.

Then my dissertation appeared. I had switched themes; now the title was *Heinrich Eulenboeck: From the Irony of Tradition to the Realism of Irony*. Over 740 pages I unpacked the history of a lone satirist and late-born master of every technique in the repertory of Western painting who only achieved artistic expression in old age.

Of course I was also obliged to laud the farmhouses. In the meantime these had also found their admirers: to some colleagues they represented proof that simple beauty was not yet passé, to others, enigmatic satire. I thoroughly explored both possibilities and avoided taking sides: the very richness was rooted in the ambivalence, which is to say that the artist was being ironic about irony itself and mocking mockery on the way to profound emotion in the sense of the Hegelian upward spiral.

'When do we break it up?' I asked again.

We were in a hotel room in London. Rain was pounding against the window, breakfast sat untouched on the trolley from room service, and Saddam Hussein was reviewing a parade on television.

Heinrich's ivory cane was leaning against the wall next to the silver walking stick I had given him recently – by now he needed not just the one but both to walk.

'You're so young. You don't understand a thing.'

'What don't I understand?'

'Any of it – you can't understand.'

'But what?'

I stared at him. I had never seen a grown man cry before, and I was stunned: I had never expected such a thing. Of course I had known that he would no longer be able to step back again, but what was so terrible about that? Try as I might, I just didn't get it.

He was right. I really was still very young.

Six months after Heinrich had decided to remain the painter everyone believed him to be, to keep on exhibiting, giving interviews, selling pictures and being famous, my father came to visit.

We were working in the studio. I was sitting in front of my new PC writing my essay 'Realism as a Critique of Ideology in the Work of Heinrich Eulenboeck', while Heinrich was scratching away at his sketch pad with a shaky hand. He could do this for hours on end, and sometimes he even achieved some drawings. Then the phone rang, and Arthur, without explaining how he had got this number, announced that he was in the neighbourhood and could come by.

'Now?'

'Yes.' As always, he sounded surprised that I should be surprised. 'Not a good time?'

Half an hour later, as he was standing on the doorstep, I thought he looked tired and unkempt; he was sweating and he hadn't shaved. Heinrich greeted him in the fashion of a Grand Seigneur, saying 'Welcome!' and 'I have heard so much about you,' and 'What an honour, what a pleasure,' to which my father reacted with restrained but ironic courtesy. We sat down at the table; the housekeeper served us with food she had hastily warmed up in the microwave. Arthur's eyes flashed while Heinrich talked about Warhol – 'a commercial artist!' – Lichtenstein, Beuys and Kaminski. Unfortunately he'd become accustomed to trotting out the well-worn phrases from his interviews even when there was no microphone in the offing. He gave a lengthy description of his meeting with Picasso, and given that I knew he'd never met him, I had to get up and leave the room in order not to interrupt him.

When I came back, he was just describing the vernissage that his New York gallerist Warsinsky had recently organized for him: who had been there, what the critics had written, which pictures had sold and for how much. His moustache bobbed up and down, his lower lip trembled, and whenever he wanted to emphasize what he was saying, he knocked on the table.

To change the subject, I asked Arthur what he was working on right now. I knew he didn't like the question, but it was better than listening to Heinrich.

'Probably going to be another detective novel. A classic locked-room mystery. For people who like riddles.'

'So is there a solution?'

'Of course! But nobody will find it. It's very well hidden.'

'Is that the case with *Family* too?'

'No. That's a story in which the solution really is that there's no hidden solution. No explanation, and no meaning. That's the whole point.'

'But that's exactly what it's not! Or rather it is, but only if you tell it in a way that makes it so. Every existence, if you look back on it, is made up of terror. Every life becomes a catastrophe if you summarize it in the way you do.'

'Because that's the truth.'

'Not the whole truth. Not exclusively. Afternoons like today, places like this . . .' I gestured vaguely towards the window, the sea, our table, him, me and Heinrich. 'Everything passes, but that doesn't mean that there's no such thing as happiness, not by a long chalk. It's a matter of moments, the *good* moments. They're worth everything.'

Arthur was preparing a retort, but Heinrich got there first. He had a question, he said. What was meant by that piece of lunacy that he himself didn't exist? That's what the book said. It said in it that one didn't exist. But he did. He was sitting right here!

'Undeniably,' said Arthur.

But seriously, this was absurd!

Heinrich's outburst surprised me. I hadn't known he'd read *My Name Is No One*, we'd never talked about it.

'If it's absurd, there's no point in getting upset about it,' said Arthur. 'It's only a book.'

'No excuses. Are you trying to say I don't exist?'

'And if I did?'

'You can't!'

Arthur looked at me. 'Is this really necessary?'

'What are you talking about?'

With a circular gesture he pointed, exactly as I had already done, to the window, the sea and the table, to himself, to me, to Heinrich.

For a few moments we were all silent. I heard Heinrich's whistling breath and hoped that he hadn't understood.

'A life doesn't last long, Ivan. If you're not careful, you squander it in stupidities.'

'You should know.'

'Yes, I should.'

'Leave my house!' said Heinrich.

'Do you paint his pictures too?' asked Arthur.

There was a long silence.

Then: 'Leave my house,' Heinrich whispered.

Arthur laughed out loud. 'It's really unbelievable! You paint his pictures and nobody notices?'

'Out!' Heinrich got to his feet. 'Out!' His voice shook, but when he was determined, it still had both strength and authority. He pointed at the door. 'Out!'

As I accompanied my father to the hall, I was searching for some suitable remark, some sentence I could utter. 'When will I see you again?' I asked finally.

'Soon.' It didn't sound very convincing. He laid his hand on my shoulder, and a moment later he was gone.

I take off my overalls and wash my hands. The water runs bright and clear, collecting a swirl of colours as it falls. I feel a trace of sadness, a trace of pride, a trace of concern, as I always do when I finish a painting. But what could happen? Whenever it's a question of the authenticity of a Eulenboeck, there's one person who has the last word, and that person is the chairman of the Eulenboeck Trust, the sole heir of the artist, namely me.

The title of this picture has been listed among his works for years: *Holiday Snap No. 9*. I mentioned it already in an essay at the end of the nineties, and since five years ago there's been a dossier in the archives of the National Gallery detailing the provenance of a painting depicting a French marketplace with a Niki de Saint Phalle sculpture. Archives take security precautions against people who want to steal things, but there's nobody to stop someone smuggling something in. In another six months John Warsinsky's gallery will offer *Holiday Snap No. 9* for sale, but not before the chairman of the Eulenboeck Trust has alerted the most important collectors to it. They will all study the dossier to check the provenance, then the Eulenboeck Trust will be asked to make a statement as to its authenticity. Everyone knows the chairman of the Trust is also the seller, but this doesn't bother anyone, it's part of the game, and indeed who would be bothered by it anyway: nobody's losing. After a thorough check, the Trust will give the painting its seal of authenticity – on the one hand an account of its impeccable provenance, as it passed directly from Eulenboeck to his heir, and on the other because the leading Eulenboeck expert, namely me, has already described it as a too-little-known masterpiece years ago.

Nonetheless I am careful. I've twice refused a certificate of authenticity to paintings I'd done myself, and another time I said that an obvious fake by some hack was genuine. I'm considered a difficult and erratic authority. Collectors fear me as much as the gallery owners do, people often are up in arms over my unpredictable verdicts, and I'm not infrequently put down as incompetent. No one is going to get suspicious.

Down on the street a man is pushing a wheelbarrow full of sand. Three young men in baseball caps are coming towards him. They stop and look back at the wheelbarrow, as if sand were something interesting, then they lean against the wall with that curiously casual nervousness that only the under-twenties have, and light cigarettes for one another. Two cars drive past, then one, then another two – at precise intervals, like Morse code. What if you could read the universe? Perhaps that's what is behind the terrifying beauty of things: we are aware that something is speaking to us. We know the language. And yet we understand not one word.

How sad that you don't hear me, poor Heinrich. People who communicate with the dead like to assert that they could feel there was someone there. I never had this feeling. Even in the unlikely event that you have an afterlife, invisible, freed from your body and all earthly burdens, our concerns are a matter of indifference to you. You're not standing next to me at this window, you're not looking over my shoulder, and if I talk to you, you don't answer.

So why am I speaking to you?

He already didn't understand me any more while he was still

alive. In the final six months he was almost always in bed; some-times he would be seized by rage for no reason at all, and then he would have to laugh quietly. Along the way I painted *A French Film Is Being Shot*, *Great Day of Judgment* and *Market Scene in Barcelona*. From time to time he would appear behind me and watch. *Market Scene* didn't interest him: a dramatic moment in an auction house, the audience staring raptly at the auctioneer, who is in the process of lowering the hammer on a monochrome blue canvas by Yves Klein. *Day of Judgment* made him grin to himself: a crumpled page of newsprint, apparently ripped out of the Arts section of the *New York Times*, every detail rendered realistically, on the right a hymn of praise for a biography of Billy Joel, and on the left a hatchet job on a book of poems by Joseph Brodsky. Only *A French Film Is Being Shot* made him cluck with pleasure: an altarpiece, way at the bottom the lighting technicians, the grips and the extras, on the step above them a semicircle of camera people, then above them the actors, transfixed in worship, and right at the top, flanked by two mighty producers doing double duty as archangels, the director in his dark glasses. I never liked it, even while I was working on it I found it dull, and even technically it held no attraction, being far too close to simple caricature, but it became by far his best-known picture among the general public – not least because the director looked like Godard. Warsinsky sold it for a million, four years later I bought it back for a million five, in order to sell it under the table to a collector from Turkmenistan for three million. I hope I never see it again.

At some point he never got up again. The television stayed on, he stayed in bed and kept talking quietly to himself. Mostly he was telling a story that dated from his youth, over and over again: there was a drinking session in it, a test of courage among soldiers, and a game of Russian roulette. I heard it every day while I fed him chicken soup, while I helped him on the toilet, while I plumped up his pillows and covered him up like a child. He became thin, his eyes clouded, and all of a sudden he had also forgotten his stories. I often sat by his bed and wondered if the man I'd known was really still hiding in this crumpled, shrunken body.

For there were still some moments of clarity. Once I found him sitting up; his head turned towards me, he seemed to recognize me, and he asked when we were flying to Paris. He advised me to dedicate myself to my own painting again too. He actually said that: my own painting again *too*. Then he sank back into himself with his deceptively wise tortoise smile, a little trickle of spit ran down his chin, and when I changed the sheets, the look on his face was so blank it was as if he hadn't uttered a word in ages.

Another time he suddenly asked for his bank account number. I had to write it down on a piece of paper, because he wanted to call the bank, and when I said that it was impossible at two o'clock in the morning, he began to scream and beg and threaten me. When I did bring him the phone, he had no idea what to do with it.

I often heard his voice in my dreams. When I woke up and heard him snoring beside me, I would be certain that he really had spoken to me, but whenever I tried to remember what it was he'd said, all I knew was that he'd asked for something and I'd said yes. But to what, I no longer knew.

As he lay dying, I sat at his side uneasily, painfully moved, and asked myself what this moment demanded. I wiped his brow, not because it was necessary but because wiping someone's brow in this situation seemed the right thing to do, and again there was something he wanted to tell me: his lips formed words, but his voice would not obey, and by the time paper and pencil had been located, he was too weak to write anything. For a while his eyes stared at me as if he were trying to transmit thoughts by sheer willpower, but it failed, his eyes broke contact, his chest sank, and I thought, This is what it looks like, this is how it is, this is what happens. This.

Since then, unknown paintings by Eulenboeck come onto the market quite regularly. In the hands of another heir, things could have taken a bad turn, but he had no family. No aunt from overseas and no distant cousin surfaced; luckily there was only me.

I must be on my way, looking after an estate is a full-time job. Today I still have a date for coffee, a dinner, and then a second dinner: conferences, projects, more conferences. I look down at the street again doubtfully, where the three young men are just starting to move. A fourth, blond, wearing a red shirt, is coming towards them, and the three of them surround him.

I turn away from the window and look at *Holiday Snap No. 9* as if I were seeing it for the first time. The colours I used are more than thirty years old, as is the canvas: one of several I bought during Heinrich's lifetime and set aside in his studio. He handled them at the time: if a forensic expert ever examines them, he'll find the master's fingerprints.

I unlock the door, go out, and lock it again behind me. The better part of the day is already over, the rest will consist of administration and talk. The elevator grinds its way down towards the bottom.

I step out onto the street. It's hot. The four young men up ahead are no more than silhouettes, the brightness makes it hard to get a clear look at any of them. I just have to make it to the subway, and it'll be cooler down inside. I wish I could call a taxi, but unfortunately there are no phone kiosks any more. Sometimes it would be an advantage to have a mobile.

Something's not right. They're fighting. The three of them have got the fourth in the middle, and now one of them is grabbing his shoulder and giving him a shove while another catches him and shoves him back again. He's surrounded. And I have to get past them.

Meanwhile I can hear what they're saying, but I don't

understand it, the words make no sense. My heart is thumping in an odd way: suddenly I no longer feel hot, and my head is clear. It must be the atavistic responses triggered by the proximity of violence. Should I go back the other way or keep going as if nothing were happening? It looks as if they'll pay no attention to me, so I keep walking towards them. 'I'll kill you!' one of them yells quite openly and shoves the one in the middle again, and one of the others yells something as he shoves him back, like '*I'm* going to kill you,' but it could be something else too, and I want to call out to the one in the middle that he should pack it in, there are three of them, there's only one of you, give up, but he's big and strong and has a large chin, and – I give him a sideways glance as I go past – oxlike, empty eyes. And because it can't just stay that way, with a shove and then another shove and no escalation from there, one of the three lashes out with his fist and hits the one in the middle on the head.

But he doesn't fall down. That's not the way things happen in reality, someone doesn't fall down right away. He just bends over and covers his face with his hand while the one who hit him whimpers and clutches his fist. It could look quite funny, but it doesn't.

I'm already past them. They've paid no attention to me. I hear a scream behind me. I keep going. Don't turn around. Another scream. Just keep going. And then I do turn around.

My pathetic curiosity. See, see everything, so see this too. Now it's only the three of them standing there, the one in the middle has disappeared, like some magic trick, I think. They seem to be dancing, one of them forwards, the other one backwards, and it takes a few seconds for me to understand that the one in the middle hasn't disappeared, he's lying on the ground, and they're kicking him and kicking him and kicking him.

I stand still.

Why are you standing still, I ask myself. Vanish, so that they don't realize you're a witness. That's exactly what shoots through my brain: don't be a witness! As if I were dealing with the Mafia and not with some adolescents. I check the time, it's shortly before four, and I tell myself that I must move on quickly, this kind of thing must happen all the time, as you can see if you have a secret studio in the worst neighbourhood in the city.

They're still kicking the one who's on the ground. From here, he's just a huddled shadow, a bundle with legs. Keep going, I command myself, don't get curious, disappear! So I keep walking, step by step – fast, but not at a run.

But it's in the wrong direction. I'm walking towards them again. Never have I felt so strongly that I'm not one person but several. One person who's walking and one who's giving futile orders to the one who's walking, telling him to turn around. And I realize that it's not just that I'm curious. I'm going to interfere.

I'm just reaching them. It's taken longer than I expected because with every step I take, time stretches out longer: I cover half the distance that separates me from them, then half of the distance that remains, and then half of that again, like the tortoise in the old story – and suddenly I'm almost certain I'll never get there at all. I see their legs and heavy shoes flashing forwards and backwards, I see their arms rising and falling. I see their faces clenched with exertion, I see a television antenna glinting high above them, I see a plane way above that, I see a colourless beetle running its tiny way along a crack in the asphalt, but I see neither cars nor other pedestrians, the five of us are alone, and if I don't interfere, no one else is going to do it.

Now would be a really good time to have a phone. I keep walking. The half of the distance still remaining will have its own half, and that half yet another one, and I grasp that time is not only endlessly long but also endlessly dense, between one moment and the next lie an infinite number of moments; how can they possibly pass?

They're paying no attention to me, I could still turn around. The boy on the ground is holding his arms over his head, his legs are bent, and his torso is hunched. I realize that this may be the last moment I could actually steer clear of this thing. I stand still and croak, 'Leave him alone!'

They pay no attention. I could still turn back. Instead of a reply, what I hear is the person inside me, the one who's not listening to the other one who's begging him to keep quiet, again saying loudly, 'Leave him alone! Stop that!'

They pay no attention. What do I do? Interposing myself between them is out of the question, absolutely no one could expect that of me. Relieved, I'm on the point of turning around, but at that very moment they stop. All three, simultaneously, as if they've rehearsed it. They stare at me.

'What?' says the biggest of them. His face is shadowed with stubble, he has a thin ring in his nose, and his T-shirt says *Bubbletea is not a drink I like*. He's panting as if he'd just finished a heavy workout.

The one next to him – this one's T-shirt says *Morning Tower* – also says 'What?', in a shaky drawl.

The third one just stares. His T-shirt displays a screaming red Y.

The one on the ground lies motionless, breathing hard.

It's the critical moment. Now I have to say the right thing, find the right words, a sentence that will ease the tension, make things better, break them up, clear the air. Fear is supposed to make you think faster, but that's not happening here. My heart is thumping, there's a roaring in my ears, and the street seems to be turning slowly on its own axis. I didn't know it was possible to be this afraid, it feels as if I'd never in my life been frightened before, and I'm just learning what fear is right now. Things were all fine just a moment ago, I was upstairs, behind a steel door, surrounded by safety. Can the switch happen at such speed, can the worst be so close at hand?

And I think, Stop asking yourself things like this, you don't have time, you have to say the right thing! And I think, Maybe there are moments when there are no right words any more, moments when words have no meaning any more, when they fall apart, when they lead nowhere, because whatever you say is simply irrelevant. And I think, Just stop thinking! And I think . . .

Now *Bubbletea is not a drink I like* is coming at me, repeating 'What!' but not the way it sounded before, not as a question and not in surprise, but as a naked threat.

'He's done,' I say. 'He can't even move any more. He's finished.' Not bad, I think, so I did actually manage to find something to say. 'You guys are much stronger. He doesn't have a chance, there's no point any more.'

'And who are you?'

That didn't come from *Bubbletea is not a drink I like*, it came from Y. I hadn't expected that of him. He'd struck me as harmless, a hanger-on, a bystander, almost a friend.

'I'm . . .' But my voice is inaudible. I clear my throat, now it's better. '. . . no one.' The ancient response given by Odysseus, tried and well tested in situations like this one. 'I'm no one!'

They stare.

'If he dies, you'll get sentenced to life.'

I realize immediately that this was a mistake. First, he's not going to die, and second, nobody under twenty gets sentenced to life. An entire army of juvenile lawyers, juvenile judges and juvenile counsellors makes that impossible, nobody's life gets ruined that young any more, as I know from my brother the priest. But if I'm in luck, they won't know this.

'The police are certainly already on their . . .'

Things come together again: street, sky, voices, shadowy figures above me and me on the ground, leaning against the wall of a house. My head hurts. I must have fainted.

Stay sitting down! You've done enough. In the name of all the saints and all the devils and all that is beautiful in the world, stay sitting down!

I get to my feet.

How strange: usually people in danger turn out to be smaller, more gutless, more pitiful than they thought they were. That's normal, that's usual, that's what you expect of yourself. You're convinced you'll be revealed as a coward at the first opportunity. And now this. Ivan Friedland, aesthete, curator, wearer of expensive suits, is a hero. I could have done without it.

I'm up on my legs. With one hand I'm supporting myself against the wall, with the other I'm struggling to find my balance. This time I don't have to say a word – the sheer effrontery of my getting up at all is enough: they don't back off.

'So who are you?' Y asks again.

'If only I knew.' People have used jokes to get themselves out of bad spots like this.

'Are you nuts?' asks Y.

And *Bubbletea is not a drink I like*, as if surprised by this realization, says, 'Knock it off, Ron. The guy's nuts.'

Then I notice that something has opened in *Morning Tower*'s hand, something small and silvery and wicked. Things have turned serious. Even if I'd thought they were serious already – I was wrong, they weren't. They are now. 'Do you want to kill him?' I ask. But it's not about him any more.

'Ron!' says *Morning Tower* to *Bubbletea is not a drink I like*. 'Shut up!'

'No, Ron!' says Y. '*You* shut up.'

It must be me who's confused, they can't all be called Ron. To cover up the pounding of my heart, I ask exaggeratedly loudly if it's money they want.

But they just stare and say nothing, and I get the feeling I've made another mistake. The pain throbs in my forehead. Maybe I should show them some cash. My jacket, its thin fabric tailored by Kilgour in London, is so wet I might have just climbed out of the water. I move my hand towards the wallet in my inner pocket, realize that their looks have changed, try to complete the gesture so that there won't be any misunderstanding, and know, even as my fingertips brush the leather, that this was yet another mistake: *Y* ducks away, *Bubbletea is not a drink I like* takes a step back, *Morning Tower*'s hand shoots out and touches me, and as I am pulling out the wallet, pain shoots through my chest, my head and my arms, flames outwards, piercing through asphalt, parked cars, houses, sky and sun, filling the world, becoming the world, then turns back on itself and is inside me again. My wallet lands on the ground, but I flap my arms, and keep my balance, and don't fall.

I look at the three of them. They look at me: calmly, almost as if they're curious, and their rage had suddenly dissipated. Not dumb, not angry, just confused. I think *Bubbletea* may even be trying to smile at me. I try to smile back, but I don't manage it, I'm feeling very weak.

Y picks up my wallet, looks at it in a questioning way, and drops it again. Then they run. I look after them until they disappear around the corner.

The boy at my feet moves. He stretches, moves softly, holds out his arms, turns around, and tries to stand up. His face is swollen and bloody, but still he doesn't seem to be that badly hurt. No, he's not going to die. He probably won't even have to go to the hospital. He rolls forward, gets his elbows on the ground, and pushes himself shakily onto his feet.

'Everything's okay,' I say. 'Don't get upset. Everything's good.'

He blinks at me.

'Everything's good,' I say. 'Everything's good.'

He takes a few wobbling steps towards my wallet, picks it up, and looks inside. His right eye is closed, the eyelid is twitching, blood is running out of one ear. There's absolutely nothing written on his red T-shirt.

'Shit,' he says.

'Yes,' I say.

'I really gave it to Ron last week, and now they caught up with me when I was alone.'

'Yes,' I say.

'They're coming back,' he says. 'They're coming, they're coming back, they're on their way here already. They're coming back.' Deep in thought, he pockets my wallet, then turns away and wobbles off.

Did he say they're going to come back, did he really say that? Cautiously, step by step, I cross the street. I must not fall down. Once I lie down, I won't be able to get up again. Every breath I take is like a jab, and each time I extend my leg, bolts of pain shoot through me. There in front of me is the door, that's where I have to go, behind it the elevator is waiting, up there is my studio, secure behind its secure steel door, they can't get in there, it's safe in there, I'll be safe if they come back.

The street is so wide. I must not faint, it's only a few more steps.

On I go. He took my wallet!

And on I go. If they really are all called Ron, it won't be hard to find them. But maybe they were just doing it to confuse me.

And on I go. Can the heat be melting the asphalt, is that possible? My shoes are sinking in, and little waves are running across the sticky mass.

And on I go. There, the door, the key in my trouser pocket, the key has to go in the door, the door needs the key, but I still am not there yet. Why is there no one here? No car, no one at a window, but perhaps this is good, because if someone were here, it could be the three of them again, he said they'd come back. The door. The key. It must be the right one, the one for the front door, not the one for the studio, and not the one for my apartment, because that's not where I am, where I am is here.

And on I go. Just a few more steps. A few. And again a few. Keep going. A few more. A few steps. The key. The door. Here.

It slips, scrapes across the metal, the keyhole is dodging me, to the right then to the left, my hand is shaking but I can feel it, get the key in, turn it, the door opens, into the house, the elevator, I push the button for the fifth floor, the elevator jerks.

A man is standing next to me, a moment ago he wasn't here. He has a hideous gap between his teeth, and a battered hat. He says, 'Jaegerstrasse 15b.'

'Yes,' I say. 'That's here. That's the address of this house. Jaegerstrasse 15b.'

'Jaegerstrasse 15b,' he repeats. 'Fifth floor.'

'Yes,' I say. 'We're going to the fifth floor.'

We've already got there, the elevator stops, the door opens, the man is no longer there, I get out; now everything depends on getting the second key into the lock. I'm in luck, the door opens, I go in and lock it behind me. Then I take hold of the bolt – for a moment it doesn't seem to want to move, but then it does slide sideways with a squeak, and the door is blocked. I've done it, I've reached safety.

I want to sit down. The chair is over against the opposite wall, but relief gives me strength. I walk and I walk, and eventually I get there. What I really want to do is sleep, long and deep, until everything is better.

I touch my stomach. My hand comes away wet, my jacket is wet, my trousers are wet too, I cannot remember when I ever sweated this much. I hold my hand in front of my eyes. It's red.

And there he is again, with his hat and the gap between his teeth, and even as I'm looking at him, I guess that he's about to disappear again.

'Go to your brother,' he says, 'help him. Jaegerstrasse 15b, fifth floor. Go!'

Instead of answering that it isn't my brother here, it's me, I blink in the direction of *Holiday Snap No. 9*, and there he is again, looking in from outside, no mean trick to keep his balance on the window ledge up on the fifth floor! I can read his lips: *Jaegerstrasse 15b, fifth floor*, and I want to cry, 'You there, I know where I am!' but it's too much of an effort and now he's already disappeared again.

I'm cold.

In fact, I'm shivering. My teeth are chattering, and when I hold my hand up in front of my eyes, I see it's trembling. Heinrich comes in with his moustache and his stick and his cane, and goes over to the window. Behind his head an aeroplane moves through the streaks on the windowpane like a little fish swimming through water, and already we're in a meadow, and I'm smaller than I was a moment ago, and Papa and Mama are saying that I should drink water, and I ask Papa if he wasn't Heinrich just now, and he wants to know if I'm really not thirsty, and I say, Yes, I'm really thirsty and a little way off Eric is sitting in the grass looking so exactly like me that I feel I'm him. I dig around in the blades of grass, find a worm, and pick it up, it coils itself across my palm, Papa bends over my shoulder, and the feeling of safety remains even as I look around the studio. The worm on my hand isn't a worm, it's blood, and Heinrich says, You have to get out of here, or it'll be too late.

Do you remember Eric's call, I ask. He said his secretary had mixed up Martin and me, and she called the wrong person. Do you remember?

You really have to get out of here, Ivan.

If she hadn't mixed us up, then I would have met him for lunch today and I wouldn't have come here and none of this would have happened, isn't that curious?

Very curious, but you've got to get out of here. Otherwise it'll be too late.

Too late . . . so why didn't I give him my watch? A TAG Heuer, four thousand euros, bought in Geneva two years ago. If I'd given it to him, I wouldn't have had to reach into my inner pocket. I look at the watch hands. Ten past four. Ten past four. Ten past four. Eleven past four.

All well and good, says Heinrich, but I'm advising you to get out of here.

Where to?

Out.

But where to?

The main thing is out.

Out *there*?

Out anywhere.

It's easy for him to say, but it's true, it was a mistake to come back here. This building is empty except for one floor, the warehouse, but I've never seen a soul even there. I'll have to crawl to the door, past *Holiday Snap No. 9* and the sniggering children, across the rectangle of light the sun is casting on the floor, the door is several yards further on, that's where I'll have to straighten up to reach the bolt and the handle, and then I'll be out.

So I push myself out of the chair, sink to the floor, and start to crawl. I've still got the strength, I'm managing, I'll be able to reach the door. First I have to get past the chest of drawers; the bottom drawer, which is partway open, holds my brushes, all my brushes, but I don't know at this particular moment how I'm going to find the right one. It's not easy, there are a lot of them, and besides I'm not *looking* for a brush!

But what am I looking for, then?

It'll come to me. Past the chest of drawers. Cold floor against my cold hands, cracked floor against my cracked hands, rough floor against my rough hands, keep going. I must not look at the painting, so that I don't attract the attention of the children, and I have to stay clear of the rectangle of light.

But what was that about? The thing with the rectangle of light, what was that?

I no longer know. Help me, open the door, I can't manage the thing with the bolt. Someone will find me down on the street, someone will call a doctor. And what if the doctor asks what I was doing in a neighbourhood like this? But why would he ask, what does he care about my studio and a handful of forged paintings that you can't even call fakes, they're genuine, you're the fake, poor Heinrich, help me with the door! I have to get out before I faint.

If you know this, you also know that you're alone here.

Yes, I know this. And?

Ivan.

Yes?

If you're alone here.

Yes?

Then I can't help you with the bolt.

No?

Ivan.

Yes, I understand. Yes. So I have to. Keep going. But when I'm downstairs and the three of them come back, what do I do? Is there some way they can get in, do they have a key? Maybe when they took my wallet, they took my keys too.

If they'd taken them, then they'd be here now, not you.

How so?

Because you'd have no key.

But what would they want here?

Good question. Maybe you should keep on crawling.

But –

It's urgent.

But –

It's really urgent, Ivan.

I've never noticed how big this studio is. Looking at the window from down here, there's much more sky, much more blue than usual. I assume it's still hot outside, but I don't feel it, I'm cold. Now it hurts a lot again. If you don't have to breathe in, things would be easier, you can limit it but you still do have to breathe a little bit, and it burns like fire. It's the pain that's keeping me conscious. I'm so tired and things keep going dark for a moment, but then I breathe in again and in that moment it hurts so much that I'm awake again, do you understand?

Ivan, I'm not here.

You never were. Since that afternoon we went to the hypnotist. Always somewhere else. But aren't you impressed? Your son, the hero.

I'll never hear about it, Ivan. No one will, if you don't make it to the door and outside. Keep crawling, don't get stuck in the grass.

Do you remember the two of us in the sandbox? You built towers and I knocked them over, and then you weren't the one who cried, I was, until Papa came and said, 'Eric, stop that!' and it wasn't even you who'd done it.

The grass is so high. But what if they do come back? The thin man is standing there again, pulling at his hat and saying, 'Jaeger-strasse 15b, fifth floor!' He raises his hands as if to command a hearing, and bobs up and down nervously. 'That's where you'll find him, that's where your brother is.'

No, I say, that's where I am, and there is here.

But he's not listening to me, he's in such a hurry to impart the information all over again: 'Jaegerstrasse 15b, fifth floor!' He hops and waves, all trace of calm has evaporated, he's actually fading already and I know I won't see him again.

It's freezing cold, but I'm safe. The three of them won't find me. The door is barred, and even if they have the key, the grass is too thick. Everything rises and falls, forwards and backwards, all of it in waves, to and fro. This building will not be here for ever, and even the blue out there won't always be blue. Only I will always be here, I have to be here, there has to be me, because without me all this wouldn't exist because there'd be nobody to see it. The cold floor, hard beneath my temple. And a rocking, as if I were on a boat again.

Do you remember when we went to Tangiers, you and I and Mama and Papa, and the evening ferry took us across the straits? We were six years old and when we left Algeciras the air was redolent with the smell of flowers and sweetish petrol, the stars shimmered around a coppery moon, and Papa is carrying both of us in his arms, and Mama is following along behind, and there's a fat man, all unshaven, asleep on the deck, his mouth wide open, and I have an intuition that I'm going to remember him all my life, but then the ferry stabbed its way out to the open sea, and the coast became a flicker of light, and next to us were pale cliffs and the sounds of the waves. The four of us belong together, it will always be like this, and I know, as I lay my head on his shoulder, that I'm about to fall asleep although I don't want to, it's night everywhere, nothing but stars close above our heads, more of them than ever, Africa will soon appear, only the pain when I breathe in reminds me how hard the ground is, and it's cold again, everything keeps going up and down, and think about how excited the two of us were the first day, naturally they sat us next to each other so that everyone would notice that we look exactly alike, and our parents stand behind us against the wall, and the teacher says is there one of you or are there two, and the question strikes me as so hard that

I turn around to Papa and Mama, but they smile and say nothing, as if to make clear to us that from now on we have to be the ones to answer, and look, there's a bird fluttering past the window, I don't see it, just its shadow in the rectangle of light, I've never seen a bird fly so slowly, we'll be in Africa soon, and then it's morning again, I could go after it, I'd really love to know

Seasons

1

The flowering apple tree was close to the wall, and you could see into the house through the window. On the main floor were the salon, the living room, the former media room, now empty, and the library. If you climbed higher you could see through the fanlight into the entrance hall and from still further up, directly into the study with the desk and the pale patch of wall where the little matchstick man had hung until recently. Anyone who still had the strength for it could keep climbing all the way up onto the roof.

Marie wouldn't have dared go up there on her own, but along with Georg and Lena it was possible, because if there were three of you, none of you wanted to be a coward, and sometimes Jo came too. You had to set one foot in the fork of the branch and the other on the upper edge of the window frame, and then it was really important not to look down. Just don't think about it, close yourself off inside, or you'd feel in your stomach how far down it was, you'd start to sweat, you'd seize up with fear and hang there like a sack. The right way was to grab the tin gutter, get a swing going, push one knee against the wall, and barrel forward until you could work your fingers in between the roof tiles and pull yourself up. Then you could sit there with your back pressed against the slope of the roof and your heels in the gutter, looking over the top of the tree and the house where Georg lived all the way to the street beyond the next one. Ragged clouds were being driven across the sky, pulled and crushed and torn by the wind. As soon as they dissolved, the sun stood there like a blazing fire – even when you squeezed your eyes tight shut, it burned its way through to your eyeballs.

Georg often talked about his father being a policeman, and how he was allowed to play with his pistol at home, but no matter how often he announced he was going to, he never actually produced it. He also told stories about robbers, murderers, con men and crocodiles. A crocodile could lie there motionless for hours on end, looking like an old tree trunk, and then suddenly it lunged and snapped its jaws. He'd been in Africa and in China, in Barcelona and in Egypt.

They talked about what could have happened to Ivan. Maybe he'd gone to America. People often took secret trips to America, sometimes they went by ship, and sometimes even an aeroplane, people over there wore big hats and boots.

'Or maybe China,' said Lena.

'China's too far away,' said Marie. 'And besides, they speak Chinese there.' She felt the sun on her skin, she heard the rustling of the apple tree and the soft buzz of a bumblebee close by her ear.

'Can't he learn Chinese?' asked Georg.

'Nobody learns Chinese,' said Marie, because it was too hard, and there was no point, how could anyone find words in all those brushstrokes? And what if even the Chinese were only pretending they could? It was possible – she did the same, pretending she understood what her father was talking about when he kept explaining to her that the big crisis had saved him.

'And if he's dead?' asked Georg.

Marie shrugged. How warm the tiles were. You could doze off, but you mustn't, you had to keep your heels stuck tight in the gutter so as not to slide off the slope of the roof. 'If he's dead, they'd have found him.'

'He could be in the forest,' said Georg.

'What sort of forest?'

'The forest. Where the wolves are.'

The bumblebee landed somewhere, paused for a moment or two, then flew off again. Marie blinked. A cloud was looking like a bicycle with a man on it who had a hat but no head.

'Does space up there just keep on going?' asked Lena. 'Or does it end somewhere?'

'Maybe there's a wall,' said Marie.

'But even if there is,' said Georg, 'you can always keep flying. You could make a hole in the wall. It can't come to an end. It can *never* come to an end.'

'But if the wall is solid,' said Lena. 'Really, really solid?'

'You could still make a hole in it,' said Georg.

'The most massive wall in the whole world?'

'Then imagine you have the pointiest tool.'

For a while none of them said anything. The buzzing of the bumblebee rose, then fell, then rose again.

'Matthias is stupid,' Lena said eventually.

'Yes he is,' said Georg.

'Why?' asked Marie.

'Marie and Matthias,' sang Lena. 'Matthias and Marie. Marie and Matthias. Matthias and Marie.'

'When's the wedding?' asked Georg.

Without opening her eyes, Marie made a fist and punched him. She hit him smack in the middle of his upper arm, and Georg let out a scream. Marie didn't like Matthias that much, and of course both of them knew this. It was just the usual talk up on the roof.

Once Mama had caught them as they were climbing down. She had worked herself up into a terrible state. Georg and Lena had been forbidden to visit for a while, as had Jo and Natalie, even though Natalie had never ever been up on the roof. Marie had given her solemn word never to do anything so dangerous again, but she had crossed her fingers in the pocket of her jeans so it didn't count, and luckily Mama soon forgot about it again. Mama forgot things quickly. She hadn't been home a lot recently, there were costumes to try on and people to meet, and lots of telephone calls, and she had to have regular meetings with the divorce lawyer, a courtly gentleman with a beard, big ears and eyes like a seal.

Her father came twice a week and took her to the zoo or the cinema. She wasn't that interested in animals, and the films were always the wrong ones – he simply didn't get what you wanted to see if you were eleven. Sometimes she also went to visit him in the presbytery. It was a secret that he was living there, she wasn't allowed to tell anyone, not her grandparents, not Ligurna, not anyone at school, and most of all not Mama.

The presbytery smelled of mothballs and cooking. Her father slept on a couch next to the TV under a picture of Jesus looking as if he had a toothache. Her father always wore jeans and a red-checked shirt, and sometimes he wore a baseball cap that said *I ♥ Boston* on it. When she asked him when he washed the shirt, he got cross and said that he had two others just like it. He no longer owned a computer, or a phone, or a car, and only one pair of trainers. She had never known him to be in such a good mood.

'The crisis!' he cried as they were walking around the zoo. 'Nobody saw it coming. It's like the end of the world. And eight months ago nobody was even dreaming of it!'

They stopped. A gnu with empty eyes returned Marie's glance.

'Real estate derivatives. If only we'd predicted it, we could have made billions! But nobody predicted it. The exchange rates are in free fall, not even the banks can borrow money.' He clapped his hands. 'And everyone knows it, they all keep talking about it, nobody wonders about it, do you understand? Nobody has any questions! Do you understand?'

Marie nodded.

He squatted down. 'Everyone's losing money,' he said in her ear. 'Everyone's losing everything, do you understand?'

Marie nodded.

'Nobody's asking about their own money now. They're all expecting it to be gone, they're reckoning on it because it's happening to everyone. It's a miracle. Not one client is asking what's happened to his investments.'

Marie knew the way you were supposed to look so that it seemed you were understanding everything. She used this look in school, and it was often enough to get her good marks. And she always put it on when her father decided to tell her things that were important. He believed that the two of them were alike and that she understood him better than anyone else did.

'Marie,' he said. 'You understand me better than anyone else does.'

Seeking help, she looked over at the gnu.

'If, for example – it's just an example, Marie! If you've made losses, and you were expecting that – but then suddenly no one's asking questions any more!'

'Are we going to go see the tigers?'

He leapt up and clapped his hands again, so loudly that a woman who was passing, pushing a pram, looked at him reproachfully. 'And Kluessen's in the hospital! It may be a long time, he could even die, who knows! I'll soon be done with the son. Who could have seen it coming!'

He put his hand on her shoulder and pushed her forward. She wasn't surprised that they were heading for the exit. She wasn't going to see the tigers today either. Her father never went to see the tigers.

'Finally!' called Georg when he saw them coming back. He was sitting on the garden fence wearing his Robin Hood cap, he'd tied on a quiver, and he had a bow in his hand. He'd obviously been extremely bored.

'Are they sharp?' asked her father.

'Not sharp, pointed. No, they're not pointed.'

'They look pointed.'

'But they're not.'

Her father paused for a few seconds before saying, 'You're not allowed to shoot with pointed arrows. It's too dangerous.'

'They're not pointed,' Georg said again.

'Honestly!' said Marie.

'Is that true?'

Both of them nodded. Georg even laid his hand on his heart. But her father didn't see this because he was looking absentmindedly at the other side of the street.

'I've never liked this house.'

'Me neither!' said Marie.

'Were you ever in the cellar?'

'There's a cellar?'

'No. There isn't, and you're not going down there!'

'Is it true that you lost all that money?' asked Georg.

'The crisis. Completely unexpected. No one saw it coming. Do you watch the news?'

Georg shook his head.

'Do you know what derivatives are?'

Georg nodded.

'And what *mortgage-backed CDOs* are, do you know that too?'

'Yes.'

'Really?'

Georg nodded.

'Be careful with the arrows.' He gave the house across the street another anxious look, then stroked Marie's cheek and left.

'They really aren't pointed!' Georg called after him.

'Promise!' called Marie.

As she was watching her father go, she thought of Ivan again. It was only recently that she'd grasped that maybe the riddle would never be solved. Never, which meant: not now and not later and not even much, much later, not in her whole life and not even after that. She often found herself thinking how he'd once explained to her in the museum why artists painted ugly stuff like old fish, rotten apples or boiled turkeys: it wasn't because it was about the things themselves, it was about painting the things, so – here he had looked at her solemnly and spoken very quietly, as if he were betraying a secret – so what they were painting was painting itself. Then he'd asked her if she understood, in the same voice her father always used when he asked her the same question, and she'd nodded the same way she always nodded. Her uncle had always seemed a little weird to her, because he looked so exactly like her father and had the same voice and yet was someone else. Things were sometimes strange. People painted fish in order to paint painting, bicycles fell over when you set them on their two wheels but were perfectly stable on these same wheels when you rode off on them, there were people who looked exactly like other people, and sometimes someone disappeared from the world just like that, on a summer day.

'Hit it!' Georg handed her the bow. Over on the other side of the garden an arrow was embedded, quivering, in the target. 'But careful, they're very pointed!'

For a while they took turns shooting. Although it wasn't a large bow, it was hard to pull; sometimes Marie hit the target, but more often it went wide. Georg had more practice. Her fingers were soon hurting from the bowstring.

Lena came by, climbed onto the fence, and watched. Her mother had let her go out for an hour. A man in an expensive leather jacket had come, she said, and had brought her chocolate.

Georg shot and scored. Marie shot and didn't score. Georg shot and didn't score, Marie shot and didn't score, Georg shot and didn't score, Marie shot and scored, a window was thrown open in the house next door, and a woman called over that she hoped these weren't pointed arrows. All three of them swore they weren't.

Gradually the gathering dusk made it hard to aim. The tree seemed bigger than before, but its contours were getting blurred, and it became more difficult to focus on it. Marie aimed one more time and the taut bow trembled, because her arm was already exhausted. She held her breath. The moment stretched out and stretched out, as if she could stop time with the bow. And still it stretched out. Then she shot. The arrow drew its path in the half-light, brushed the trunk, and vanished into the grass.

She said goodbye to Lena and Georg and went across the street. How come evenings smelled different from mornings? Even noon had its own particular smell. The shadow of a bird flew up out of a bush and she jerked back: a fluttering, a cawing and swirling, and it was above her head, already gone into the upper air. She tipped her head back. If Ivan was really dead, then he was up there too now, and the clouds wouldn't obstruct his view, because the dead could see through everything.

The gravel path crunched under her shoes. Through the kitchen window she saw Ligurna stirring a pot, with the phone clamped between her cheek and her shoulder. The window was open, it would have been easy to listen in. But it usually wasn't worth the effort; grown-ups rarely talked about anything interesting. Should she climb the tree again? Not as far as the roof, she didn't dare do that on her own, but maybe as far as the study window? But then this seemed too dangerous as well. It was hard to see the branches in the dark, you could fall, and if unexpectedly a witch was sitting in the tree, you'd be helplessly in her power.

She went through the hall and up the stairs to the dining room. Her plate was already waiting for her: a piece of brown-red meat with some sauce, rice, a little mound of peas and a glass bowl of pudding on the side. She touched the meat. It felt warm, squishy and stringy, alive and dead at the same time. She opened the window and threw it out. She did that a lot. An animal would get it outside; at least it had never happened that food she'd thrown out in the evening was still there the next morning. She was never allowed to leave anything on her plate. If she failed to eat something twice in a row, Ligurna reported it to Mama, who then came and took her hand and asked if she was worried about something, or stressed, or if she had something she didn't want to tell her.

Of course she had, because it felt good to have secrets. Mama knew nothing about the money that Marie had hidden in the nursery: three hundred and twenty euros, folded and squashed flat under the foot of her bed. Part of it was from her pocket money, and part of it from Grandfather's wallet, which he always left lying around carelessly in the hall. It was important never to take too much, twenty at the most, never a fifty. As soon as a fifty went missing, the grown-ups noticed. They never missed smaller amounts. Mama also didn't know that the brooch she'd been hunting for for so long was buried next to the apple tree; Marie and Lena had been playing Treasure Hunt and then couldn't find the place again. Nor did she know that Marie had already forged her signature on excuse notes to her teacher twice, so that she could go fishing with Georg. Unfortunately they hadn't caught any fish, because neither of them could bring themselves to stick a worm on the hook.

Besides there was so much Mama didn't know about this house. Some things you just couldn't explain to her.

Two months ago Marie had come home from school, set down her bag, and lain down on her back on the carpet, to listen to the rain – sometimes she'd lifted up her hands, closed one eye, and looked at the outlines of her fingers against the white of the ceiling. She had called Lena and Georg, but neither of them was at home, then she tried Natalie, who already had her own phone, but she hadn't answered either. So she'd gone up to the top floor. There was a whole room full of empty suitcases up there; in earlier times Marie could spend hours just opening and closing them, loving being able to get into them and sit down, or climb from one into the next, but when you'd turned eleven, the excitement wore off.

In the room next door were cupboards with bed linens, hand towels and all sorts of embroidered stuff; she'd locked herself in there and listened for some time to the drumming of the rain on the roof. Then she'd gone out into the hallway again and opened the door to the little bedroom next door. In it were a table and a chair; the wallpaper was ancient and had bleached-out brownish rectangles on it. The window was dirty; Ligurna obviously never cleaned in here. Marie had actually wanted to go in, but then she'd closed the door carefully and gone back downstairs.

Only when she was back in her room with the desk lamp switched on and her arithmetic notebook open did she turn ice cold with fright. There had been someone sitting at the table – hunched forward, his head turned towards the door and propped up on his elbows, hands pushed deep into his hair. She'd seen, but hadn't been able to take it in at first; only in her memory did it become clear. The one thing she couldn't recapture was the face.

How could you explain something like that to your parents? Not even Ligurna would have believed it.

She ate the peas, the rice and the pudding. Then went to Mama's door, knocked, and walked in.

'Why don't you knock?' Mama was lying on the bed learning her script. 'Well, come here and sit down. Will you help me run lines?' She held out the sheets of paper to Marie.

There were only three pages. The first one went:

```
7/4, INTERIOR, DAYTIME - ELKE'S APARTMENT
Elke and Jens next to each other at the table.


              ELKE
     It can't go on like this, Jens.


  Jens, looking worried, shakes his head.


              ELKE
     You know it and I know it.


              JENS
     And Holger knows it too.


              ELKE
     Don't talk about Holger.


              JENS
  How am I supposed not to talk about him?
             He's between us.


              ELKE
  He's my husband. The father of my children.
```

                              JENS
                        And what am I?
                  Elke looks him in the eye.

                              ELKE
                   You're everything, Jens.

'Elke is full of contradictions,' said Mama. 'Sometimes I feel
close to her, then she's a total stranger again.'

'Why does the world exist?' asked Marie.

'Elke wants to be free. That's the most important thing to her.
But she also knows she's responsible. She's trying to live this
contradiction.'

'God made it, but where did God come from? Did He make
Himself?'

'Did I already tell you who's playing Jens?'

'When people say God made everything, that's not an explanation. Why does something exist?'

'Why does something exist?'

'Yes, why?'

'Mirso Kapus.'

'What?'

'That should be "Excuse me?" Mirso Kapus is playing the lead.
You know him from TV.'

'I don't watch TV. I watch DVDs. Lena's cousin burned us a
copy of *Star Wars* yesterday.'

'Nobody can say why the world exists, the world doesn't need a
reason. Mirso Kapus won the biggest TV award.'

'Things would be so much simpler if it didn't exist.' Marie
crawled under the bedclothes. 'All the people and cars and trees
and stars. And all the ants and bears and the sand in the desert and

the sand on other planets and the water and Georg and the Chinese and everything else. There's so much of it!'

'Elke can grow and develop. The story can go in all sorts of directions.'

It wasn't totally dark under the bedclothes; a little light could make its way in. 'Can I sleep here?'

'Not today. I've got to learn this thing.'

'But it's only three pages.' Marie tugged on the blanket a bit so as to be able to breathe better. Through the crack she could see Mama's dressing table with the mirror, she saw the picture with the teddy bear that had hung until recently in her father's study, and she saw one corner of the window.

'Three pages or twenty or a hundred – that's not the point,' said Mama in irritation. 'You have to come to grips with a role, find your way into it.'

Marie closed her eyes. Her limbs felt heavy. She heard Mama murmur, 'He is my husband, the father of my children.' Then she must have gone to sleep for a while, because Mama shook her gently and then she was holding her hand and feeling her way along the hall. In the nursery Mama helped her off with her shirt, jeans and underwear, pulled on her pyjamas, put her into bed, covered her up, and gave her a kiss, so that her hair tickled her cheek. And all the time Marie was thinking that she hadn't had to brush her teeth, Mama had forgotten, sometimes you got lucky. Then the door closed, and she was alone.

Pale spots of light from the streetlamps flickered on the blanket. She heard the apple tree scraping against the wall. She heard the wind. She pulled the covers over her head so that now all she heard was the rustle of the material, but if you lay still, really really still, and didn't breathe, then you stopped hearing anything at all, there was no more world and there was almost no more Marie. This must be sort of what it was like to be a stone and lie there while time passed. A day, a year, a hundred years, a hundred thousand years. A hundred times a hundred thousand years.

All the same, a day was a long time. So many days still until the holidays came around, so many more until Christmas, and so many years until you were grown up. Every one of them full of days and every day full of hours, and every hour a whole hour long. How could they all go by, how had old people ever managed to get old? What did you do with all that time?

2

The trees were already a riot of colour, but the leaves had not yet started to fall. Marie was coming home from school with her backpack slung over one shoulder and her mobile in one hand when she saw that there was a man waiting at the garden gate.

'Marie?'

She nodded.

'Do you have some time?'

Arthur was tall and pale and stood leaning slightly to one side, as if he had back pain. His hair was a mess. He held the car door open for her; the seats smelled of new leather, and there was no dirt on the floor, not even the tiniest scrap of paper.

It had been two months since Marie had received his letter. It was the first proper letter she'd ever had in her life, and Ligurna had simply laid it next to her plate, as if it were nothing special. But Ligurna had given up being interested in what went on in the household: since Mama had given her her notice, the food tasted even worse than before and dust was collecting on the furniture. They weren't going to be able to hold on to the house for very much longer either, said Mama, even with help from the grandparents it was too expensive. Mama was sad about this, but Marie was not. She had never liked it.

The envelope had held a single sheet, on which the handwriting was astoundingly legible. Unfortunately, wrote Arthur, they still didn't know each other, but she could get in touch with him at any time. Under this was an email address, and under that was his signature.

Dear Arthur, she had replied, *thank you for your letter, this is Marie, how are you? This is my email address. With warm regards, Marie.*

The answer came a week later. He wanted to know what day her birthday was, what class she was in, and whether she liked school or not, who she sat next to, what the name was of her dumbest teacher, which TV programmes she liked best and liked least, if she liked arithmetic, if she liked her father, if she liked her mother, what she thought of Ivan and Martin, what her favourite colour was, if rain made her depressed, how often she thought about Ivan's disappearance, if she thought people should be allowed to eat meat, if she thought Wednesdays were better than Mondays, and, if so, were they always better or only sometimes, and if she thought it was better to be subject to a king, a president or no one at all. He asked about balloons and books, he asked about teddy bears and dolls, he asked about her friends. He asked why she had answered his questions so far, he asked her not to feel compelled to answer them, he thanked her for answering him, and ended with a brief salute, without having given away a single thing about himself.

She had only recently been given her own phone. It lay in her hand, red, smooth and cool to the touch, flat at the back, the entire front forming the screen, but she wasn't yet used to typing without keys. You kept touching the wrong place, the spell-check programme kept on replacing the words you'd written with others that made no sense, but she typed and she typed. She was thirteen now, questions weren't a problem any more. When two days had gone by without a reply, she wrote, *Dear Arthur, did you get my email, how are you? Can we meet? With warm regards, Marie.*

The car ran almost soundlessly as she looked around. She didn't know this part of town and had no idea where her grandfather was taking her. Plaster was peeling off the walls and the street was littered with discarded cans.

'In the meantime, has there been any word?' asked Arthur.

She immediately realized he was talking about Ivan. 'No, but there was an article recently.'

She began to search on her phone. Bookmarks, lists of links, ah, here it was: www.Art-Review-Online.com/sebastianzollnersopinion/eulenboeck. She cleared her throat. She liked reading aloud and was always pleased when her turn came in school, even if she pretended she found it embarrassing, because who wanted to be seen as a suck-up. She pronounced everything right, she rarely made mistakes and hardly even stuttered when she came to the hard words. She would never be as beautiful as Mama, or become an actress, but her voice was faultless.

What does it say about our fragmented society that Heinrich Eulenboeck of all people is our country's artist of the hour? Are we in such need of a dandy for the middle classes, are we really so terrified of uncertainty, that we find it necessary to encase ourselves in the protective armour of irony? Obviously the answer is yes. Few artists in this crisis were able to maintain their prices; almost none of them were able to increase them. Scared collectors preferred to tread lightly and invested in bricks and mortar or gold nuggets they could keep in a safe in the cellar. Blue-chip painters became as rare as pink elephants. So how did this artisanal, rock-solid classical irony suddenly feel itself being snatched out of the hands of dealers and auction houses like hot cakes?

'Let's face it,' says the chief curator of the Free Gallery in Bochum, Hans-Egon Eggert, 'it's all about the new estate executor and his battle plan: do a hard U-turn race to cash in.' The background: since August of last year, Ivan Friedland, the go-get-'em heir of the Old Master, has vanished without a trace. 'Friedland's main claim to fame was his tending of Eulenboeck's reputation,' continued Eggert. 'But now the focus of attention has shifted.' Karl Bankel, the director of Hamburg's Koptman Museum, is even more critical: 'Looking after the opus of an important artist is a highly complex task. Very few people are up to it. Ivan Friedland was not. His successor is even less so.'

In the art world it was always an open secret that Friedland owed his position not to any particular competence, but to an intimate relationship with the venerable old prince of painting. His controversial activities unsettled collectors, but kept prices within moderation. Under Eric Friedland, who was at first the provisional and then the permanent successor of his brother, this policy has changed: suddenly Eulenboeck's paintings are appearing in every possible exhibition of this-or-that private collection: Art Forum Rottweil, the Telefonica Art Centre in Madrid, the Bingen Artists' Union, the Project Space of the City Bank in Brussels and the Ebersfeld Savings Bank Foundation, you name it. What was once an artificial shortage of paintings has become an absolute torrent, and even articles of merchandise – or, as we say, *merch* – have now been sighted in museum shops: cups, sheets, tea towels, all decorated with the beloved rural landscapes of Eulenboeck's early period. For some time now the major museums on both sides of our beloved Atlantic have been retreating from this artist. But shame on anyone who sees a possible connection between all this and Eric Friedland's supposedly precarious business circumstances. Already there's word on the Rialto that prices are stagnating. One does not need to wear the mantle of a prophet to guess that he who flies high may plunge to disaster – and who can feel sympathy, when the body of work, in the opinion of connoisseurs, lacks all substance and is mere gruel? But once the vagaries of momentary fashion no longer cloud our eyes, perhaps we shall be ripe for another art, a delicate, more subtle, but nonetheless courageous art, an art that no longer looks back to the past but forward to the future. It will be the Hour of the Quiet Ones, far from hype, far from hysteria, the hour – to take but one example – of *Krystian Malinovski*. His work is not that of a profiteer in this crisis, it overcomes it. When asked how he imagines a time when . . .

'But it's all contradicting itself, isn't it?' Marie looked up. 'First he says he's important, then he says – '

'Don't worry about it.'

'Should I keep reading?'

'It's enough.'

'Papa says pictures just can't bring in the kind of money to make his debts disappear. Papa says art isn't worth that much. But he says it still keeps the bank away. They take every cent, but they let him live as long as there's money coming in. That's why he's living in the presbytery, but I'm not supposed to say that. Where do you live?'

'I travel a lot.'

'Are you still writing?'

'No.'

'Why didn't you come before now?'

'I have things to do.'

'What kinds of things?'

'Nothing.'

'You do nothing?'

'It isn't that easy.'

Arthur turned the car and headed for an almost empty parking lot. Big clowns' faces made of paper and all sorts of artificial stuff grinned above an entryway, and behind them you could see the outlines of a roller coaster.

'A fair,' said Marie, disappointed. 'Wonderful.'

They got out. A man was leading two boys by the hand, a woman was pushing a pram, some young men were drinking out of beer bottles, and a man and woman were standing arm in arm in front of a shooting gallery.

'Why did you go away back then?' she asked.

'People will tell you life is all a matter of obligations. Maybe they've already told you. But it's not always the case.'

Marie nodded. She had no idea what he meant, but she hoped he wouldn't look at her and realize this.

'You can live without ever having a life. Without entanglements. Maybe it doesn't make for happiness, but it takes the load off.'

'Why don't we . . . ?' Marie pointed to the maze. Mazes were never hard. Just keep following the right-hand wall and don't take your eyes off the ground: provided you don't get distracted by the mirrors, you'll be back out in no time.

She pulled out her phone. *Go figure*, she typed, *I'm at the fair*. While Arthur was paying, she headed for the entrance. The door opened with a hum.

What the hell fair? asked Georg.

Is there a carousel? wrote Natalie.

Tell me where to come, wrote Jo.

She groped her way along the wall. A pane of glass let her see the booths and the semicircle of the Ferris wheel, and the roller coaster. A small boy was licking an ice cream cone and stared right through her as if she were invisible.

Very funny, she texted.

Not funny at all, Jo replied. *I love fairs. Wish I were there too.*

So where was Arthur? Okay, she'd been in this situation before, this was how it was when her father took her to the zoo. She was doing it for him, he was doing it for her, both of them would much rather have just stayed at home. She kept feeling her way along the wall, then around the corner, then around another corner, then around yet another corner, and then she should have found herself at the exit. But she wasn't at the exit, she was standing in front of a mirror, and there was no way forward.

But we were going to go to Matthias's birthday party, wrote Lena.

Later, she replied, and tucked the phone away, because she had to concentrate.

There was a splash of blue on the floor. She went past the mirror and around a corner, and then around yet another corner, and finally she saw the turnstile at the exit, but she was looking at it through glass, because the way was clearly leading in the opposite direction, left, then left again, back towards the entrance. There was the blue splash again, and next to it a bent stick of metal, one end rounded like the head of a walking stick, and the other filed to a sharp point. She bent down. No question, the splash was the same splash. But there was no mirror in front of her; could the splash have moved? And where had the metal stick come from? So – right and then right again, and here was the blue splash once more. Something wasn't adding up. Do it again: right, and then again right, and the blue splash was there, but now the stick of metal had disappeared. She went in the opposite direction.

Left, then left again, and she was facing a wall of glass and could go no further. She turned back and reached the entrance. It was locked.

She touched it, shook it, knocked. Pointless. She knocked harder. Nothing. She banged with her fist. More nothing.

She stepped in front of the sheet of glass through which she could see the fair, and tried to wave at the man in the booth who was collecting entrance fees. But the angle was impossible – she couldn't see him and he couldn't see her. Maybe call Emergency? But she'd paid her entrance fee, she'd just make herself look ridiculous. She went left, then she went right, then left again and right again, then past the glass partition twice, and three times past the wall of mirrors, and then she was back looking at the splash of blue. On the other side of the glass a man went down on his knees and looked right at her. She flinched. Only then did she recognize Arthur.

She banged on the glass. He laughed and banged back: he obviously thought the whole thing was a joke. She pointed left and then right, and put her hands in the air to tell him she didn't know how to get out. Arthur stood up and wandered out of her field of vision. Her throat tightened, and in her fury she felt the tears begin to come. Just as she was starting to call Emergency, someone tapped her on the shoulder.

'Right here,' said Arthur.

'Sorry?'

'The way out. It's right here. In front of you. What's wrong, why are you crying?'

It was true, the exit was just a few feet away. One turn to the left, then another to the right, and the turnstile was smack in front of her. Why hadn't she been able to see it? She whispered that of course she hadn't been crying at all, wiped away her tears, and ran out into the open air.

Arthur pointed to a tent. Small, blue, with a red curtain over the entrance, and electric lights blinking over it like stars: *Your future*, they said, *in the cards.*

'I'd rather not,' said Marie.

'Come on,' said Arthur, 'maybe it'll be good news.'

'And if it's bad news?'

'Then you just don't believe it.'

They went in. A reading lamp threw its yellowish light onto a wooden table with a dirty felt cloth. Behind it sat an old man wearing a pullover. He was bald, except for two tufts of hair over the ears, and he was wearing spectacles. In front of him lay a pack of cards and a magnifying glass.

'Come in, come closer,' he said without looking up. 'Come here, take your cards, read your fortune, come right up.'

Marie looked at Arthur, but he was standing there with his arms folded, saying nothing.

'Come closer,' said the soothsayer mechanically, 'come here, take three cards, read your fortune.'

Marie went to the table. His glasses were incredibly thick, and his eyes behind them were almost invisible. Blinking, he held up a little pack of cards.

'Choose twelve, and read your fortune.'

Hesitatingly, Marie picked up the deck. The cards were greasy and much handled, and like no cards she was familiar with. There were strange figures on them: a falling star, a hanged man, a knight on a horse holding a lance, a masked figure in a boat.

'Take twelve,' urged the soothsayer. 'Take them. Twelve euros for twelve cards. One euro per card.'

Arthur put fifteen euros on the table. 'Have you been doing this a long time?'

'Sorry?'

'Have you been doing this a long time?'

'Before this I did other things, and before that still other things, but they didn't go so well.'

'Hard to believe,' said Arthur.

'I packed entire halls.'

'Big halls?'

'The biggest.'

'So what happened?'

The soothsayer looked up.

'What happened?' Arthur asked again.

The soothsayer blinked, and held his hand up to his forehead. 'Nothing,' he said finally. 'Bad times happened. Bad luck happened. The years went by, they happened. A man is not who a man was.'

'And yet a man is finally who a man is,' said Arthur.

'Who a man is?'

'Who a man was.'

'What do you mean?'

'Just a joke.'

'What kind of joke?'

Arthur didn't reply. Marie looked at the cards she was holding and waited.

'We don't have much time,' said Arthur.

The soothsayer nodded, groped for the money, found it, tucked it away, hunted around in his pocket, and laid three coins ceremoniously out on the table. 'Take your cards,' he said to Marie. 'From the middle, or the top, or the bottom. Whatever you want. Close your eyes. Listen to your inner self.'

'Twelve?' asked Marie.

'Lay them out here. One next to the other. Right here on the table.'

'I have to take twelve?'

'Right here. One next to the other.'

She gave Arthur another questioning look, but he was staring at the soothsayer in a most peculiar way. How was she supposed to pick the cards? She could choose any single one of them individually, or she could take a whole dozen right out of the middle of the deck. Uncertainly, she twisted the whole packet in her hands.

'Doesn't matter a damn,' said Arthur.

'Excuse me?' said the soothsayer.

'If it works, it works, no matter how you pick the cards,' said Arthur. 'And if it doesn't work, so what?'

'Your future,' said the soothsayer. 'Your fate. Right here on the table, please.'

Marie pulled a card out of the middle of the deck and set it on the table, face down. And another. And then another. And then, from different parts of the pile, nine more. She waited, but the soothsayer didn't move.

'Done,' she said.

The soothsayer blinked in her general direction. His mouth gaped open. He pulled a green silk kerchief out of his breast pocket and blotted his brow.

'Done!' she said again.

He nodded, then he counted as he briefly touched each card with his finger. 'Twelve,' he said softly, half to her and half to himself, poked at his glasses, and then arranged the cards neatly in a semicircle.

'No matter what it costs,' said Arthur. 'It's just a matter of making the effort. With everything you've got.'

'Excuse me?' said the soothsayer.

Arthur didn't reply.

The soothsayer began to turn over the cards. Something horrifying emanated from the images; they struck Marie as primeval, brutal, indescribably ugly. They seemed to announce sheer power, a world in which no creature ever befriended another creature, in which anyone could do absolutely anything to another person, and in which it was suicidally stupid to believe anything anyone said. There was a figure captured in mid-leap in a dance, and on another card was a great round moon, ringed in clouds. The soothsayer bowed forward, his head almost touching the table, and his bald spot was unmistakable. He picked up the magnifying glass and examined one card after the other.

'The Three of Swords. All standing on their heads.'

'There aren't three,' said Arthur.

The soothsayer raised his head. His eyes shimmered in a tiny flicker behind his glasses.

'Count them again!' said Arthur.

There were five swords. Marie could see that at a glance. The soothsayer's index finger wandered from one sword to the next, but his hand was shaking and the swords were so narrow that he kept missing them.

'Seven,' he said. 'Standing on their heads.'

'That's not seven,' said Marie.

The soothsayer looked up.

'Five!' she called out.

'Five swords,' said the soothsayer, and set his finger on the next card. 'Five swords, standing on their heads, beside the Sun and the Lover.'

'That's the Moon!' said Arthur.

The soothsayer took off his glasses and mopped his face with the green handkerchief.

'Sun and Moon must never be mixed up!' said Arthur. 'They're polar opposites.'

'Polar whats?' asked the soothsayer.

'In the Tarot. They're polar opposites, or so I'm told. It's really not my thing. Don't you have a hearing aid?'

'They always make that whistling noise and you can't understand a thing.'

'A hearing aid that whistles must really mess up hypnosis.'

'No,' said the soothsayer, 'if it whistles, you can't do it.'

'But reading cards goes okay?'

'The prices to rent a stand are too high. Bunch of crooks. Not enough customers. I used to fill entire halls.'

'The biggest?' said Arthur.

'Excuse me?'

'Do please go on!'

The soothsayer lowered his head until his nose was only a fraction of an inch above the cards. He pulled one of them out from the middle of the pack. It displayed a fortress and a bolt of lightning, and there were people frozen in the wildest contortions.

'The Tower,' said Arthur.

'Excuse me?'

'Is that the Tower?'

The soothsayer nodded. 'The Tower. In combination with the Five of Swords, standing on their heads. Plus the Moon. It can mean . . .'

'But it isn't!' exclaimed Arthur. 'That is not the Tower.'

'So what is it?' asked the soothsayer.

'You can't see a thing,' said Arthur. 'Am I right? You don't hear a thing, and you can't see a thing any more.'

The soothsayer stared at the table. Then he slowly set his magnifying glass aside.

'Goodbye!' cried Arthur.

The soothsayer said nothing. They left.

'But you paid him anyway,' said Marie.

'He gave it his best shot!'

'What was it all about? The Tower, the Five of Swords, and was that really the Moon or was it actually the Sun? And what did it mean, anyway?'

'That he couldn't read a thing.'

'But my future!'

'Seek it out yourself. Seek out the one you want.'

She wondered why Arthur seemed so relieved. She would have liked to take a trip on the ghost train, but he suddenly seemed to be in a hurry. They walked to the car park. He hummed to himself quietly all along the way, and was still smiling as he unlocked the car.

'I have a house,' he said as they drove off. 'It's by a little lake, and there isn't another house to be seen in any direction. When I'm there, I can work all day. It rains a lot. I thought nature would do me good, but that was before I knew that nature mostly consists of rain. Sometimes I take a trip somewhere, and then I come back again. For a long time my work was a cut above average, then it wasn't any more, and now all I do is read other people's books. Books that are so good, I could never have written them myself. You asked what I do – well, that's what I do.'

'That's how you spent all your time?'

'It went quickly.'

'Where are we off to now?'

Arthur didn't answer. For a time they drove in silence.

Then he braked and parked the car. Marie looked around. She'd been here with her class before, and not too long ago, on a school outing.

'Are we going to the museum?'

'Yes.'

Marie sighed.

They got out and went up a marble staircase and then down a long corridor.

'I've got to get back soon,' she said. 'Homework.'

'Do you get a large amount of it?'

She nodded. It was Saturday, and luckily they never got assignments over the weekend. 'Yes, a very large amount.'

What gives with Matthias's birthday party??? wrote Lena.

Yeah yeah yeah later, wrote Marie.

Pictures hung one smack against the next, some of them just had lines, others had blotches, and on some of them you could see actual stuff: landscapes, buildings, even faces. There were whirling things and whiz-bangs and torrents and explosions of colour. Anyone who was interested in this sort of thing, she thought, would certainly be interested here. But she wasn't that person.

'I really have to get home.'

Arthur stopped in front of a picture. 'Look at this.'

She nodded. It had a gold frame and it featured the sea. There was also a ship.

'No,' said Arthur. 'Look at it.'

The sea was blue the way all seas are blue, under a cloudless sky and a big sun. The ship was being followed by a whole swarm of seagulls.

'No,' said Arthur. 'Really look!'

In fact, the sea wasn't all blue. There was foam on the waves, and the water had darker and lighter areas. And the sky had lots of colours in it too. Right on the horizon there was a sort of misty transitional space, and around the sun everything dissolved into a thick impasto of white. When you looked at it, it was like being dazzled. And yet it was all just bits of colour.

'Yes,' said Arthur. 'That's it!'

The ship had a long keel, five smokestacks and portholes that sparkled. Little lines of flags fluttered in the wind, people were crowded onto the decks, and the stern sported an anchor on its own substructure.

Out in front, in the bow, was a piece of sculpture: one of those oversized bent watches, like the ones Marie had seen on slides in school, some very famous artist had made them but she couldn't remember his name. She looked at the little plaque

247

on the wall: *Sea Voyage with Expensive Sculpture. H. Eulenboeck,* 1989.

She stepped even closer, and immediately everything dissolved. There were no more people any more, no more little flags, no anchor, no bent watch. There were just some tiny bright patches of colour above the main deck. The white of the naked canvas shone through in several places, and even the ship was a mere assemblage of lines and dots. Where had it all gone?

She stepped back and it all came together again: the ship, the portholes, the people, even though she'd just seen that none of it was even there. She took another step back, and now it seemed as if the picture were telling her that whatever it was communicating to her had nothing to do with what it was actually portraying. It was some kind of a diplomatic message that seemed to be contained within the brilliance of the light, the vast expanse of the water or the distant trajectory of the ship itself.

'Fate,' said Arthur. 'The capital letter F. But chance is a powerful force, and suddenly you acquire a Fate that was never assigned to you. Some kind of accidental fate. It happens in a flash. But the man could certainly paint. Think about that, and don't ever forget it. The man could paint.'

'Who?'

'Ivan.'

'But that's not by Ivan.'

Arthur stared hard at her. She waited, but he didn't say a word.

'Can we go now?' she asked.

'Yes,' he said. 'I'm going to take you home.'

3

As Marie and Matthias reached the presbytery, Eric and Martin were fighting again. There was nothing unusual about this, it was pretty standard.

'Good that I'm moving out!' yelled Eric.

'I'm not stopping you. What I truly don't need here is some kind of fanatic. How can anyone even begin to assert – '

'That God performs miracles?'

'God does *not* perform miracles. The minute you start with miracles, you cannot begin to explain why He fails to make them most of the time. If He saves you, why didn't He save everyone else? Because you're more important?'

'Maybe.'

'You're not serious, are you? You mean He sent a complete economic crisis just to rescue you from the mess you'd got yourself into? You're not just saying that, you actually *mean* it?'

'Why not? Why shouldn't it have come just to save me personally, why not?'

'Because you're not that important!'

'Obviously I am. Otherwise it wouldn't be – '

'That's a totally circular argument!'

'You people always say that His ways are not ours to know. You keep telling us that no one can predict how He will steer our fate and by what means.'

'And Ivan? Did he disappear just so that you could grab his paintings and use the proceeds to pay the interest?'

'You may not say any such thing!'

'*You* were the one who said it!'

'I never said that!'

'It follows implicitly from what – '

'We were twins. You don't understand. I'm not just me, and he's – well, he wasn't just him. In a certain way we were always just one person. It's hard to explain.'

'Every day!' said Martin to Marie. The acolyte held out the white shirt to him, and he panted as he slipped his arms into the sleeves. 'Every day he explains to me that God watches over the world and over him in particular. Every day!'

'He didn't want to baptize me!' cried Eric. 'I had to go to another parish. My own brother didn't want to baptize me!'

'Every day he stands in front of me in that check shirt of his and says that God sent a financial crisis just to save him.'

'Go play with your cube, and leave me in peace.'

'The cube isn't a plaything.'

'No, it's a serious sport, really hard stuff!'

'Save yourself that tone of voice! I'm back at number twenty-two again!'

'On which list?' asked Marie. She knew the answer, but she also knew how much Martin liked repeating it.

'The national one!'

The acolyte put the stole around Martin's shoulders. He was an unprepossessing young man with whom she'd had a brief conversation the week before. It hadn't been easy, because at first he'd been so shy, but after she'd smiled at him twice, he'd immediately asked her to go out with him. She'd tried to say no as nicely as she could, but he was stricken anyway, and since then he'd avoided her. Martin had got to know him at the Catholic Youth. There was a hole in his right nostril from which a ring had recently been removed, and his name, if she remembered correctly, was Ron.

Marie put her arm around Matthias's neck. She felt him flinch; he found it awkward whenever she touched him in front of her father. He was afraid of him, you couldn't reproach him for that.

It wasn't easy having a boyfriend. Sometimes she wished she'd waited, but Lena already had one, Natalie had one, and even Georg would have liked to have a girlfriend. In desperation he'd even asked Marie, but she'd had to laugh, the thing was too absurd. She'd been together with Matthias, who was already sixteen, a year older than she was, for a month now, and she'd already slept with him three times. The first time it was strange and a bit exhausting, and the second time it just seemed really dumb, but the third time, at his house, while his parents were away and the dog kept scratching pathetically at the door, suddenly made her understand why people made such a fuss about it all.

The acolyte stepped back. Martin was now in his full vestments. Immediately he looked thinner and radiated worthiness.

'Is Laura coming too?' asked Eric.

'She's shooting,' said Marie. 'They've enlarged her role in the new season.'

'So what's it like, this series?' asked Martin.

'Very good,' said Matthias. 'Really interesting.' Marie poked him with her elbow. Both of them had to grin.

It was a year ago when she'd begun to draw. Nobody knew, she was still too inept in the way she laid down her lines, the shapes of things were not yet under her control, but she had no doubt that she would get better. Later she intended to study graphic arts alongside her major, which would be medicine, and then she'd pick up another language, or maybe three or even four, but not more: she still wanted to be able to read books and take trips to distant continents, Patagonia was a must-see, as was the coast of North Africa, and she also had to get to China.

'So, let's do this.' Martin opened the door. Outside the snow was coming down in big, slow-falling flakes.

It was only a few steps to the church. Martin went first, followed by Ron, then Eric, with Matthias and Marie bringing up the rear. She stuck out her tongue to taste the snow. The white cold stifled all noises. She tucked her arm into Matthias's.

'Can we go to my place afterwards?' he whispered in her ear.

Maybe that was a good idea. His parents were off on another trip. They would have the house all to themselves, and yet she wasn't sure. She liked Matthias and didn't want to hurt him, but maybe what she needed was a different boyfriend. She tipped her head to one side so that her hair brushed his cheek. 'Maybe.'

Eric looked back at them uneasily. Marie was too young to be running around arm in arm with a boy, let alone a pathetic one. It was far too early. If things kept on going like this, they would soon be kissing each other. How was he going to stop it?

He had to pray more often. Praying always helped. If he'd prayed more in the past, he'd never have got himself into such difficulties. All of his hunches had proved true: people were under constant surveillance, the cosmos was a system of signs arranged so as to be legible, nights were infested with demons, and evil lurked in every corner. But he who entrusted himself to God had nothing to fear. It was all plain and simple, and he couldn't understand why his brother got so cross every time he talked about it. He'd always understood Ivan, but things with Fatso were eternally complicated. It was simpler to talk things over with his new friend Adrian Schlueter, who'd explained to him that God was obliged to forgive anyone who went to Confession: the Lord Himself was bound by His own Sacrament.

So Eric went every day to Confession. He had already been in every church in the city, he knew where you got stuck in a queue and where you were next up right away, where the priests were approachable, where they were inquisitive, and where even after the tenth time they didn't recognize you; he knew which churches were better to avoid because there were demons staring down off their façades, hissing swear words and trying to prevent you from getting in. Confessing every day demanded its own discipline. Sometimes you'd done nothing wrong and you had to invent it, but it was worth the effort: you could go through life devoid of sin, as weightless as a newborn, without any fear of the Last Judgment.

He looked up. Flakes of snow were dancing against the grey of the sky. It had started to snow the previous evening, and lying on his lumpy sofa he had been unable to sleep because of the sheer silence. He had spent the night visualizing his desk, his business cards, his phone setup, his computer, his company car – everything that would be his again soon.

It was only two months since he'd bumped into Lothar Remling. Much boxing on the shoulders, loud cries, football talk: Unbelievable, whooped Eric, apropos of absolutely nothing, the game! Remling replied that you couldn't believe how the idiots had frittered the whole thing away, and then he started talking about how these were high times for Remling.Consult, governments had been pumping so much money into the system that nobody knew what to do with it all, could you have imagined such a thing even a year ago! Then he asked how things were going for Eric, and Eric was about to answer that he was up to his ears in new projects and working himself into exhaustion, but then suddenly, to his own astonishment, he said he wasn't doing anything.

Nothing?

Absolutely nothing. Totally, absolutely nothing. All day. He had withdrawn from the world and was living in the presbytery. With his brother. The priest.

Totally crazy, said Remling. Are you for real?

Eric said he'd realized things couldn't go on like this. Everyone needed to declare time out once in a while. Sit and think. As for him, he dipped into the Bhagavad Gita. Meditated. Went to Confession. Spent time with his daughter. Was also administering the art collection of his dead brother. Of course he'd be making a comeback, but there was no hurry. It was so terribly easy to lose sight of the essential.

The essential, said Remling. Yes, exactly, that was what it was all about.

Then he had asked for Eric's number, and Eric had told him he didn't have a mobile any more, but he could be reached at the presbytery.

And Remling had actually called three days later, and they'd met to eat, and two days later they'd met again, and then again that same week, and everything was in the bag. No, Eric had said, he didn't need a lawyer to take care of the contract, his future was cradled in the hands of God, and Remling had exclaimed that all this was so cool.

Eric had no doubt whatever that he was on the fast track to glory at Remling.Consult. As regards experience, he had it nailed, he knew every trick in the book, he had built one of the biggest asset-planning companies in the country. The fact that it had been torpedoed wasn't his fault, no one had foreseen the crisis, no one had been able to know what was bearing down on them, everyone who worked for him had said the exact same thing. He met twice a week with Maria Gudschmid and Felsner for tea, and they went around in a circle saying Who Could Possibly Have Known?! Which was why the investors had accepted their losses, and why Kluessen's son had decided not to sue. The only fly in the ointment was his one-time chauffeur, who'd written a letter to the state prosecutors, but the accusations it contained were so off the wall that nobody had wanted to pursue the thing. The sale of the almost one hundred paintings and almost one thousand sketches that had been found partly in Eulenboeck's studio and partly in Ivan's apartment, when combined with reproductions of Eulenboeck's farmhouses on pens, children's crayons, pyjamas and cups, had become so profitable that he could pay off the interest on the bridging loan. But such a shame that so many pictures had gone missing: there were three dozen paintings described exactly in Ivan's records – nobody had ever seen them, nobody knew a thing about them, it was just as if they'd never existed. Now the boom was unfortunately a bust, Eulenboeck's prices were shrinking, and the licence agreements were all eroding, but the worst was past. He wasn't going to jail. God had decided that one. And his instincts had sharpened themselves, and he was thinking faster than he ever had – it had been genuinely helpful that he'd had to restrict his budget for medications – he now took only the essentials, those things that made it possible to stand more or less upright and get through the day.

And that's what he'd said to Sibylle. He hadn't seen her for four years, she'd lost weight, and she looked exhausted. He'd told her what he'd told Remling: Bhagavad Gita, Confession, no mobile, time out, hand of God. He'd talked about the crisis that nobody could have foreseen, he'd talked about the presbytery and about the divorce. He'd talked about the fact that he would never again be a complete human being since the day his twin brother had died. Sibylle had asked if Laura was okay again, healthwise, and he'd said, Thank God, yes! And now he was going to move in with her. His income was down to the bare minimum it took for sheer survival, he had no means to pay for an apartment of his own, but he absolutely had to get out of the presbytery, no matter what. It was no place for a pious human being of any stripe.

Eric bent down and scooped up a handful of snow. It was still so powdery that it was almost impossible to shape it into a ball. He wanted to hurl the crumbling lump at somebody, but couldn't see any particular target. Marie suddenly seemed too grown-up to have snowballs thrown at her, and he didn't want to target her disgusting boyfriend either – if he hit him in the face, it would be really embarrassing. And he couldn't snow-bomb Martin any more either, now, when he was wearing his priest's outfit. So he took aim at the acolyte.

He hit him in the back of the head, and the snow dusted itself into a halo. The young man spun around, with the momentary look of an animal on the attack, then his face softened into an effortful smile.

There was something odd about him. The first time he'd come into the presbytery and met Eric's eyes, he'd begun to giggle hysterically. He still could barely talk to Eric without turning pale and beginning to stutter. Eric guessed he must have been commissioned by someone to spy on him, but it just didn't matter any more. He was under the protecting hand of God.

They went into the church. The organ advanced triumphantly from one chord to the next, and the congregation was bigger than before. The five old women who always came were here, along with the friendly fat man, the sad young woman, and Adrian Schlueter. But this time there were also a few old friends of Ivan's, including a Belgian painter with a pointed beard and a silk shawl, and a cousin none of them had seen in ages, and Eric's secretary Kathi, who was now installed at the Eulenboeck Trust to oversee merchandising. Martin's mother was here, and next to her, upright and calm, was Prelate Finckenstein. In the front row, face hidden behind dark glasses, maybe out of grief and maybe out of a desire to pass unrecognized, sat Ivan and Eric's mother.

Ivan had been missing for four years now, and in the previous week he had officially been declared dead. Eric had insisted on this Mass, he had begged, cursed and finally threatened to intervene with the bishop. Martin had defended himself as long as he was able. Ivan had never been baptized, and besides which, Masses for the souls of the dead were absolute rubbish – why would the Almighty, All-Knowing God change His view of a single human soul because that soul's survivors sang a few songs? Or, to put it better, any Mass for the dead would have been rubbish if there really had been an all-knowing God and any sense in theology. Which was why he'd finally given way.

The congregation rose to its feet. 'The Lord be with you,' said Martin. Since he had come to understand that faith was never going to alight on him, he'd felt free. Nothing was ever going to help: never in this life was he going to be thin, and never in this life was he going to escape the power of reason.

'And with your spirit,' murmured the congregation.

Martin spoke about his brother. He wasn't a novice, so the sentences flowed freely, without his having to think about them: Ivan Friedland had lived and painted, he had researched, he had seen much in the world, because the act of seeing was his passion. He had behaved badly to no man, and he had dedicated his work to a greater artist, whose authority he had been the first to acknowledge. Much was to have been expected of him, but an untimely fate had cut short his life, only God knew how. He would never come back.

Martin folded his hands. The acolyte took a ragged breath, rubbed his face, made little coughing noises, and sniffled in a way that could drive anyone mad. The boy was doing his best, but he just wasn't suited for this job, someone had to find another solution for him. Perhaps Eric could help, he still had all these connections.

As Martin heard himself speak, he closed his eyes. He imagined the snowflakes falling outside. If the weather report was to be believed, they were going to keep falling for days, big machines would be working at full power to clear the streets, chemicals would be sprayed around with abandon, but the snow would keep falling on the pavements, on the parked cars, on the gardens, trees, roofs and antennas. For a few days to come, the world would be a thing of beauty. He noticed that he was getting hungry again.

'And now,' he said, 'the Profession of Faith.'

MEASURING THE WORLD

Daniel Kehlmann

'Nothing less than a literary sensation' *Guardian*

At the end of the eighteenth century, two brilliant and eccentric young scientists set out to measure the world.

Alexander von Humboldt swashbuckled his way across the globe: navigating ocean and jungle, eating with cannibals, swimming with electric eels, lowering himself into volcanoes and scaling the highest mountain known to man.

Carl Friedrich Gauss, on the other hand, stayed at home, using the power of thought to battle his way into exotic mathematical realms and the landmark realization that space is curved.

Measuring the World brings these two geniuses to life, capturing their balancing act between loneliness and love, absurdity and greatness, failure and success.

'Pulsing with fictional energy ... Here for once is a popular hit as sophisticated as it is engaging' *Sunday Times*

Quercus

www.quercusbooks.co.uk

ME & KAMINSKI

Daniel Kehlmann

'The novel barrels along like a top-of-the-range BMW on a deserted autobahn ... The comedy has a touching, tender precision' *Independent*

Sebastian Zöllner, an underachieving art critic, has pinned his hopes of advancement on writing the biography of the reclusive artist Manuel Kaminski. Inept, charmless, and with scant knowledge of art history, Zöllner is hardly the man to rediscover a lost genius. But he has made one crucial discovery about his subject: that Kaminski's long-lost love, Therese, is still living, contrary to what the artist himself had been led to believe.

'An accessible and humorous road trip into the worlds of art and journalism, satirising both' *New Statesman*

Quercus

www.quercusbooks.co.uk

FAME

A novel in nine episodes

Daniel Kehlmann

'A real beauty of a book' Jonathan Franzen

Imagine being famous. Being recognized on the street,
adored by people who have never even met you, known the
world over, wouldn't that be great? But what if, one day, you
got stuck in a country where no one spoke your language
and you didn't speak theirs. Where no one knew your face
and you had no way of contacting your home and family.
How would your fame help you then? What would happen
if someone got hold of your mobile phone? If they spoke to
your girlfriends, your agent, your director and started making
decisions for you. And when no one believed that you were
you any more, when you saw a lookalike acting your roles
for you, what would you do?

'Brilliant' *Independent* 'Extraordinary' *Guardian*
'Ingenious' *Daily Telegraph*

Quercus

www.quercusbooks.co.uk